Praise for Jeffrey Siger

A Deadly Twist
The Eleventh Chief Inspector Andreas Kaldis Mystery

"Followers of the series will relish a reunion with Kaldis and a group of friends in an engrossing procedural. New readers will discover the gorgeous aspects of Greek life in a mystery that uncovers the corruption of the country."

—Library Journal, Starred Review

"As always, Siger keeps readers turning the pages with ingenious plot twists and delicious description of the Greek isles, while the compelling Andreas remains an engaging, multifaceted lead character."

—Booklist

"Siger balances the conflict that fuels the plot with vivid descriptions of the culture, food, and glorious settings of this off-the-beaten-track Greek island. Endearing supporting characters add to the fun. Travel buffs will be enchanted."

—Publishers Weekly

"Reading Kaldis's amiable eleventh case is like visiting old friends."

—Kirkus Reviews

"Required reading."

—New York Post

"Reading a novel in this series is always a treat. There is so much to like: great characters, an intriguing story line, and a wonderful setting. Enjoy... A-Rating."

—Deadly Pleasures Mystery Magazine

"Uncanny ability to predict crises that are addressed in his novels a year or two before they become harsh realities."

—*BookReporter*

Island of Secrets
(First Published as *The Mykonos Mob*)
The Tenth Chief Inspector Andreas Kaldis Mystery

"Siger seasons Kaldis's investigations with abundant slices of Greek history and island mores, along with [wife] Lila's consciousness-raising conversations. Armchair travelers will have fun."

—*Publishers Weekly*

"A perfect setting and first-rate storytelling."

—Ragnar Jónasson, bestselling author
of the Dark Iceland series

An Aegean April
The Ninth Chief Inspector Andreas Kaldis Mystery

Best Books of 2018 in Crime Fiction by *Library Journal*

"The great man behind Greece's crime mysteries."

—*Greek City Times*

"Vivid local color, agreeable central characters, and exciting action scenes make this a winner."

—*Publishers Weekly*

"The ninth case for Siger's Greek detective, brimming with suspense and a distinct sense of place, continues to deepen the back story of its band of heroes."

—*Kirkus Reviews*

"Siger's ninth atmospheric mystery vividly depicts the political and economic issues involved in the European refugee crisis. VERDICT: Fans of Adrian McKinty's Sean Duffy books and other police procedurals that handle violence and political issues with black humor will welcome this outstanding crime novel."

—*Library Journal*, Starred Review

"This latest outing also offers a perspective on the Balkan Peninsula and the thorny issue of asylum seekers. A fast-paced international series."

—*Booklist*

Santorini Caesars
The Eighth Chief Inspector Andreas Kaldis Mystery

"[This is a] novel that's both a rock-solid mystery and comments incisively about so many issues besetting Europe and the world today."

—*Huffington Post*

"The eighth case for Siger's police hero has a timely plot and a handful of engaging back stories about its detective team."

—*Kirkus Reviews*

"As always, Siger provides readers with an action-packed plot, well-developed characters with lots of attitude, breathtaking Greek scenery, and a perceptive take on the current political and economic problems affecting Greece. International-crime fans need to be reading this consistently strong series."

—*Booklist*

Devil of Delphi
The Seventh Chief Inspector Andreas Kaldis Mystery

2016 Barry Awards nominee for Best Novel

"Siger brings Chief Inspector Andreas Kaldis some very big challenges in his seventh mystery set in troubled contemporary Greece... The final plot twist proves well worth the wait, but it won't take readers long to get there as they will be turning pages at a ferocious clip."

—*Booklist*, Starred Review

"Though the reader is always several steps ahead of the police here, Siger's sublimely malevolent villains make the book a page-turner."

—*Kirkus Reviews*

"A killer named Kharon (for the mythological ferryman who transports the dead across the River Styx) and bomba, or counterfeit wine, complicate the lives of Chief Inspector Kaldis and his team. The seventh book in Siger's Greek procedural series features a strong sense of place and a devious plot."

—*Library Journal*

Sons of Sparta
The Sixth Chief Inspector Andreas Kaldis Mystery

"Siger paints travelogue-worthy pictures of a breathtakingly beautiful—if politically corrupt—Greece."

—*Publishers Weekly*, Starred Review

Mykonos After Midnight
The Fifth Chief Inspector Andreas Kaldis Mystery

"From the easy banter of its three cops to its clutch of unpredictable villains, Kaldis's fifth reads more like an Elmore Leonard
caper than a whodunit."

—*Kirkus Reviews*

"Acclaimed (particularly by Greek commentators) for their realistic portrayal of Greek life and culture, the Kaldis novels are very
well constructed, and this one is no exception: not only is the
mystery solid but the larger story, revolving around the political
machinations of the shadowy global organization, is clever and
intriguing. Fans of the previous Kaldis novels would do well to
seek this one out."

—*Booklist*

Target: Tinos
The Fourth Chief Inspector Andreas Kaldis Mystery

"Thrilling, thought-provoking, and impossible to put down."
—Timothy Hallinan, award-winning author
of the Poke Rafferty thrillers

"Nobody writes Greece better than Jeffrey Siger."
—Leighton Gage, author of the Chief
Inspector Mario Silva Investigations

"*Target: Tinos* is another of Jeffrey Siger's thoughtful police procedurals set in picturesque but not untroubled Greek locales."
—*New York Times*

"A likable, compassionate lead; appealing Greek atmosphere; and
a well-crafted plot help make this a winner."

—*Publishers Weekly*, Starred Review

"An interesting and highly entertaining police procedural for those who wish to read their way around the globe and especially for those inclined to move away from some of the 'chilly' Scandinavian thrillers and into warmer climes."

—*Library Journal*

"The fourth case for a sleuth who doesn't suffer fools gladly pairs a crisp style with a complex portrait of contemporary Greece to bolster another solid whodunit."

—*Kirkus Reviews*

"Siger's latest Inspector Kaldis Mystery throbs with the pulse of Greek culture… Make sure to suggest this engaging series to fans of Leighton Gage's Mario Silva series, set in Brazil but very similar in terms of mood and feel."

—*Booklist*

Prey on Patmos
The Third Chief Inspector Andreas Kaldis Mystery

"A suspenseful trip through the rarely seen darker strata of complex, contemporary Greece."

—*Publishers Weekly*

"Using the Greek Orthodox Church as the linchpin for his story, Siger proves that Greece is fertile new ground for the mystery genre. Sure to appeal to fans of mysteries with exotic locations."

—*Library Journal*

"The third case for the appealing Andreas will immerse readers in a fascinating culture."

—*Kirkus Reviews*

Assassins of Athens
The Second Chief Inspector Andreas Kaldis Mystery

"Jeffrey Siger's *Assassins of Athens* is a teasingly complex and suspenseful thriller... Siger and his protagonist, Chief Inspector Andreas Kaldis, are getting sharper and surer with each case."
—Thomas Perry, bestselling author

"Siger is a superb writer... Best of all, he creates the atmosphere of modern Greece in vivid, believable detail, from the magnificence of its antiquities to the decadence of its power bearers and the squalor of its slums."
—*Pittsburgh Post-Gazette*

"This is international police procedural writing at its best and should be recommended, in particular, to readers who enjoy Leighton Gage's Brazilian police stories or Hakan Nesser's Swedish inspector Van Veeteren."
—*Booklist*, Starred Review

"With few mysteries set in Greece, the author, a longtime resident of Mykonos, vividly captures this unfamiliar terrain's people and culture. Mystery fans who like their police procedurals in exotic locales will welcome this one."
—*Library Journal*

Murder in Mykonos
The First Chief Inspector Andreas Kaldis Mystery

"Siger's intimate knowledge of Mykonos adds color and interest to his serviceable prose and his simple premise. The result is a surprisingly effective debut novel."

—Kirkus Reviews

"Siger's view of Mykonos (where he lives part-time) is nicely nuanced, as is the mystery's ambiguous resolution. Kaldis's feisty personality and complex backstory are appealing as well, solid foundations for a projected series."

—Publishers Weekly

"Siger...captures the rare beauty of the Greek islands in this series debut."

—Library Journal

"Siger's Mykonos seems an unrelievedly hedonistic place, especially given the community's religious orthodoxy, but suspense builds nicely as the story alternates between the perspectives of the captive woman, the twisted kidnapper, and the cop on whose shoulders the investigation falls. In the end, Andreas finds more than he bargained for, and readers will be well pleased."

—Booklist

Also by Jeffrey Siger

The Chief Inspector Andreas Kaldis Mysteries
Murder in Mykonos
Assassins of Athens
Prey on Patmos
Target: Tinos
Mykonos After Midnight
Sons of Sparta
Devil of Delphi
Santorini Caesars
An Aegean April
Island of Secrets (First Published as *The Mykonos Mob*)
A Deadly Twist

ONE LAST CHANCE

A CHIEF INSPECTOR ANDREAS KALDIS MYSTERY

JEFFREY SIGER

Poisoned Pen
PRESS

Published by Poisoned Pen Press, an imprint of Sourcebooks
P.O. Box 4410, Naperville, Illinois 60567-4410
(630) 961-3900
sourcebooks.com

Library of Congress Cataloging-in-Publication Data

Names: Siger, Jeffrey, author.
Title: One last chance : a Chief Inspector Andreas Kaldis mystery / Jeffrey
    Siger.
Description: Naperville, Illinois : Poisoned Pen Press, [2022] | Series:
    The Chief Inspector Andreas Kaldis mysteries ; book 12
Identifiers: LCCN 2021042289 (print) | LCCN 2021042290
(ebook) | (trade paperback) | (hardcover) | (epub)
Subjects: LCGFT: Novels.
Classification: LCC PS3619.I45 O54 2022 (print) | LCC PS3619.I45 (ebook)
    | DDC 813/.6--dc23
LC record available at https://lccn.loc.gov/2021042289
LC ebook record available at https://lccn.loc.gov/2021042290

Printed and bound in the United States of America.
VP 10 9 8 7 6 5 4 3 2 1

To Rick, Steven, Carli, Danny, and my ever-expanding band of grandnephews and grandnieces.

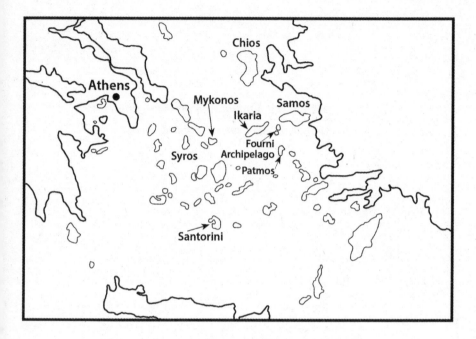

Aegean Sea
(Depicting Relevant Islands)

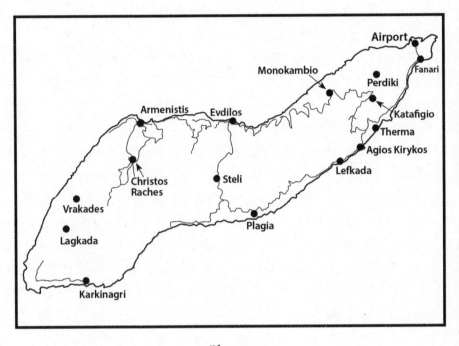

Ikaria

Chapter One

Magdalena Zaoutis knew every pebble, rut, root, and pothole on the mountain path from her ancestral cottage down to the local spring. She made the trek every day, whether she needed water or not. She'd been doing it for more than a hundred years, first with her mother when she was four, later with her own children, grandchildren, and their children and grandchildren. She saw no reason to stop now.

Many of her family members had moved to the Greek mainland, other islands, or foreign countries to escape the harsh subsistence common on the northern Aegean island of Ikaria. But making a life away from this place, now known to the world as "the island where people forget to die," came at a price, and Magdalena wore black as a sign of her continual mourning for the husband, four children, and three grandchildren who'd passed away while she lived on.

Longevity was the great blessing—or curse—of a life lived on Ikaria. The average lifespan for men and women extended ten years longer than elsewhere in Greece, and one in three residents made it into their nineties. Living past one hundred was not uncommon, and those who made it to centenarian status enjoyed a special camaraderie forged through a shared century of maintaining the traditions and observances of their uniquely rigorous island way of life.

Magdalena was cheery by nature, not one to dwell on unhappy thoughts, but today she felt particularly sad. The hardest deaths for her to endure, other than those among her family, were of childhood mates who'd also made it to the century mark, or close to it. In each passing she saw a bit of her own past die with them. Their deaths were to be expected, of course, but over the past weeks, so many of her friends from other parts of the island, indeed some of the healthiest, had passed on within days of each other. She wished there were no more funerals to attend, except perhaps for her own.

No, not yet.

She'd survived the pandemics of 1918–1920 and 2020–2022. It was not yet her time.

She heard the somber tolling of the church bells echoing up from the village through the craggy rock and pine tree ravine running by her stone home. In spring, this deep, narrow gorge carried rushing water from the mountain that loomed above her cottage. But for now it brought news of life events for those who understood the cadence of the bells. Today they spoke of another soul leaving Magdalena's world. *Who?* she wondered. Surely she would know the deceased, or at least someone in the family. She knew all the families, except of course for the newcomers, but few of them stayed past summer.

One of her grandchildren would tell her who had passed on, along with other news from the island grapevine. She no longer walked to town to keep up with the gossip. They wouldn't allow her to make the journey. If they could, they'd have stopped her from making her daily trip to the spring.

She smiled, then sighed. *I know it's because they care about me. But I can't stop now. I have more to do.*

———

Greece's General Police Headquarters, better known as GADA, sat close by the heart of Athens's bustle, down the block from Greece's Supreme Court, across the street from the stadium of one of Greece's most popular soccer teams, and next door to a major hospital. GADA's Special Crimes Unit, headed by Chief Inspector Andreas Kaldis, charged with investigating potential corruption and other matters of national concern, occupied the eastern side of the fourth floor.

Andreas sat at his desk reading a report when a compact, five-foot-three, redheaded ball of energy poked her head through the doorway. "Morning, Chief."

Andreas smiled at his administrative assistant. "Morning, Maggie."

"May I speak with you?"

Andreas's smile faded as he put down the report. "For you to even ask means it must be serious."

Maggie stepped into the office and shut the door.

"Now I know it's serious. Please don't tell me you're retiring."

"What, and give up the endless joy of tormenting you? No such luck, Chief."

They'd been doing their variation on a vaudeville act since he'd returned to GADA from a brief stint as police chief on the island of Mykonos. The luck of the draw had landed him with Maggie Sikestis, GADA's mother superior and source of all wisdom on its many secret ways.

"Okay, then what is it?" He gestured for her to sit in one of the two chairs across from him.

She sighed as she sat, her eyes welling up with tears.

Andreas jumped up and hurried around his desk to sit in the

chair next to her. He reached to take her hand. "What's wrong? Are you ill?"

In the way of Greek women, she gestured *no* with a quick upward lift of her eyebrows.

"Is it Tassos?"

Tassos Stamatos, Andreas's mentor since his days on Mykonos, reigned as Chief Homicide Investigator for the Cycladic Islands from its capital island of Syros. Tassos and Maggie had been an item since the moment Andreas had unknowingly rekindled an old romance between his widower friend and the never-married Maggie.

Again she gestured no, drawing in and letting out a deep breath as she did. "We're both fine. It's my *yaya*."

"Your *grandmother*?"

"Don't sound so surprised," sniped Maggie. "You might think I'm old enough to be your mother, but I come from sturdy Ikariot stock."

"Sorry, but you've said your mother passed away, so it never occurred to me that your grandmother might still be alive."

Maggie shut her eyes. "My mother died in an automobile accident. Otherwise she'd still be with us."

Andreas squeezed her hand and waited for her to continue.

She looked up at him. "Yaya passed away early this morning. I brought my suitcase to the office. I need to leave early so that I can make it to the airport in time to catch the flight to Ikaria."

"Absolutely. Take off as much time as you need."

She squeezed his hand. "Thanks, Chief."

"You do realize that Lila will insist we attend the service."

"How sweetly you put that, making it seem as if you otherwise wouldn't think of coming."

Andreas blushed. "You know we'll be there."

"There's no reason for you to come. The funeral is tomorrow

morning, and my flight's the only one that will get me there in time for the service. The only alternative is a ten-hour ferry ride."

"We have friends with boats and planes who can get us there sooner."

Maggie shook her head. "I know you'd find a way to be there, and I love you and Lila for that, but to be perfectly honest, if you came, I'd feel obliged to make sure you're properly looked after. Frankly, I don't need that additional burden at the moment."

Andreas nodded. "Whatever you say." He patted her hand and smiled, "I must say, though, it's interesting how you managed to convert my heartfelt gesture of compassionate support into a thoughtless imposition."

"It's a gift." At last, she gave him a smile.

"How old was your *yaya*?"

"She'd have turned one hundred and five next month."

Andreas crossed himself. "God bless her soul."

"She was a feisty, upbeat lady until the end, even after burying all her children. She blamed their deaths on leaving Ikaria. Even my mother's death in a car accident she blamed on her moving to Athens." Maggie shook her finger and spoke in a creaky voice: "Maggie, if your mother had listened to me and stayed where she belonged, she'd have been walking, not riding in an automobile."

Andreas laughed. "Sounds like a special lady."

Maggie sighed, "She was. And had a good run."

"We should all be so blessed."

"Amen."

"At least let me make arrangements to get you to the airport."

"No reason to put you out."

"You won't be. I'll get Yianni to drive you."

Yianni Kouros had been Andreas's right-hand man since their days together on Mykonos, when Yianni was a brash young bull-of-a-rookie cop.

"How will you possibly function with both of us out of the office at the same time?"

"I'll leave one of those incessantly chatty television news shows running in the background until Yianni gets back. That way it will seem as if you never left."

Maggie feigned a scowl. "You're going to miss me when I'm gone."

Andreas leaned over and kissed her on the cheek. "Already do."

Chapter Two

Athens's Venizelos International Airport was a half hour or so from GADA, but Yianni made it in twenty minutes.

"Who's going to stop me?" he said to Maggie when she suggested he drop below 160 kilometers per hour.

"Hopefully, not the good Lord."

Yianni accompanied Maggie through check-in and security, then waited with her until her flight was called to board. After hugging her goodbye and wishing her *kalo taxidhi* for a safe trip, he reached into his pocket and pulled out a brand-new surgical mask.

"I know they're no longer required, but wear it, just to be on the safe side."

Maggie took it and patted him on the cheek. "You're a good boy."

On the shuttle from the terminal to the plane Maggie studied the faces crowded into the bus. She hadn't been on a plane since the pandemic first hit and wondered if her fellow passengers held the same mixed feelings as she did about flying. She guessed it only natural to question whether it was the prudent thing to do.

Though Ikaria was only 130 miles by air from Athens, Maggie hadn't seen Yaya for more than two years. The times simply hadn't allowed it. But they'd spoken often, and whenever Maggie raised the possibly of Yaya coming to live with her in Athens, where medical care far exceeded that available on the islands, she'd given the same answer. "Don't worry, we Ikariots are used to living isolated from the rest of the world."

Arguing that point with Yaya was useless, for she epitomized her island's fiercely independent roots. Reputedly inhabited since 7000 BCE, Ikaria's rugged mountainous terrain, lack of decent ports, brutal winds, and reputation as the poorest island in the Aegean discouraged virtually all but pirates and conquerors from paying it much mind. Indeed, in 1829, when Greece obtained its independence from the Ottoman Empire, Ikaria remained under Ottoman rule. Not until 1912, when Ikariots tossed out the Turks, did it join modern Greece—following five proud months as the independent country of the Free State of Ikaria, complete with its own flag, anthem, and postage stamps. But joining Greece did little to change the Ikariots' historical skepticism toward outside help, in that for much of the twentieth century, the Greek government gave little more than sporadic assistance to the island, and used it as a place of banishment for thousands of political dissidents.

Today, tourism drives Ikaria's economy, fueled by its international reputation as one of the world's five Blue Zones, where a hardy, long-living population thrived on a lifestyle and diet that regularly saw Ikariots living to an advanced age.

Once nestled in her window seat, Maggie shut her eyes and thought back to the many summers she'd spent with her mother visiting Yaya at her mountainside cottage. Maggie's mother and grandmother were born on that property, as were Yaya's mother, grandmother, and more generations of the family than Maggie could trace. The one-room house in which Yaya had lived was built in the time of pirates, when that scourge of the Aegean raided islands for booty, slaves, and women, often slaughtering those inhabitants they didn't spirit away.

Like many such houses, Yaya's was built with an eye to security from marauders. It stood on the inside of a ravine, fashioned out of stone to camouflage it from invaders scanning the hillsides for signs of life, and laced with hidden passages and false walls in case the house was detected. There was also a newer, two-story house on the property, built in the early part of the twentieth century—after the time of pirates—on ground away from the ravine and overlooking the sea. It offered more space and conveniences, but when Yaya became matriarch of the family, she chose to live in the one-room *chyto* where her ancestors had been born, leaving the larger, modern home to the younger generation.

Maggie'd had all those places to explore, in addition to a vineyard, orchards of lemons, oranges, grapefruit, figs, apricots, almonds, and olives, tended gardens filled with squash, beans, tomatoes, eggplants, peppers, beets, onions, and potatoes, wild-growing oregano, thyme, rosemary, chamomile, basil, and more, plus a stone shed for Yaya's goats and pigs.

It had been a barefooted young girl's paradise.

———

Maggie fell asleep soon after the plane took off, waking forty-five minutes later as it neared the island. Travelers arriving by sea often described Ikaria's profile as an overturned ship set atop the azure sea. But from the sky, looking down at its mountainous spine, sharp slopes to the south, and isolated plains to the north, she had a different thought: How did such a stark and stony landscape, at the mercy of harsh winds, thunderous storms, and roiling seas regularly assaulting it across 400 kilometers of open water, manage to support so much lush greenery?

Ikaria looked like an elongated version of the American state of New Jersey turned on its side, but was less than one-tenth the size of the state of Rhode Island. Its population of 8,500 lived among seventy inhabited villages and towns dispersed over three municipal units around the capital town of Agios Kirykos to the south, the former capital of Evdilos to the north, and Raches to the west.

Ikaria National Airport ran north-south, spanning nearly the width of the island between the seas at its eastern tip, in the rural area of Fanari. With a runway too short to comfortably accommodate most jets, its modest terminal retained the flavor of its mid-1990s origins.

The first person Maggie saw when she stepped inside the small terminal was Tassos. He stood smiling by a statue representing Ikaros, or Icarus, the mythical son who hadn't heeded his father's warning not to fly too close to the sun on his wax wings. As legend had it, Ikaros fell to earth and perished on rocks off the southern coastline, midway along the island that now bore his name.

"I didn't think you'd be here until tomorrow morning," she said, giving him a big hug and kiss.

He took her roller bag. "A friend on Syros is from Ikaria. He has a fast boat, and I convinced him it was time to pay a visit to his family. We're heading back tomorrow after the funeral." He paused. "Unless, of course, you'd like me to stay longer."

She wound her arm through his and squeezed. "That's wonderful of you to offer, but I've got a lot of family stuff to sort through with my cousins. You'd be bored to death."

"When are you planning to return to Athens?"

"After the *Trisagio* service."

"Nine days after Yaya's passing?"

"Yes, on *Enniamera*."

"Maybe I can come back before then…if it's okay with you?"

"I'd like that." She squeezed his arm tighter. "By the way, why are we standing here?"

"I thought we're waiting for your luggage."

"I only have this bag."

"For more than a week's stay? I'm impressed."

"I had no choice. The hike up the hill to Yaya's house is a killer, and I'm long past the day when I could rely upon some big strong Greek Adonis coming to my rescue to carry my bag."

"I think you just dated yourself and insulted me."

"Reality's a bitch," she said with a smile.

Tassos chuckled.

"Do you have a car? Taxis are hard to come by at the airport if you haven't arranged ahead. I planned on calling a cousin to pick me up if I couldn't find one."

"Don't worry, we're covered."

A marked police car waited outside the terminal entrance.

"How did you manage this? Wait, don't tell me. Someone on the Ikaria police force owed you a favor. It seems everywhere we go you're owed a favor."

"I've learned that if you're nice to people, they'll be nice to you in return."

"I sense for you it's more like, 'Be nice to me because I know where your bodies are buried.'"

Tassos shrugged. "With some folk that's the way it has to be, but not with this island's chief of police. I helped train him, and a few years back recommended him for this position."

"And he considered that a favor?"

Tassos grinned. "His wife's a local, and she wanted to come home."

"I like him already."

A slim, tousle-haired young cop jumped out of the front seat, took the bag from Tassos, and put it in the trunk.

"Thanks, Dimitri. This is my friend, Maggie. She works with Special Crimes out of GADA, so be careful what you say around her."

Dimitri smiled. "A pleasure to meet you, Miss Maggie. So sorry about your *yaya*'s death."

"Thank you," nodded Maggie. "Do you know where I'm going?"

"Tassos told me to your *yaya*'s."

Maggie looked at Tassos. "I'll be there tonight along with the rest of the family watching over Yaya's remains until the funeral."

Tassos nodded. "I figured as much. That's why I booked a room as close to her house as I could find, just in case you wanted to get some sleep before the funeral. You won't be getting any at her house tonight."

She sighed. "I know."

They slid into the back seat as Dimitri started the engine.

"Do you know where it is?" she asked Dimitri.

"I was born and raised here, which means I know your *yaya*'s house."

"You knew her?" asked Maggie.

"Everyone did. Her hospitality was legendary. Her door was always open to generations of locals who loved hearing her tell stories of the island's past."

Maggie smiled and sighed. "I'm named after her, but no one calls me Magdalena."

Dimitri nodded. "She still had such a quick wit and sharp tongue for her age."

Maggie stared at Tassos. "Don't you dare say a word."

Tassos raised his hands in surrender. "I'm not that brave."

———

The twenty-minute drive from the airport to the port at Agios Kirykos followed a paved two-lane road that, on Ikaria, qualified as a highway. Eleven kilometers beyond the airport, the road split into two branches; one continued along the south coast toward Agios Kirykos, and the other went north toward Evdilos, the island's second port and center of northern and central Ikaria, before winding on to coastal western Ikaria.

Ikaria's roads were a notorious adventure for drivers and pedestrians alike. Narrow and winding snakelike around hills, mountainsides, and ravines, with barely a guardrail to be found, whether paved or unpaved, they presented treacherously harrowing experiences for the uninitiated. Some roads narrowed to close to seven feet wide when they passed through a village, squeezed between a house on one side and a sheer drop-off on the other, making horn-honking around corners a necessary survival tool.

The island's many unpaved roads seemed more suitable for goats than vehicles, and all were subject to the harsh vagaries of nature. A few years back, a portion of the main road along Ikaria's southern coast had washed away, forcing travelers to employ boats or wildly circuitous detours to get beyond the closure. Ikariots accepted such long-lasting inconveniences as yet another challenge to endure and overcome as part of their arduous, self-reliant way of life.

Maggie rested her head against Tassos's shoulder as the car wound southwest between the blue of the sea and the many greens, browns, and grays nature had bestowed upon her ancestral island. Her thoughts drifted to Yaya's tales of the island's once-vast forests. Ancient oak, pine, fir, plane, and cedar trees that had long ago fallen victim to indiscriminate logging, a voracious charcoal industry, and, in more modern times, those who saw forests as an impediment to their plans for developing or farming the land. Much of what had once been dense forests had been razed for development or overrun by impenetrable scrub brush.

A remembrance of Ikaria's heavily wooded past still could be found in the six-square-mile Randi Forest, the oldest forest in the Balkans. Within its boundaries grew three-hundred-year-old holm oaks, the last remaining link to a species dating back five million years. They survived only because the European Union had designated the preserve a protected ecosystem.

As Maggie saw it, the passing of the age of pirates had not ended the looting of her island, but only given rise to a more insidious breed of plundering profiteers.

Suddenly, she giggled.

"What's so funny?" asked Tassos, patting Maggie on her arm.

"I'd just had an anti-capitalist thought and realized that if ever there was a place to have one, it's here."

"Yep, Red Rock is certainly the place for that."

"I'm not sure calling it Red Rock would go over well with the locals."

"But that's its nickname. Besides, I thought Ikaria was proud of its leftist heritage."

"It's how they earned the nickname that grates on them."

"I've no quarrel with why they're pissed off at the nickname, but you have to admit the political climate on the island is distinctly leftist."

"How could it not be after what the national government put it through after the dreadful starvation years of World War II— and then four more years of civil war between nationalists and communists?" said Maggie. "But there's more to the story. Lots of the thirteen thousand communists banished to Ikaria after the civil war were educated—doctors, lawyers, teachers, and creative types. The government wouldn't let them live with locals, and their movements were restricted, but with so many needing places to stay, and the government offering little assistance in the way of food and shelter for the exiles, they ended up living in virtually every unoccupied house on the island. Many of those homes were in desperate need of repair, so the exiles fixed them up. Over time, locals came to regard them as welcome guests, not criminals, and after their banishment ended, many came back as tourists to visit the friends they made during their years of exile."

"Sounds like the law of unintended consequences at work. The government picked Ikaria as a place of containment for those with unwelcome political views, but instead created a sanctuary and breeding ground for dissident thinking."

Maggie pointed to a graffiti-covered retaining wall bearing the symbols of splinter political parties, revolutionary groups, and die-hard soccer fans. "And its progeny are still with us."

"Indeed," said Tassos. "Welcome home."

———

A few kilometers west of Agios Kirykos, Maggie leaned forward and pointed toward a sign on the right marking a hiking trail. "Here we are."

"You must be kidding," said Tassos. "Do you really expect us to lug your suitcase up that mountain?"

"Not *us*, me. I'm used to it."

"I can't let you do that."

"Stop being macho."

"My heart's fine. I'll do it."

"I won't let you risk it."

"Uh, may I interrupt?" said Dimitri, pulling up to the sign.

"Don't bother. I'm not going to let you carry it either," snapped Maggie.

"Well," Dimitri continued, "it's more than a kilometer up to your *yaya's* house. I think it would be easier if you allowed me to drive you there."

"Drive? How can you do that?"

"I suspect you haven't been back for a while. A couple years ago, a developer built half a dozen vacation homes on the mountain to take advantage of the view of the sea. He built an access road to get his equipment up there, and improved it a bit to attract the sort of upscale buyer who would never buy a house requiring a long, steep hike to get there."

"So much for taking advantage of the island's healthy lifestyle," said Tassos.

"The road runs within a hundred meters of your *yaya's* home, and the walk from the road to her house is a lot easier than this one." He nodded toward the path.

"I can't believe it," said Maggie.

"The island's growing," said Dimitri. "It's always attracted tourists with roots on Ikaria, but now it's drawing those who see it as a fountain of youth. Plus, it's become a magnet for young people from Athens over the summer."

"Why's that?" asked Maggie.

"A lot of reasons. It's a lot cheaper than, say, Mykonos. The surfing is great, and they're allowed to camp on the beach. Plus—and this is unofficial—no one hassles them when they smoke dope."

"Sound like modern-day hippies," said Maggie.

"Straight out of Athens alternative-lifestyle neighborhoods, like Exarchia."

"Whatever the reason, I vote for driving there," said Tassos.

Dimitri pulled back onto the road and, 150 meters along, turned right onto a narrow dirt lane.

"It looks barely wide enough for two donkeys to pass each other," said Maggie.

"I think the developer described it as 'a quaint pathway to paradise.'"

"Has he sold all the units?" asked Tassos.

Dimitri nodded. "But not to native Greeks. Foreigners are the ones with money these days. Greeks with money tend to want to spend their holidays on 'sexier' islands."

"They should only know what they're missing," said Maggie, squeezing Tassos's hand.

The road wound up the hillside toward a cluster of two-story stucco homes angled so that their broad picture windows had unobstructed views of the sea.

"I can't think of anything less in keeping with Ikaria's historical camouflage-where-you-live architecture than those…fishbowls," said Maggie, shaking her head. "Yaya must have hated them."

"As an adjacent property owner, she probably could have stopped them, if she'd wanted to," said Dimitri. "But she wasn't like a lot of Ikariots or, for that matter, islanders in general. She wasn't jealous of her neighbors. Once, when I stopped by to say hello and check on her, I asked what she thought about the new construction. She said she didn't love it but didn't let it bother her either. 'Progress,' she said."

"God bless her," said Tassos. "Sounds like the sort of philosophy that gets you past a hundred."

Dimitri stopped about fifty meters before the new houses at a narrow path off to the right. "Here we are." He popped open the trunk and went to get Maggie's bag while she and Tassos climbed out of the back seat. "Your *yaya's* place is a hundred meters down that path. I'm happy to carry the bag there for you, if you'd like."

"Thank you for the offer, Dimitri," said Maggie, turning toward Tassos, "but I'm sure my big, strong Adonis can handle it from here."

Tassos laughed as he gripped the roller bag by its handle and started toward the path. "I think I've just been hustled."

Maggie stepped in behind him, gently pinching him on the butt. "Admit it, you love it."

———

Maggie and Tassos strolled hand in hand along a path running through Yaya's vineyard and orchards, past the two-story house where some of Yaya's great-grandchildren now lived with their parents, to the edge of a steep, rocky ravine. They carefully made their way down the side of the ravine on rough-hewn stone steps that opened onto a broad ledge. Tucked back on the ledge against the side of the ravine and extending back into what looked to be a cave, stood Yaya's cottage. Every visible bit of the cottage, except for its front door and two small windows, was made of stone, with not a hint of color to be seen. Camouflage, indeed.

"What's down there?" said Tassos, pointing to more stone steps leading down into the ravine.

"Can't you see it?"

"See what?"

"The goat shed."

"All I see are rocks."

"That's all you're supposed to see. There's a much narrower ledge down there, and if you look closely, you'll see two huge boulders slanted back against the face of the ravine."

"Yeah, I see them."

"They form the entrance to a stone goat shed that extends back along the side of the ravine beyond the two boulders."

Tassos shook his head. "I don't see a thing."

As if on cue, a black-and-white goat made its way out from beneath the boulders.

"Amazing," he said with a smile.

"I know. Ikariots are masters of disguise."

"Maggie," screamed a black-clad, gray-haired woman from the cottage doorway.

"Who's that?" asked Tassos.

"One of my mother's closest childhood friends." Maggie and the woman hugged and kissed. "This is my friend, Tassos."

"A pleasure to meet you," nodded Tassos.

She nodded back and said to Maggie, "Come, the family will be excited to see you."

Maggie turned to Tassos. "Are you coming in?"

"Just to offer my condolences." Tassos put Maggie's bag off to the side of the doorway. "Dimitri's waiting for me back at the car."

Maggie stepped inside the cottage to a chorus of greetings and an avalanche of hugs and kisses. A long single room, now packed with mourners, served as living room, dining room, kitchen, and bedroom. A modest bathroom had been added after the civil war years, along with running water and electricity. Telephone service had only arrived with the cellphone.

At the far end of the room, resting on chairs, sat the open coffin, surrounded by women in black chanting among themselves, while men huddled together off to the side, reflecting on memories of Yaya. The plastered walls around them were adorned with various icons, a faded photographic portrait of Yaya and her husband at their wedding, and identically framed photographs of each of her children when they were young.

Maggie made her way to the coffin, stood silently for a moment, said a prayer, crossed herself, and kissed Yaya on the forehead.

"How are you doing, my love?" whispered Tassos, coming up behind her.

Without taking her eyes off Yaya, she said, "As well as can be expected. Yaya led the life she wanted for a very long time. And in good health right up until the end. You can't ask for more than that."

"No, you can't." He paused. "She must have really loved you."

"Why do you say that?"

"She kept a photo of you." Tassos pointed to a photograph on a small table.

Maggie laughed.

"What's so funny?" barked a thin, white-haired gentleman, shuffling toward the coffin and shaking his cane at the two of them.

Maggie smiled. "My friend here saw the photograph on the table and thought it was me." She turned to Tassos. "It's Yaya, forty-plus years ago."

The old man squinted. "You do look a lot like her." Then he squinted at Tassos. "I think I know you."

"It's possible. We're both from the Cyclades and old enough to have bumped into each other many times."

"It was more than a bump."

Tassos shrugged. "Could be."

"Have you ever been arrested?" said the old man.

"Not yet, but there's always time." Tassos turned to Maggie and spoke in her ear: "I think I better leave now before he connects me to something uncomfortable in his past."

"Don't be silly."

"Remember, I worked for the Junta…can't imagine Ikariots having fond memories of those days."

"You'd be surprised," she whispered. "A lot of desperately needed infrastructure projects got underway here under the Junta. Besides, it's all in the past."

"*Tassos*," exclaimed the old man. "I thought I recognized you."

"Here we go…" Tassos turned to face the old man. "I'm flattered you remember me, sir."

"You're as glib today as you were as a prison guard for the Junta." He spat on the word Junta.

"I'm afraid you have me at a disadvantage, sir. To whom do I have the pleasure of speaking?"

"Mihali Bursakos, but you wouldn't remember me. I was only in Giaros Prison for a couple of weeks."

"I'm impressed at your memory, but may I ask why you remember me?"

"Because of the way you treated your communist prisoners." The man moved closer.

Tassos forced a smile but said nothing.

"We were beaten and abused, as refugees are today."

Tassos casually moved away from Maggie. "Whoa. I didn't go in for any of that back then, and I still don't."

"Yet you worked for a dictatorship that imprisoned us because of our political views."

"What can I say? It was my job. But I did nothing I'm ashamed of." Tassos braced for what might happen next.

"I know." The man smiled and patted Tassos on the shoulder. "You always treated us with respect, never struck us, and I once saw you stop a guard from beating a prisoner."

Tassos let out a deep breath. "I'm amazed you remember that some fifty years later."

"When your life is in the hands of your jailers, you remember those who treated you fairly."

"That's very nice to hear. Thank you."

Mihali nodded, turned, and hobbled toward the gathered men.

"I think I better leave before someone remembers me in a less-flattering light," he told Maggie, sotto voce.

"A wise move, my love."

He kissed her on the cheek. "Call me if you want to get some rest. My room's in the village at the bottom of the hill."

She kissed him back. "Don't wait up."

———

Late into the evening, somber visitors kept passing through the cottage to pay their respects to Yaya, many bringing food and drink for the mourners. Descendants of Yaya and her contemporaries each told tales of her impact on their lives, some eliciting smiles, others tears, but all serving as a blessing to her memory.

A little past midnight, Maggie sat alone by the coffin, gently stroking Yaya's hand, lost in memories. She sensed someone standing behind her and turned to see who was there. "Mr. Mihali. Why are you still here? You must be exhausted. Please go home and get some rest."

"Your *yaya* was very special to me. I thought of her as my best friend. Many of us did." He fixed his eyes on Yaya's face. "I can't believe she's gone. Always so cheery, always looking forward to making new friends."

Maggie pointed to a wooden chair next to hers. "Please, sit down."

Mihali carefully lowered himself onto the chair. "She once told me how much she loved having young friends." He smiled. "Like me in my nineties. But I know she missed her many old friends who'd passed away decades ago."

"She was blessed to have friends like you."

Mihali sighed, "So sad." He patted Maggie on the shoulder. "I only wish her final days hadn't been so difficult."

Maggie blinked. "What do you mean? I thought she passed away peacefully in her sleep."

"She did, but the last two weeks saw many Ikariots close to her age pass away unexpectedly, and that upset her."

"She never said anything about any of that to me," said Maggie.

"I'm not surprised. Those of us up in years who value our independence don't like sharing 'end-is-near' thoughts with our families. That only starts them pestering us to move in with them or to a care facility."

Maggie nodded. "That sounds like Yaya."

"What bothered her was how many of those who died were in good enough health to be living relatively independently." He looked into the coffin. "Just like her."

Maggie let go of Yaya's hand and turned to face Mihali. "What are you trying to tell me?"

Mihali shrugged. "Nothing more than what was on her mind."

Maggie fixed her eyes on Mihali's. "I'm more interested in what's on *your* mind."

Mihali sighed, then met her stare. "No one can recall so many elders passing away over such a brief period. Not even during the pandemic."

"Suggesting what?"

"I'm only telling you what I know. Whether the deaths are anything more than coincidence, I cannot say. But I know your friend is a policeman, and Yaya always spoke proudly of your work at GADA. You are in a far better position than I to determine if more than coincidence is at play."

Maggie stiffened, maintaining her stare. "Do you know the names of those who died?"

"Some, but there may have been others."

Maggie reached into her bag, pulled out a notebook and pen, and handed them to Mihali. "Please write down the names, and the names of any family members you think I should speak to."

Maggie watched him carefully write out the names. "You have exceptionally good handwriting."

"Thank you. It's a habit formed over many years as a pharmacist. Doctors have such horrible handwriting...I suppose it's an act of resistance. Creating order from chaos."

Maggie smiled. "That sounds like my relationship with my boss. Are you still practicing?"

"No, but my granddaughter has a pharmacy in Evdilos near where I now live, and she allows me to stop by and bother her." He handed Maggie her notebook and pen. "These are the four I know of who passed away before Yaya."

Maggie leaned in toward Mihali. "You might claim not to be suggesting anything, but I'm sure you appreciate that what you're telling me is alarming. Is there anything more you think I should know?"

He bit at his lip. "They all died alone at home in their sleep."

"Anything else?"

He looked back at Yaya's coffin. "None had an autopsy."

Chapter Three

Rural Greek burials took place as soon as possible after death, usually within a day or so, and without embalming. Families relied on the women of the community to prepare the body for viewing and burial. In virtually no other aspect of Greek life was the role of women as dominant as in the matter of funerals. Not only in cleansing, preparing, and dressing the body, but as anguished mourners, sobbing, crying, shrieking, wailing, hair-pulling, and lamenting over the deceased.

Maggie had tried dozing off in a chair by the coffin, but mourners seeking to outdo one another in demonstrations of their grief kept jarring her awake. She considered going to the main house to sleep, but felt she'd be abandoning Yaya. So she tried to snatch as much of a nap as the mourners would allow, reflecting as she did on her conversation with Mihali.

It must be coincidence. Perhaps a common infection? She couldn't imagine foul play. Violent crime was literally unheard of on Ikaria. And certainly not crimes committed against its most revered citizens.

She drifted off again, until a rooster let loose with his morning call.

"That's it," said Maggie to no one in particular, jerking awake and pushing herself out of her chair. She looked at the old woman next to her. "If anyone comes looking for me, please tell them I'm up at the main house taking a shower and getting ready for church."

The old woman nodded, but not in a way that had Maggie thinking she understood. Not that it mattered. Anyone looking for Maggie could find her easily enough.

The cicadas were well into their morning song when Maggie, dragging her rolling suitcase, made her way up the uneven rocky steps to the top of the ravine. She marveled at how Yaya had managed to make that trek so many times each day for so many years, often carrying much more than Maggie carried now. Once at the top, she stopped and stared off toward the sea, still tinted rose from the rising sun.

Hard to imagine Yaya gone…and so suddenly.

Of course, it always felt sudden.

She shook her head and walked toward the main house. Mihali's conversation had aroused her curiosity, and now she sensed it working its way into her thoughts of Yaya's final days. For now, though, she had to put such thinking out of her mind and focus on the funeral. After all, that's why she was here—not to be distracted by an old Greek man's conspiracy theory. And certainly not on Ikaria, ground zero for that sort of thinking.

She stepped up her pace and, upon reaching the house, found her cousins awake, dressed, and eating breakfast. By the time she'd showered and changed clothes, her cousins had left to join the procession that would accompany Yaya's coffin up from the cottage and through the family's orchards and vineyard to the new road, where a vehicle waited to carry Yaya to church.

Maggie decided to wait in front of the main house for the procession to pass by, rather than pushing her way into the crowd massed by the cottage. Many people had loved Yaya, and this was their day to honor her.

She heard the sounds of the procession before seeing six of her young male cousins emerge from the ravine carrying their *yaya*'s coffin. Once the pallbearers had passed, Maggie stepped in behind the coffin to join her family and held the offered hands on either side of her.

The path to the new road wended its way through an ancient olive grove. Yaya had played among those same trees as a young girl. Maggie wondered what she might have pondered while roaming this land. Likely the same sort of things all little girls wondered: What would her life be like? Who would she marry? How many children would she have?

That's when it hit her. Her grandmother was passing through these familiar sites for the very last time.

Maggie burst into tears and did not stop crying until the coffin was aboard the vehicle and on its way to the church, leaving her and the other mourners to find their own way there.

"Hey, need a ride?" shouted one of her cousins from his car.

"No, thank you," dabbing at her eyes with a handkerchief. "I can use the walk."

She did her best to compose herself as she watched the line of cars slowly follow Yaya's coffin down the hill.

She'd just started making her way down the road when she felt an arm slide under her own.

"I hope you don't mind me leaning on you, but my walking legs aren't as steady as yours," said an old woman, clad head to toe in black.

"It would be my honor," said Maggie, patting the woman's hand. "But why don't you ride in one of the cars?"

"Tradition calls for me to walk."

Maggie nodded. "You look familiar."

"I'm Calliope. Last night you asked me to tell anyone who might be looking for you where to find you."

Maggie nodded. "Sorry, I should have recognized you."

"You've had a lot on your mind, I'm sure."

"Thank you for coming last night and staying as long as you did."

"I take it as my obligation."

Maggie turned slightly to get a better look at Calliope's face. "Are you family? If so, I owe you an even bigger apology."

Calliope chuckled. "No, not family, but I feel an obligation to stay with those I prepare for their final journey."

"I'm sorry, I don't understand what you mean."

"I was her *savanotria*. I bathed and prepared her after she passed away."

A thousand questions raced through Maggie's mind, but this was not the time or place to ask them.

Maggie glanced up at the sky. *Or is it?*

———

Tassos stood outside the stone-and-stucco church at the heart of the village, waiting for Maggie and the coffin to arrive. The line of cars parked along the road running past the church had narrowed the road down to a single lane, requiring patience by drivers heading in opposite directions. But no horns honked, no one shouted, and everyone managed to figure out a way to get past without disturbing the mourners.

Tassos's mobile rang. He looked at the caller ID. "Top of the morning, Andreas."

"You're sounding chipper for someone at a funeral."

"I'm inspired by the thought of possibly making it to a hundred."

"Good thinking. How's Maggie doing?"

"I'm guessing she's exhausted from her all-nighter with the family, but I haven't heard from her since we said goodbye at her *yaya's* house. I'm waiting for her and the procession to arrive at the church."

"Please pass along Lila's and my love and condolences. We tried reaching her, but her phone must be off."

"Give her mine too," said Yianni, chiming in on Andreas's speakerphone.

"Will do." Tassos paused. "The procession's arriving now."

"Well, I'll let you go."

"No need to hang up. Maggie's not here yet, and nothing's going to start for a while."

"You sound lonely."

"Nah, it's just been a weird morning."

"How so?"

"I was having coffee at a *kafenion* when an old-timer tried to get me to buy a chance at his lotto game."

"With all the computerized instant-payoff games out there, I didn't think any of those guys were still hustling their private rackets."

"This guy had a novel angle for his. He was selling blind chances for five euros each, and if the ticket you bought turned out to contain the winning numbers, you and he split the pot fifty-fifty."

"That doesn't sound so weird," said Yianni.

"The weird part was what he meant by 'the winning numbers…'"

"And?" asked Andreas. "Are you waiting for the drama to build before you deliver the punchline?"

"The winning ticket is the one that contains the date and hour of the day when the next Ikariot over ninety dies."

"*What?*" shouted Andreas. "That's beyond weird. It's sacrilegious."

"What a sicko," said Yianni. "How the hell does he get away with that? I'd think he'd have been run off the island by now."

"I told him the same thing, in tougher language. He took offense, and said he used his half of the pot to buy flowers for the deceased, and kept not a cent for himself. That way, no one ever passed on without at least some tribute paid to their memory."

"Wow," said Andreas. "So much for misjudging a saintly man."

"Tell me about it. I was so embarrassed I bought four tickets and told him to keep all the winnings for himself if one of mine happened to hit."

"How did he ever come up with that idea?" asked Yianni.

"He said he's been doing it for years. Until a few weeks ago, the tickets only contained a date. Then so many of the elderly started dying that he had to add the hour of day in order to sell enough tickets to cover the cost of a nice wreath."

"I've got to admire the guy's improvisational dedication," said Andreas.

"You've got that right. Hey, I gotta run. I see Maggie, and she's waving for me to join her. It looks like they're getting ready to carry the coffin into the church."

"A bit of advice. I wouldn't mention the old-timer's game to Maggie. She's got enough on her mind as it is, and despite his good intentions, it's likely to upset her to think people are willing to bet on when others might die, especially since one of them turned out to be her *yaya*."

"Good point," added Yianni from the background. "What she doesn't know can't hurt her."

"Or me. Bye."

———

The priest appeared from behind the intricately inlaid wooden *iconostasis* separating the main part of the church from the altar area, said a few private words to the family, and began the service. Age-old prayers and blessings joined a background chorus of crying, moaning, and wailing, along with the wafting scent of scores of burning candles in sand-filled brass stands close by the open coffin. No one else said a word except when called for by the service. This was a time for showing respect to the soul that remained with the body for three days after death.

At the conclusion of the church service, the pallbearers huddled around the coffin, gripped it, and lifted together. They turned so Yaya's body lay with her feet facing east and exited the church feetfirst, opposite from how the coffin had entered. The priest led them, taking care not to retrace the steps taken into church. Behind the coffin walked the family, followed by a far larger crowd of mourners than had squeezed into the small church for the service.

The pallbearers slid the coffin into the rear of the funeral van. Behind it stood a pickup truck filled with flowers, and a line of cars waiting to accompany Yaya to the site of her grave. Maggie's mother and father rested on that same shaded, hillside plot overlooking the sea, and someday Maggie would too. At least that was the plan, though hopefully not for many decades.

For Maggie, the ride from the church was a long blur of sobbing against Tassos's chest. At the cemetery, he kept one arm snugly wrapped around her shoulders while she clutched his free hand in both of hers. Wailing among the crowd of women huddled around the coffin came in waves when the pallbearers removed the lid, and subsided only long enough to hear the priestly blessing and prayer for Yaya's soul. As the pallbearers sealed the coffin, the cries resumed and then hit a crescendo when they lowered it into place.

Maggie stood by Yaya's grave until most of the other mourners had left, then went to pray by her parents' graves. Thoroughly drained, all she wanted to do was go to bed, pull the covers over her head, and have a good cry. She was in no mood for the socializing that inevitably followed a funeral. But her cousins had booked a local taverna to host the traditional post-funeral meal of fish soup and fish: the family's way of thanking those who'd paid their respects.

She shut her eyes tightly, then drew in and held a deep breath. She slowly let it out and opened her eyes. She could see her Yaya smiling, as she always did when passing along her favorite bit of advice to her grandchildren:

Traditions must be observed, for they are how we stay engaged with those who've passed on, and provide an honorable path forward to those who shall follow them.

Maggie sighed. *I know, Yaya. It's time to re-engage.*

———

Maggie and Tassos stood at the edge of a paved two-lane road bordering an open porch attached to a three-story stucco-and-stone building. A sign over a bright red door identified it as a taverna with roots dating back to 1950.

Tassos said he took that to mean it likely had opened as the village's leftist taverna. Though Greece's civil war ended in 1949, animosities remained, and all across the nation, former combatants and their supporters had created their own places to congregate where they could spend their time among like-minded folk. He called it "a midtwentieth-century version of the twenty-first-century chat room."

The door opened directly into a large room filled with worn square-top tables grouped together in long parallel rows lined with tattered, woven-seat taverna chairs, and packed with guests who'd come to pay their respects to Yaya and her family.

Maggie's female relatives waved for her to join them at a line of tables filled with women. She turned to Tassos, but he put his finger to his lips before she could speak.

"Go, sit with your family. It's a tradition. I'll sit with the men and make believe I'm a revolutionary."

Maggie smiled. "You are a revolutionary. You just don't know it yet." She kissed him on both cheeks and went to her cousins' table.

Tassos looked around for a place to sit and saw Mihali waving to him. "Come, I have a place saved for you."

Oh no, thought Tassos, *another trip down Junta-memory lane.*

As soon as Tassos headed for the table, Mihali rose and lifted his glass. "A toast to the only good Junta man I ever knew."

Tassos forced a smile as he sat next to Mihali. "Am I supposed to thank you for that introduction?"

"Why not?"

An old man sitting across from them waggled a finger at Mihali. "The only good Junta member is a dead Junta member."

Tassos turned to Mihali, "How's that for an answer to your question?"

"Forget about him, he's senile, but in the old days he was a wild-eyed apologist for 17 November. Sometimes he acts as if they're still around."

"It you're talking about Greece's most notorious and violent homegrown terrorist organization—which I'm certain you are— may I remind you that it took its name from the final day of the student uprising that led to the overthrow of the very Junta you're bent on tying me to."

"Don't be so dramatic. He's harmless. Besides, we both know 17 November is dead. Its leadership captured, convicted, and put away decades ago."

Tassos leaned in toward Mihali. "Maybe we're not talking about the same 17 November. The one I have in mind got away with murder, kidnapping, and robbery *for almost thirty years,* assassinating over twenty prominent Greeks and foreigners in more than one hundred attacks—starting with the CIA's section chief in Athens. It was only after Greece was under terrific pressure from the worldwide community to guarantee a terrorism-free 2004 Olympics that the government announced arrests and claimed it had put an end to their reign of terror."

"Like I said," insisted Mihali, "17 November was crushed two decades ago."

"Yeah, crushed. Funny, though, isn't it, how in post-Olympics years, so many new terrorist organizations have sprung up and remain active?"

"My nephews would take care of you properly," shouted the other man, waving his finger wildly at Tassos.

Tassos stared at Mihali. "What the hell is he talking about?"

Mihali stuttered, "N-nothing. Don't worry, he's just ranting."

"Xiros, shut up," shouted another man, shaking a fist at the old man.

Tassos fixed his eyes on Mihali. "Did I hear him correctly? He just called the old man Xiros. Does that happen to be his surname?"

Mihali looked away.

Tassos leaned in closer. "Xiros is the surname of three brothers from Ikaria convicted as key members of 17 November. One of whom has shown a propensity for escaping from prison."

Mihali shrugged. "The old man's brother was their father."

"As I recall, the father was an Orthodox priest."

Mihali shrugged again. "Children."

Tassos whispered, "How many other friends and relatives of that family are at this table?"

Mihali bit his lip, blinking. "A few."

Tassos's lips now nearly touched Mihali's ear. "If you don't straighten this out here and now, I promise you I'll make the rest of your days so miserable you'll think your Junta experiences were a holiday."

Mihali began to tremble. "I—I'm not a well man."

"Then you'd better get rid of that target you just put on my back."

Mihali took a quick swig of wine and waved both hands at Xiros. "My friend Tassos wasn't part of the Junta; we were in prison together. He was liked by everybody. I was just teasing him. It was a bad joke."

Xiros squinted at Mihali. "Do you swear on your family's honor that what you just said is the truth?"

Mihali swallowed. "Yes."

Tassos spoke up. "Truth is, I spent more time in prison in those days than he did. And his joke-telling wasn't any better back then than now."

Xiros raised his glass to Tassos. "Welcome to the island of the oppressed."

Tassos nodded back, "Thank you," then whispered to Mihali: "Sorry you had to lie on your family's honor."

"I didn't lie," he said with indignation. "I swore it was a bad joke."

Tassos smiled. "Well played."

Mihali looked disconsolate.

Tassos put his arm around the man's shoulder and spoke into his ear again. "Sorry, but you left me no choice. I've seen the bodies of 17 November's victims. There's no upside to attracting its sympathizers' attention, especially if you're a cop."

"I didn't mean to put you in danger."

"I know," said Tassos, patting Mihali's shoulder. "But these days people are particularly edgy and looking for someone to blame for all the hell they been through. There's no telling what might set them off, which is why I do what I can to stay off their radar."

"I guess I'm too old to worry about such things."

"How old are you?"

"Ninety-one."

"A mere babe in the woods."

"At this table I am."

"Really?"

"Half a dozen here are older than I am, including Xiros. He's ninety-nine."

Tassos glanced across the table at Xiros actively engaged in a heated debate with the man next to him. "That's almost enough to get me to reconsider my politics."

Mihali pushed a glass toward Tassos and raised his own. "To the revolution."

"Which one?" smiled Tassos, picking up the glass.

"Does it matter?"

Tassos smiled, "*Yamas*, to our health."

"*Yamas*."

———

Maggie struggled to overcome her exhaustion and stay engaged in the many conversations bouncing back and forth across the table. There were a lot of stories about Yaya—most of which she'd already heard—and much bragging about children and grandchildren. Nothing unusual, nothing exciting, nothing to keep her awake. She looked toward Tassos, hoping to catch his eye and signal him to be her excuse for leaving early. But he was deeply engaged in conversation with Mihali and never looked her way.

She slowly gave up the battle to keep her eyes open and drifted off into the din of conversations surrounding her.

Her eyes bolted open when she felt someone take her hand.

"Sorry, I didn't mean to wake you, but you were beginning to lean in toward the table, and I didn't want you to hurt yourself."

Maggie blinked at the woman holding her hand. "Calliope? I thought you were sitting at another table."

"I was, but the cousin sitting next to you came over to my table to chat with friends. I noticed you'd fallen asleep and was worried you might fall, so I took your cousin's seat."

Maggie smiled. "You're a very caring soul."

"Thank you."

"I'm embarrassed to ask, but how long was I asleep?"

"Only ten or fifteen minutes."

"Amazing. I could have sworn I was awake the whole time." Maggie rolled her shoulders. "Well, I actually feel better now, more awake."

"Sleep does that. It's key to a long life. Naps are important."

"Yaya always told me the same thing, but they're almost impossible to take when you work in an office."

"That's the dilemma we all face. Earning a living or living a life."

"It's not quite that simple," said Maggie. "Many had to leave Ikaria to find work elsewhere so that they could support their families back home."

Calliope smiled. "I know. I was one of those who left to do just that. But as soon as I was old enough to retire, I came straight back to our island."

"What did you do?"

"I worked in a hospital."

"Is that where you learned what you do now?"

"No, that came later, when I returned to Ikaria. I did many things in the hospital, mostly administrative, but all aimed at keeping patients comforted and alive. Now I prepare souls for their final journey. To honor those I could not save."

Maggie gave her a quick hug. "You're a special lady."

"So was your *yaya*."

Maggie pressed an index finger across her lips. "Since you knew her, may I ask you a question?"

"Sure."

"How did she seem in the weeks leading up to her death?"

Calliope shrugged. "I didn't see her during that time, so I can't answer your question. All I can say is that she seemed healthy the last time I saw her."

"When was that?"

"About a month ago."

Maggie looked down at the table.

Calliope leaned in closer to Maggie. "What's on your mind, dear?"

Maggie sighed. "I guess I'm just having a hard time accepting that she's gone. Yaya always seemed so alive and cheerful. To hear she wasn't her normal self in her final days came as a surprise."

"I wouldn't know anything about that. I was only called upon to bathe her and perform the intimate tasks necessary to prepare her for her funeral."

"What sort of tasks?"

"I had to insert absorbent material into the body's orifices to prevent bodily fluids from seeping out."

Maggie shuddered.

"Are you okay?"

"Yes, that's just more information than I want to think about."

"I understand." Calliope swallowed. "If you want to know the state of her health when she passed on, I think you should ask your family about the hospital or clinical treatments she'd been receiving."

Maggie blinked. "What treatments?"

"The ones where she received her IV."

Maggie leaned in. "Are you talking about an intravenous injection?"

"Yes."

"For what?"

"I didn't see the IV, but I did see IV needle bruising on her arm. And, if I may say so, from the size of the bruise, whoever performed the procedure wasn't very good at it."

"Why would she have an IV?"

"No idea, but as I said, maybe a family member knows."

Maggie started rocking back and forth in her chair. Raising the subject with her cousins would likely set off a barrage of questions for which Maggie had no answers, and risked firing up suspicions and finger-pointing of the sort that devastated families. She needed to know a lot more before daring to take that chance.

Calliope put a hand on her arm. "I'm sure there's an explanation."

Maggie let out a deep breath, and looked straight at Calliope. "What's yours?"

She sighed. "All I can say is that anyone could have an unexpectedly difficult time inserting an IV." She looked around to see if anyone was listening, then whispered to Maggie, "But this was the third occasion in two weeks that I'd prepared a body with the same sort of botched IV insertion."

Maggie jerked up in her chair.

Calliope shook her head. "And every one of those poor souls was over ninety."

Chapter Four

Andreas sat in his office, staring at the pile of reports on his desk. Maggie had been away less than a day, and he already missed her. The temporary secretary who'd taken over for her was a nice guy with good skills, but Maggie knew precisely which reports to show Andreas, and which to simply file away. Every report was marked URGENT or bore some equivalent alert intended to draw his unit into an investigation. The complainants ranged from neighbors reporting on neighbors to politicians reporting on rivals, as well as some folk claiming space aliens lived among us.

As Andreas saw it, the space alien reports often had a more legitimate basis for laying claim to his time than those trying to draw him into obvious personal disputes best left to civil courts or elections. At least with space aliens there was the possibility that what the complainant took to be out-of-this-world behavior was grounded in earthly criminal activity.

Maggie had a knack for seeing through it all and sparing him wasted time. But she wouldn't be doing that for him today. Or for a week. At least.

Yianni poked his head through the doorway. "Do you have a moment, Chief?"

"I'm up for anything that keeps me from looking through these reports." Andreas flashed the open-hand curse sign at the pile on his desk.

"I'll take that to mean we both miss Maggie, but if cursing makes reports go away, I'll try it on the pile on my desk." Yianni settled his big frame onto the sofa across from Andreas's desk. "So, here's my problem. It's tied into the undercover operation we're running on foreign involvement in domestic drug trafficking. It appears we have some new characters in the mix."

"Space aliens?"

"Huh?"

"Forget it. A bad joke."

"Our guy on the inside just learned that Greeks are providing foreign traffickers with protection."

"That's no surprise. We always knew there had to be Greeks involved."

"But not our own drug-enforcement guys."

"What?"

"You heard me right."

"Damn. I thought we'd put those days behind us."

"It makes it hard to see how we can coordinate with drug enforcement if their own people are dirty."

"How high up does it go?"

Yianni shrugged. "No idea. Our guy doesn't even know the names of the two pointed out to him as being dirty."

"Then how do we know they're government agents?"

"Our guy was part of a trucking crew of three sent to the port in Piraeus to pick up a container. With customs and police buzzing all around the port, a new guy in the crew started bitching about getting caught. The driver told him not to worry, they were protected. He pointed at two men standing by the customs shed and said, 'DEA.'"

"That's a pretty flimsy basis for charging that actual agents are involved. The driver could have been messing with the new guy."

Yianni gestured no. "Our guy's pretty savvy. It's how he stays alive. He believes the driver was telling the truth because he's been making regular pickups there for over a year and hasn't been hassled even once by anyone, including customs."

Andreas picked up a pencil and began tapping its eraser on the top of his desk. "One thing's for certain, we can't do anything to jeopardize our guy on the inside. That rules out getting him to press for IDs on the potential dirty agents."

"Then how do you suggest we identify them?"

"It would help if we knew who'd been assigned to the port on the day of the pickup. Better yet, if we had that information for every pickup the driver made there. But poking around for that kind of info in official agency records risks raising serious suspicions in the minds of the wrong people."

"Do you have a plan B?" asked Yianni.

"Find out when the driver will next be back in the port so we can film every customs, port police, and government agent having anything to do with whatever he's picking up. If we're lucky, our guy can identify the alleged dirty agents off the video."

"Do you really think that many agencies could be corrupted by this operation?"

"There's big money involved, and in financial times as hard as these, mortals can be tempted."

"I'm not," gibed Yianni.

"I'll take that as a sign of your immortality."

———

Maggie wasn't sure if her head was spinning from exhaustion or Calliope's revelation that two more recently deceased nonagenarians shared a bruise similar to Yaya's—plus a place on Mihali's list of four names.

Calliope said she had no information on the remaining two from Mihali's list because she'd not prepared their bodies, but she did agree an unusually high percentage of nonagenarians and centenarians in relatively good health had died over the past month, despite having survived the coronavirus pandemic.

Maggie was in the midst of collecting from Calliope the names and contact information of others on the island who did the same work as she did, when she felt a tap on her shoulder.

"May I lure you away from all this excitement, my love?"

"In a moment," she said, not looking up from her notebook. "Please continue, Calliope."

Tassos put up his hands and stepped back, smiling at Calliope.

"I know of four *savanotria*, but I'm certain there are others who do it."

Maggie took down the four names, closed her notebook and patted Calliope's hand. "You've been a terrific help. Thank you." She turned to Tassos. "The answer to your question is *yes*. I just have to say my goodbyes."

"I'll wait for you by the front door."

Maggie went off to circle the room and was immediately besieged by huggers and kissers offering her a parting bit of comfort, and receiving the same from Maggie in return.

By the time Maggie made it to the front door, Tassos had stepped out onto the porch. "Sorry I took so long," she said, hooking her arm around his.

"No problem. I had to move outside because my newfound revolutionary friends started waving for me to come back and rejoin their discussion on how to achieve world peace."

"Stop being such a cynic. They're just old men reflecting on their pasts. Half the stories they tell are likely made up."

"Ah, so I do have something in common with them."

Maggie hugged her arm more tightly around his. "In all but the part about being an old man."

"Bless you for that bit of flattery. So what would you like to do now?"

"Pass out on the nearest bed."

"That sounds interesting."

"Not a chance, Romeo, I'm exhausted."

"My hotel's close by. You can sleep there."

"I've arranged to stay in Yaya's cottage."

"I'm just offering you a place to nap."

"I thought you had a boat to catch."

"Not until tonight."

"If you plan on making the crossing to Syros in the dark, I hope your friend has a big boat. The waters between here and Syros can be dangerous at night."

"He's not worried. He's made the crossing many times. Besides, when it comes to dangerous crossings, from what I've seen of the traffic passing by here, I'd say crossing this road in broad daylight is far more dangerous than tonight's boat trip."

"Cars do tend to speed by."

"But it's more than that. The road is so narrow that taking one step off the porch puts you in the middle of oncoming traffic."

"That's a universal problem shared by old villages everywhere," said Maggie.

Tassos shrugged. "Whatever. I just wonder how Ikariots manage to live so damned long with roads like these."

Maggie unhooked her arm from Tassos, looked both ways, stepped off the porch, and hurried off in the direction of his hotel—with Tassos right behind her. "They've faced so many different dangers over so many millennia that learning to handle new ones is part of their DNA."

She thought of telling him about her conversation with Calliope, but then what? He might say grief was clouding her judgment, causing her to piece together a conspiracy out of readily explainable innocuous coincidences. But more likely he'd insist on inserting himself into the investigation.

Members of the tight-knit Ikariot community might be willing to open up to Maggie as a local, but having a former Junta prison guard, now chief homicide investigator, by her side, would undoubtedly doom any meaningful cooperation from the start. After all, this is the authority-wary island where a police station built in its Raches region remained unused for decades when villagers decided they could do a better job than the police at protecting themselves.

Perhaps she could tell Tassos but refuse to allow him to participate in her interviews. *No,* that would only stress him out. She'd wait until she had more information before involving him in getting to the bottom of it all.

At least that's what her instincts told her.

———

By the time Andreas arrived home to his apartment, his son and daughter were sound asleep. He found Lila spread out on a sofa in the sitting room, with an unobstructed view of the brightly lit Acropolis before her, a book on her lap, and a glass of wine beside her. She was heir to of one of the most prominent and well-to-do families in Greece, which explained to the world why a cop could afford to live with his family at the very heart of Athens's privileged society, in a penthouse apartment on the city's chicest street.

"You sure do look comfy," said Andreas, leaning down to kiss his wife.

She swung her legs out onto the floor and patted the pillow beside her. "Come, tell me all the exciting things that kept you in the office so late."

"Let's just say it's all Maggie's fault. I guess I never fully appreciated how much she does to make my life easier."

"Hallelujah. Are we having a male epiphany right before my eyes?"

"I'm serious. It took me four extra hours to accomplish the same things I do on a typical day when Maggie's in the office."

"How's Yianni faring without her?"

"He was still there when I left."

"Hm. I guess that means Toni's on Mykonos."

Andreas nodded. "He called her to complain about working late."

Lila laughed, reached for her wineglass, and handed it to Andreas. "Here, I sense you need this more than I do."

He took the glass, chugged a larger-than-polite swig, and handed it back. "Thanks." He slapped his hands on his thighs. "So, how are the kids?"

"Tassaki fell right to sleep. Sofia tried working me to let her stay up until 'Daddy gets home.' It was a nice try by a three-year-old, but I waited her out."

"And how about your day?"

"Toni and I spoke about our plans for a fundraiser for Fresh Start. It's going to be a tough sell, what with so many still coming to financial grips with the enormous economic pain inflicted by the pandemic."

"But if any charity deserves support under these circumstances, it's yours. After all, it's the crisis that's put so many adolescent girls at risk for exploitation."

Lila picked up her glass and took a sip of wine. "I think you better get yourself your own glass, and while you're at it, bring the bottle out here. If our conversation is headed toward a collaborative rant about how disgustingly ruthless humans can become when they realize how much money can be made trafficking their fellow human beings, I'm going to need a hell of a lot more alcohol to keep from screaming."

Andreas stood. "I'd prefer to avoid the rant because it will only remind me of what I contend with every day, but I'm all in on finishing the bottle." He walked toward the kitchen.

Lila called after him. "I spoke to Maggie a little bit ago. Should I call her back and say you intend on giving her a raise?"

"I wish," he said from the kitchen. "Government salaries have been frozen, if not reduced, for way too long. How did she say things are going?"

"Tassos left an hour before dusk for Syros, and she's moved into her *yaya*'s cottage. She plans on staying there for the week. Says she wants to enjoy memories of her childhood while the old place still stands."

Andreas walked in with a full glass of white wine and the remains of the bottle. "Are there plans to tear it down?"

"She's concerned that with so many cousins, there's bound to be a dispute over the inheritance. That will likely translate into a lot of arguments over what happens to the real estate and quite possibly lead to a decision to simply sell it off and split up the proceeds. Worse still would be relatives battling it out in court for years, if not decades, while the property stays vacant, unused, and deteriorating. Either way, Maggie's worried that this might be her last chance to spend time alone in the cottage with the spirit of her *yaya*."

Andreas dropped down onto the sofa, refilled Lila's glass, and raised his own in a toast. "To the irreplaceable Maggie, may her time spent in the presence of her *yaya*'s spirit bring her peace, enlightenment, and whatever else she seeks."

Lila clinked his glass with hers. "To Maggie."

———

For those who lived on Ikaria tucked behind mountains to the east, sunrise was not detected by facing that direction, but by looking for signs of sunlight striking distant islands. But to most Ikariots it didn't matter when the sun chose to make its appearance because, as with many things, time was a relative concept for them, secondary to living a stress-free life. *If it doesn't get done today, it will get done tomorrow* might well have been the motto of the island.

Dawn sunlight had not yet reached Yaya's cottage when, with coffee in hand, Maggie sat outside in the shadow of the ridgeline on the same well-worn taverna chair Yaya had perched on each morning for as long as Maggie could remember. Yaya would sit quietly, listening to the surrounding morning sounds of life and capturing the scents of all that was in bloom in the long, deep breaths she called her morning exercises.

This morning there was a slight chill to the air, enticing Maggie to draw in each breath more deeply than the one before, as if it were a remedy for too many years of breathing Athens air. She'd slept much longer and sounder than she'd expected, perhaps because she'd passed out more than fallen asleep. Her anticipated naptime with Tassos had turned into lovemaking, but the trade-off was worth it, for it reminded her that she wasn't as old as she felt. She'd returned to the cottage exhausted but in better spirits and possessed of enough nervous energy to tidy up the effects of the prior day's deluge of mourners before collapsing to sleep.

Now fully awake, she pondered what to do next.

There would be the will, and cousins making competing sentimental claims to various items of Yaya's personal property, plus who-knew-how-many predatory opportunists jumping out of the woodwork to take advantage of the situation with manufactured claims, some dating back a hundred years. All of that was to be expected.

What wasn't expected were her suspicions over the circumstances of Yaya's death. Doubts had worked their way into her mind, and she knew she had no choice but to put them to rest. The place to start was with the four *savanotria* on Calliope's list. She'd speak to the families from Mihali's list later.

Telephone calls would not work. She needed to see them face-to-face. But that would require transportation. Perhaps she could borrow a motorbike from her cousin, Spiro, who lived in the big house. A helmet too. No reason to take unnecessary risks.

Finding where the women lived should not be a problem. She'd call upon her vast network of fellow government secretaries— now working for the same pay under the politically correct title of "administrative assistant"—to get that information.

Armed with a plan, Maggie drew in and let out another deep breath, finished her coffee, and popped out of her chair. "Time to get to work."

She dressed in jeans, sneakers, a snug-fitting pullover sweater, and a well-worn brown leather bomber jacket. Not the most fashionable look, but a sensible one for a day motorbiking over Ikarian roads.

When she asked Spiro to borrow his motorbike, he offered her his car, saying, "It'll be safer."

She thanked him but said she was used to driving a motorbike in Athens and, besides, a bike would make it easier to navigate the island's roads and trails.

Spiro held out a set of keys and a helmet. "Be careful. Athens may have wilder drivers, but we have wilder roads and weather."

"It's sweet of you to be so concerned, but I've been driving motorbikes on this island since long before you were born," she pointed out.

"That's why I'm concerned. It's safer for someone of your age to be in a car."

She snatched the keys and helmet out of his hand. "Thank you, Spiro, but that's more than enough sweet concern for one morning."

"Sorry, no offense intended."

Maggie stomped over to the bike, jerked it off its kickstand, fired the engine to life, and with a taut-lipped smile to Spiro said, "None taken," before launching out across the orchard toward the road, muttering to herself, *"How's that for someone of my age?"*

———

Maggie rode east, along roads that twisted through randomly spaced patches of buildings. Some structures grouped into villages, while others stood isolated or abandoned; some flourished on vibrant greenery, while others endured hardscrabble landscapes, but practically all enjoyed some view of the sea.

Maggie's government buddies had come through with photos, locations, and telephone numbers for the four *savanotria* on Calliope's list. Maggie decided to start with the one closest to Yaya's cottage, a woman named Diony. She lived and worked in Therma, a seafront village east of Agios Kirykos with roots back to antiquity that today drew tourists to its ancient therapeutic hot springs. Archaeologists claimed Ikaria's hot springs usage dated back to long before the Romans employed them for their baths, and today they were considered some of the finest in the world.

Maggie always wondered why such a unique natural resource, coupled with Ikaria's reputation for long life, had not triggered a more vigorous effort to draw health-conscious tourists to the island. She knew that Ikaria had sued to prevent the Greek government from claiming the springs as a national asset, and that

Junta efforts a half century ago to build a major hotel just east of Agios Kirykos, near the thermal springs at Lefkada, had fallen apart amid mismanagement and corruption.

The popular explanation for why Ikaria's hot springs were never developed to their potential applied to other island communities as well: jealousy. Rather than benefiting from a neighbor's success, many would prefer seeing their neighbor fail. That attitude, coupled with the fiercely independent islander spirit, had doomed many a cooperative-minded community initiative.

As Maggie maneuvered her bike through the road's narrow hairpin curves down into Therma—stealing glimpses of the blue-green sea whenever she safely could, while picking up the scents of oregano and thyme growing wild on the surrounding hillsides—another possible explanation came to her. If ever there were a place on earth that stood for the proposition that *progress does not necessarily translate into a better or longer life*, Ikaria was it.

Perhaps Therma was comfortable with things remaining precisely as they were. It was a village of two-, three-, and four-story white stucco buildings—mainly hotels, tavernas, and other tourist-driven businesses—huddled along a small beachfront harbor, from which an assortment of similar establishments and residences fanned back toward a gorge between stone-faced, green-dotted hillsides.

Maggie parked off the beach at the western edge of the harbor, next to a stone, wood, and glass two-story building vaguely resembling a giant woodworking hand plane mounted on a broad quay. A walkway alongside the building connected to a narrow pier that led past a dozen small boats neatly moored bow-first on the east, and a cliffside natural cave snug up against it on the west. The pier ended at a protective seawall of massive three-legged concrete pylons piled on top of each other and extending halfway across the mouth of the harbor.

Maggie stepped onto the quay and headed for Therma's public hot springs, set back in the natural cave. She hadn't come for the spa, pools, or steam bath, as so many visitors did—though the relaxing thought had crossed her mind—but to speak with Diony, who worked there as an attendant.

Once inside, it wasn't hard to find her. Diony was the first to greet her, offering a broad-faced smile beneath dark eyes and jet-black hair that matched her photo perfectly.

"Hello, *kiria*, welcome to Therma Loumakia."

Maggie smiled back. "Hello, Diony."

Diony seemed puzzled. "I'm sorry, do I know you?"

"No, but a mutual friend suggested I see you."

"That's always nice to hear. Who's the friend?"

"A fellow *savanotria*. Calliope." Maggie extended her hand, "I'm Maggie Sikestes. My *yaya* passed away three days ago, and Calliope prepared her."

"I'm sorry to hear about your *yaya*, but she couldn't have had a better person to tend to her than Calliope."

"That's very kind of you to say, especially about a competitor."

Diony smiled. "I don't look upon Calliope as a competitor, nor do I feel that way about any of the others who do what we do. I'm sure they are of the same mind. We're like nurses tending to the ill. We care about our charges and respect our colleagues who do what we do."

"That's an admirable philosophy."

"Thank you. So, how can I help you? With all you've been through these past few days, you could probably use some time in our waters."

Maggie nodded. "I'm sure I could. But I'm a little rushed today. Actually, I'm here to see if you might be able to help me answer a question that's troubling me. Calliope thought you might be able to do that."

Diony pointed to two stools next to a raw concrete wall. "Please, let's sit." She stepped toward the wall and sat on a stool.

Maggie looked at the stool and wondered whether she might not be more comfortable standing.

"I know what you're thinking," said Diony. "The trick is to put the stool close enough to the wall so that when you sit, the wall supports your back."

Maggie hesitated but decided Diony seemed the type of person who would cut her answers short if she thought Maggie was uncomfortable standing while she sat. So, she slowly lowered herself onto the stool, taking care to lean back against the wall as instructed.

"If you're uncomfortable, please tell me. I can meet you after I'm done with work in a place that offers better seating."

Maggie forced a smile. "No, no, I'm fine." She cleared her throat. "I'll get right to it. My *yaya* passed away in her sleep at home one month shy of turning one hundred and five."

Diony crossed herself. "God bless her soul."

"Up until then she was in good health and hadn't complained of any illness."

Diony shook her head. "At that blessed age, the unexpected often takes our loved ones, even those in good health."

Maggie nodded. "I understand all that, but what's troubling me is this."

Diony leaned in slightly closer to Maggie.

"As far as I can tell, Yaya had not seen a doctor or been to the hospital in well over a month. Yet when Calliope prepared her, she noticed an IV bruise on her arm."

Diony blinked.

"It was a relatively recent bruise that Calliope attributed to a botched IV insertion."

Diony leaned back against the wall and shut her eyes.

"What's wrong?"

Diony did not open her eyes. "Until two weeks ago, it had been six months since I'd last been called upon to prepare some- one of your *yaya*'s age. But in these past two weeks I've done it twice, once for a centenarian man, and again for a nonagenarian woman. They were not related, and each had died in their own beds at home."

"Did either have an autopsy?"

Diony opened her eyes. "No."

Maggie leaned in closer. "You're a very caring soul. I sense something's bothering you?"

"I'm thinking of the man and woman who passed on. Both had bruises similar to the one you described on your *yaya*."

Maggie felt a chill running down her spine. "Are you sure?"

"That they were IV bruises, yes, but I have a different opinion on the reason for the bruising. At least for the bruises I saw on my two."

"What's your opinion?"

"Multiple insertions at different but relatively close times."

"Why do you say that?"

"I've seen a lot of nearly naked people pass through here. Some with IV bruises related to drug therapies for all sorts of illnesses, and others with bruises linked to their mainlining drug habits. The bruising on the man and woman I prepared struck me as resembling the bruising I'd seen on addicts."

Maggie sat up straight. "Are you suggesting they were ninety- and one-hundred-year-old drug addicts?"

Diony gestured no with a quick upward jerk of her eyebrows. "Of course not. All I'm saying is that the bruising I saw on the man and woman reminded me of bruising caused by repeated vein punctures by addicts."

"There must be another explanation."

"I'm certain there is. But medical treatments requiring repeated IVs generally involve the one-time insertion of a port device into a vein that remains there so that only a single vein puncture is required for administering multiple treatments."

Maggie bit at her lip. "Could it have been a botched IV insertion involving multiple attempts to find a vein on a single occasion?"

"I didn't see your *yaya*'s bruise, so that's possible, but the bruises on the two I prepared came from multiple insertions on different occasions."

"Which you said should have involved a port…"

"Well, not if the IVs resulted from a series of unexpected emergencies calling for a new catheter insertion on each occasion."

Maggie looked down and away. "What did the families have to say about the bruises?"

"The subject never came up."

Maggie's eyes shot back on Diony. "You mean you never told them of your suspicions?"

"Suspicions? What suspicions? All I've done is try to answer your questions over why my opinion differs from Calliope's on the potential cause of your *yaya*'s bruising. I have no reason to believe that the bruises I observed meant anything more than each had a series of IVs inserted. A not-uncommon thing for people of their age. How or why they received the IVs was irrelevant to what I'd been asked to do."

"But they had no autopsies?"

"That's not unusual. A doctor has the authority to determine the cause of death. In my experience, when someone of such advanced years dies at home in bed, without any signs of violence or accident, a doctor who knows the family will issue the necessary certification that death resulted from natural causes, thereby allowing burial to proceed without an autopsy."

Maggie sighed. "I guess I'm just looking for an explanation that doesn't exist."

"That's fully understandable. You've been under a lot of stress. Your *yaya* obviously was very important to you."

Maggie nodded, holding back tears.

Diony patted Maggie on the shoulder. "Perhaps you should spend some time with us in the hot springs. They might help."

Maggie leaned her head back against the wall and shut her eyes. "I guess it couldn't hurt."

Chapter Five

Maggie spent much of the rest of her morning immersed in hot water, followed by steam, massage, and a brief nap. Her body had relaxed. Her mind not so much.

She wondered whether she should rid her mind of her suspicions, and simply accept them as a subconscious attempt at finding ways to delay accepting that Yaya was gone. By pressing for answers to questions no one else saw a reason to ask, she kept Yaya in the present.

She left the public hot springs thinking perhaps she should give up the chase, steer her now-rejuvenated body back to the cottage, and complete her cycle of mourning there.

But first she needed a coffee.

She found a tidy *kafenion* along the beachfront and ordered a double Greek coffee, *sketos*. She wanted the high-octane version, black with no sugar, to jolt her back to life. The sea was calm and a crystal clear blue-green. A beautiful day for sailing, which explained why so few sailboats remained moored in the port. She remembered the first time she'd been on a sailboat. It was on Ikaria. A friend of Yaya's had offered to take Yaya and seven-year-old Maggie for a sail.

Yaya said she'd successfully avoided unnecessary sea cruises for most of her life, and saw no reason for changing her pattern now. But she encouraged Maggie to go, saying, "Sailing's not for me, but it could be right for you. Make up your own mind about things that might be important to you."

That was sound advice. Maggie had loved sailing ever since that day.

Maggie's thoughts drifted to her conversation with Mihali on the night before the funeral, and his mention of Yaya's final days being "difficult" for her. That was not her pattern. Nor was it her pattern to keep something that bothered her hidden from her family.

She sighed. The suspicions were back. So much for the lasting effects of a spa day. She gulped down her coffee and looked at her watch. If she hurried, she could still catch the three *savanotria* remaining on Calliope's list in time to make it home by dark. They lived on the north side of the island, in three different towns. The visits would take her on a loop around much of the island, over some tricky mountain roads. At least the weather looked good, though that could change in a heartbeat.

She paid her check and hurried back to the motorbike. The first order of business was to find a petrol station. No reason to chance running out of fuel in the mountains. That would be a surefire way of wrecking whatever modicum of calm she retained from her morning at the hot springs.

She found her petrol station in Agios Kirykos, and from there headed northeast along the main road connecting the north and south sides of the island. Her next stop lay thirty minutes away, in one of several mountain settlements that had played a central role during the sixteenth century in making Ikaria appear uninhabited and deserted to marauding pirates terrorizing the Aegean. Ikariots lived hidden in those secret villages for eighty years, during what to this day Ikariots remembered as their "century of obscurity."

For much of Maggie's ride, the road ran roughly parallel to the eastern edge of the exotic and wild Atheras Mountains, carrying her up and down hills, between villages, and through light olive to dark cypress expanses of green. Not far beyond the turnoff to the village of Katafigio, but before a horseshoe curve leading past a collection of giant wind turbines, Maggie turned right onto a secondary road that led through dense green forests into the village of Perdiki.

Today, Perdiki was a large village spread out along a plateau, sporting long, narrow stone houses amid forests of cypress and pine, and surrounded by ravines. It was also home to one of Ikaria's two folklore museums.

According to Maggie's sources, the second *savanotria* on Calliope's list lived on the western side of the village, close by the elaborate, blue-domed church of Agia Matrona and the village's centuries-old cemetery.

She found the woman at home, caring for her lively, ninety-year-old grandfather. Granddaughter and grandfather were elated at the unexpected company and launched into a full-bore display of fabled Ikarian hospitality. Maggie's toughest challenge wasn't getting her to talk but at finding a way to extricate herself from the never-ending flow of food in a manner that would not offend her hosts' overwhelming hospitality. Stuffed peppers, *saganaki*-style Greek fried cheese, *tzatziki* yoghurt dip, horta greens, beets in garlic and vinegar, apricots, and oranges were but part of what they offered her.

Maggie ended up eating far more food than she wanted, but successfully battled repeated offerings of Ikaria's famous strong red wine by pointing out how unsafe it would be for her to drink and then drive over the region's tricky mountain roads. Ultimately, her hosts offered a solution to the wine dilemma. If she drank too much, she could always spend the night with them.

That left Maggie with no choice but to invoke the ultimate weapon: fib that she'd promised her family she'd be joining them for dinner.

Amid all the hospitality, Maggie managed to ask her questions, and the granddaughter waxed on at length about all sorts of things, but nothing that shed any light on Maggie's suspicions. She'd not tended to a centenarian or a ninety-year-old, other than her grandfather, in over a year. Nor had she seen or heard of any centenarian or nonagenarian who'd died bearing bruises of the sort described by Maggie.

Maggie's next stop lay thirty kilometers away in the port town of Evdilos. Generally viewed as the island's more organized, affluent port community, it stood in contrast to the widely held image of Agios Kirykos—Ikaria's primary port and capital—as the scruffier, hardworking pugilist of a sibling to the south.

The two towns also symbolized a long-standing rivalry between Ikaria's larger, more fertile and temperate north and its less arable, rocky, and weather-besieged south. With the northern three-quarters of Ikaria essentially cut off from the south by virtually impassable mountains, jealousies and suspicions fueled political, economic, and cultural differences. Those jealousies were stoked when Agios Kirykos became the island's Administrative Center in 1866, then brought the two close to war in 1912, when Evdilos's selection as Ikaria's capital was reversed in favor of Agios Kirykos.

Tensions eased in the 1930s, when a high school built to serve all the island opened in Agios Kirykos and brought the children of both sides together. In the 1960s, a massive road construction project linked many of the island's towns and villages, finally achieving a physical union of sorts between the north and south, if never fully in spirit.

Today, two main routes linked the two sides. One essentially skirted the eastern end of the Atheras Mountain range, and the other cut north-south over the mountains roughly midway between Ikaria's east and west coasts. It was along the skirting route that Maggie set out on her journey west from Perdiki toward the village of Monokambio and on to the half a dozen other villages that lay between there and Evdilos. On a map, the road to Evdilos looked like an EKG gone wild. In reality, it signaled a merciless run of coiling and uncoiling, panic-inducing mountain roads. For the optimist, it also promised breathtaking rocky mountain vistas of the sea and beaches thousands of feet below.

This road always summoned up Maggie's pride at her island's rugged beauty, but what never failed to stir her soul was the image that met her whenever she crossed over the mountains from the south to the north: nothing but wide-open sea for as far as she looked in any direction. Yes, Chios was visible off to the northeast in places, but unlike the south, where Samos, Patmos, and the Fourni archipelago loomed ever-present, on the north side of the mountains nothing stood between her, the end of the earth, and her imagination but the deep blue Ikarian Sea.

Maggie took it easy on her drive across to Evdilos, yet she still made it in under an hour. Turned out, though, that this *savanotria* and her family were no longer living at the location Maggie had for her. Since Ikariots historically disdained formal addresses, by the time Maggie tracked down the woman's new location, another hour had passed, and when she reached the woman's home, her husband said she'd just been called out to attend to a young man who'd died in a motorcycle accident. He had no idea when she might return, but promised to ask her to call Maggie as soon as she did.

She thought of waiting, but it made more sense to leave her mobile number and push on to the final name on the list. That woman lived a half hour away in Christos Raches, a popular mountain village built high above the sea on a plateau of lush green ravines and thick oak and pine forests, bounded by orchards and vineyards, and offering views of virtually all of Ikaria.

This time Maggie had better success. The woman was at home, and only a week before had prepared a female centenarian. But Maggie's luck ended there. Her charge had no bruises or signs of an IV insertion. And like the *savanotria* from Perdiki, she'd not seen or heard of that sort of bruising on a ninety- or one-hundred-year-old who'd passed away.

Maggie had reached the end of Calliope's list. It was getting late, and her ride back to the cottage involved an hour-and-a-half trek along some difficult roads. Perhaps she should have listened to her cousin and taken his car instead of the motorbike. Thankfully, she'd be heading east and then south, not west into the blinding glare of the setting sun.

As she straddled the bike, Maggie did her best to put a positive slant on her ride back home. It would certainly be a feast for the senses, winding along twisting roads, past orchards and vineyards, through forests, around gullies, and over hillsides of green, beige, and stone. Ikaria was an internationally heralded playground for nature lovers. Geologists and hikers found heaven in rock formations that seemed to defy the laws of gravity, while birdwatchers saw it as the perfect sanctuary for their cherished quarry.

It also presented the perfect opportunity for Maggie to try and clear her mind of the nagging thought that Yaya had somehow fallen victim to foul play. Too many years of working with cops had made her suspicious of even the number of raisins in a cereal box.

Perhaps she and Tassos would take a trip. That would be nice. She started the engine.

What wouldn't be nice was Tassos's likely reaction to learning of her escapade today around the island. He'd give her a million reasons why she'd been wasting her time, perhaps even mock her for playing amateur detective. And, of course, there'd be the shouting. Men can be like that. Even the good ones.

She pushed off and drove out onto the road.

No reason to go that route. This was one escapade she'd keep to herself.

———

Maggie made it across the roughest stretch of road to the village of Steli in forty-five minutes. There she picked up a better road that put her on the mid-island route south across the mountains and east toward home. The mountain air and the late afternoon light chasing shadows across hillsides down into valleys had performed their magic. She'd stopped thinking about the circumstances of Yaya's death. An anxiety or two remained, but of the sensible kind, tied into clouds coming in quickly from the northwest. They could make her mountain-crossing treacherous if they brought rain and wind. She rode faster, hoping to outrun the potential storm, or at least reach the south side of the mountains before it hit. Her leisurely ride in the country had ended. Now she had to cover ground quickly.

She'd made it halfway up the mountainside, headed toward Plagia on the south coast, when she felt her mobile phone vibrating in her jacket pocket. Her instinct was to ignore it. She had a storm to beat over the mountain. It would be hard enough staying ahead of it without stopping to take a phone call. Besides, it was likely some jerk trying to sell her something.

Then again, perhaps Tassos was looking for her. Or maybe her boss needed to speak to her. She hadn't spoken to either of them today. Possibly her cousin Spiro had noticed the storm clouds and wanted to warn her to be careful. Or maybe something had happened to someone who needed her help.

Guilt took hold, and Maggie decided to stop at the first safe place, make a quick return call to be sure everything was okay, and promise to call back later. She pulled over at a tiny parking area offering panoramic views north toward the faraway sea.

Cloud shadows dancing rapidly across the landscape in her direction meant the storm was hurrying her way. She grabbed her phone and looked at the number. She didn't recognize it. But since she'd already stopped, she might as well call it. As she hit redial, she muttered aloud, "If it's someone trying to sell me something, I'll tear him a new—"

"Hello?" said a woman in a voice Maggie didn't recognize.

"Hi, my name is Maggie, and I just received a call from this number."

"Oh, yes, my husband told me to call you."

Maggie shook her head. She had finally put her *yaya* out her mind. Maggie introduced herself to the *savanotria* from Evdilos and explained she was calling at Calliope's suggestion, in the hope she might be able to help put to rest a question she had about her *yaya*'s recent death.

"I'll be happy to help you if I can."

"Thanks," Maggie drew in and let out a breath, firing herself up for asking questions she no longer felt necessary to ask. "Have you tended to any centenarians who'd recently passed away?"

"Yes. My friend Alki. She passed away four weeks ago." Maggie heard a sniffle. "I'm still not over it."

"I take it you knew her well."

"We met many years ago through our church, and I visited her at least once a week. All of her children had passed away before her, and I was sort of a surrogate daughter to her."

"It must be difficult for you. I know it's been that way for me."

"You'd think with someone as old as Alki I'd be prepared for her passing. But no, it came as a complete surprise."

"I felt the same way," said Maggie. "Yaya was always such a cheery and upbeat person."

"Up until a month before Alki died, I'd never known her to be happy or cheery. She was always a good and caring person, but she battled bouts of depression all my life."

"Oh, I'm so sorry to hear that."

"But out of nowhere her mood changed. I'd never seen her in such great spirits. She told me she'd found new meaning for her life."

Maggie fixed her eyes on the quickly closing clouds. "That's quite an accomplishment at any age, let alone when you're over a hundred."

"A hundred and five, to be precise. I thought the same thing. She told me that her priest had given her a reason for living."

"That's what I call truly inspiring. My *yaya* had just the opposite experience. Friends told me that during her final days she was uncharacteristically down."

"Perhaps she should have seen Papa George."

"That's the priest who inspired Alki?"

"Yes."

"One last question, if I may. Did you happen to notice if Alki had IV marks or bruising on her body?"

"Yes. On her arm."

Maggie closed her eyes. Not the answer she'd wanted to hear.

"Have you seen similar bruises on others close to her age?"

"Not recently, but I've seen IV bruising on people around her age who passed away while hospitalized."

"Any idea why Alki had them?"

"Um…no. I mean, I'm not sure."

"Did she often have IVs?"

"Not that I know of. I'd helped her get dressed many, many

times and never noticed bruise marks like that. But then again, I wasn't looking for them."

"Do you know anyone who might be able to explain her bruises?"

"Possibly Papa George."

"Why would he know?"

"He spent a lot of time with her at her home in the month before she passed away. If anyone might know, my guess would be Papa George."

"Where can I find him?"

"He's based locally in Evdilos but spends most of his time traveling around the island. His mission is to bring aid and comfort to the very old, no matter where they live."

"Sounds like a noble cause."

"If Alki's change in mood is an example of his ministry, I'd say yes."

Maggie felt the first few drops of rain. "Can I trouble you for one last favor? I'd appreciate your texting me Papa George's telephone number and where he lives. I'm standing out in the open with my motorbike, about to get drenched in the rain."

"Absolutely. I hope I've been of help to you."

Maggie started up the bike. "You have, and thank you."

They hung up. Maggie stuffed the phone back into her pocket and pulled back onto the road. The rain was slightly heavier now, but from the blurred landscape below, she could tell that harder rain, whipped by wind, was headed her way. The rest of her trip home was shaping up as neither quick nor fun. It would be a battle. There was a reason why the strongest pines and oaks bent in the face of the winds that stormed south down the far side of the mountains. About the only upside she could see to her next hour or so was that slick roads and gusty winds would require her total concentration to keep the bike upright—and thoughts of the murdered elderly from sneaking back into her thoughts.

At least for now.

———

Yianni burst into Andreas's office, "Chief, I've got it!"

Andreas stared at him. "Since you're smiling, I assume it's not something life-threatening or contagious."

Kouros ignored him and dropped onto the sofa. "I think I've got video of the two dirty drug enforcement agents we're looking for." He waved a thumb drive at Andreas.

"How did you get them on film so quickly? It's only been a day since we knew about them."

"I didn't film them. But your suggestion we catch them on video gave me an idea. I drove down to Piraeus to check out the dock area where our undercover guy said he saw them. I was hoping to find a CCTV camera that might have picked them up."

"You'd think they'd be smart enough to avoid cameras."

"They were. But only the ones in the dock area." He leaned forward and smiled. "Not the ones where they parked."

"Good thinking, Detective."

"I wish I could take the credit, but that goes to a crusty old security guard who told me I couldn't drive onto the docks. Even after I showed him my badge, he refused to let me in. Instead, he told me to park in a fenced-in area just outside the dock entrance where *official vehicles are allowed to park*. Then he added, *Don't worry, it has 24/7 closed-circuit TV coverage*."

"What a break. Like I always say, it's better to be lucky than good."

"That's not the response I was hoping for," smirked Yianni.

"Where'd you get a copy of the video?"

"From the Port Security office. I told them we were conducting a random audit on behalf of GADA's Anti-Terrorist operations into the effectiveness of port security measures, and I needed a copy of all CCTV recordings over the past three days. I figured asking for everything wouldn't tip them off to what we're actually interested in."

"How do you know the two we're looking for are on the video?"

"The videos all have timestamps and locations. I looked at the recordings of vehicles entering and leaving the parking area, then worked my way back and forth out from the approximate time our guy saw the two we're looking for. As it turned out, it wasn't all that difficult to find them. They were driving an official marked vehicle."

Andreas shook his head. "As if they had nothing to hide." He began tapping a pencil on his desktop. "So, how long until we know if our guy can identify the two in the video?"

"I'm hooking up with him sometime tonight. It's tricky, but he'll let me know when and where to meet."

"Good work." Andreas smiled. "And continued good luck."

"Thanks. Any word from Maggie?"

"Not a peep."

"Maybe we should call her just to check in. Let her know we miss her."

"I thought about that, but wondered if calling might make her feel guilty about not being at work. Besides, Lila talked to her yesterday, and I'm sure they'll stay in touch." Andreas tapped his pencil some more. "But your point's a good one. Maybe I'll call her tomorrow just to check in."

"She's probably busy with family stuff. Hearing from us will bring a welcome bit of excitement into her life."

Andreas cocked his head to the side. "You're probably right. Ikaria can't possibly offer her the thrills of working with us."

"I'm being serious, Chief."

"I am too, but thinking selfishly, that's what worries me. She might decide that the peace and quiet ways of Ikaria suit her better at this point in her life than the daily stresses and anxieties of working with you and me."

"Nah," said Yianni. "Maggie's always up for solving puzzles and getting to the bottom of things. Where else can she expect to find that sort of action than here?"

"Yeah, you're probably right." Andreas put down his pencil. "Certainly not on sleepy Ikaria."

———

The storm came in harsher and sooner than Maggie expected. Wind-driven rain began pelting her before she started down the far side of the mountain. Her helmet's visor did little to help her see more than a meter in front of the bike, and despite keeping her speed down to barely more than the minimum necessary for keeping it upright, erratic gusts of wind had her tacking more than steering.

Soaked through to the skin, she screamed at herself for being stupid enough to think she could push a motorbike over mountain roads to outrun a storm.

That's when she saw two headlights coming straight at her. Whoever was driving had taken care to avoid the treacherous edges of the road by commandeering it entirely. Surely the driver would see her and move out of her lane, or at least swerve. But the driver kept coming, even faster than before.

Maggie's heart burst into a rapid staccato as adrenaline rushed through her system and she realized she must save herself. Should she swerve left or right? All she could see through the blinding rain were two rapidly closing headlights. One edge of the road surely ran into solid rock, while the other likely plunged down a mountainside.

She dropped the bike down a gear, hit the brakes as hard as she dared on the slick road, and swerved to the right, praying not to slide off the road into a wall of rock and likely death, or over a cliff to certain death.

An image of her mother flashed through Maggie's mind, and an illusion of what final thoughts might have passed through her mother's mind as she perished in her own road accident.

The bike began sliding out from under her, and she struggled in one direction and then in another to keep it upright. She'd almost won the battle when she felt the bike's front wheel lurch off the edge of the road. She braced as best she could for impact with a guardrail or rock face, but none occurred. Instead, she had the brief sensation of flying as the bike fell forward, sending Maggie tumbling over the handlebars toward what she knew must be her death.

Chapter Six

Yianni had no idea why the undercover cop had picked a jewelry museum in Athens's Plaka District for their meeting. The century-old art deco building sat roughly equidistant from the New Acropolis Museum to the east and the Theater of Dionysus at the foot of the Acropolis to the north. It didn't seem the kind of place for such a rendezvous.

Which makes it the perfect choice, thought Yianni as he walked into the museum at the agreed-upon half hour before closing time.

An attractive young woman in a brightly colored silk scarf smiled and said, "Welcome to ILJM."

Yianni smiled. "Thank you." He looked around hoping to see his contact.

"You seem to be looking for someone," said the woman.

"Just wondering if I might recognize anyone. It's my first visit, but I understand a lot of distinguished people come here regularly."

"We consider all of our visitors distinguished." She smiled broader. "But, since this is your first visit, may I suggest you start at the top floor and work your way down."

"Uh, thank you, but I'd prefer to look around this floor for now."

She scrunched up her nose. "No, no, no. I really do think you should go to the top floor. I'm sure what's up there will interest you."

Yianni's immediate instinct was to press back at her pushiness, but instead he smiled, and nodded.

"The elevator is across from the stairs."

He took the elevator to the third floor, stepped off, and turned to enter the exhibition hall, when a door opened directly across from the elevator and a hand waved for him to come inside.

"How did you arrange this, Stavros?" said Yianni, stepping into a bookcase-lined room filled with tables covered in art books and desks packed with computers and office equipment.

His contact waved a hand around the room. "It's the museum office. My girlfriend's the manager."

"That was your girlfriend who steered me up here?"

Stavros nodded. "No reason to risk someone seeing you and me together. I doubt anyone from the crew I'm working with would ever find out I was here, but on the off chance someone did, my explanation is I'm screwing the manager. That'll earn me points in their eyes, as opposed to the bullet in the head I'd get if they suspected I was meeting with a distinguished member of GADA's Special Crimes Unit."

Yianni grinned. "And a likely black eye from your girlfriend if she ever heard your alibi. At least that's what I'd get from mine."

"I'd prefer not to test your theory," smiled Stavros.

Yianni reached inside his jacket pocket and pulled out a pack of photos. "We copied these off a video recording. They're a bit blurry, but the faces are still visible."

Stavros skimmed through the photos and handed them back to Yianni. "Yep, those are our two dirty little drug agents."

"Are you sure? You went through the photos rather quickly."

Stavros smiled. "In the undercover business, a millisecond can be an eternity. Bad guys are notoriously paranoid. They're primed to think that anyone giving considered thought to a decision is likely scheming against them. To survive in that world, you damn well better learn to make quick decisions."

"I'll keep that in mind. Do you have any idea of their names?"

"Not a clue."

"I didn't think you would. We'll try tracking them down through the license plate on their vehicle." Yianni bit at his lip. "I want you to know how much the chief and I appreciate the risks you're taking and all the great work you're doing."

"Thanks. That's good to hear from guys who have my back."

"Don't worry, we've got you covered. It's the least we can do for a cop braver than we are."

"I'm not braver," grinned Stavros, "just more into acting than you are."

Yianni laughed. "How much longer are you going to be on this assignment?"

"That's not up to me. It's up to you and your boss."

"I meant when do you think you'll have enough evidence for us to bust the bastards?"

Stavros shrugged. "Not sure, but if these DEA guys turn out to be dirty, and you bust them in a way that gets back to my bad guys, I'm disappearing and growing a beard."

"I hear you."

Stavros nodded. "If I had to bet, I'd say Far Eastern bad guys corrupted the drug agents. That crowd wants to dominate the drug trade in Greece as part of its broader plan for further infiltrating Europe."

"That's the same business model many of their colleagues have in mind for Greece's legitimate economy. They're into acquiring or controlling our seaports, rail services, energy, and whatever other major infrastructure assets are available. They see Greece as their primary gateway into the EU, and integral to their long-range planning."

Stavros frowned. "For good guys or bad guys, business is business."

"Which is precisely why we're not going to publicly bust a couple of low-level dirty government agents and lose the chance of nailing those higher up the food chain."

"That works for me. Just don't forget to give me a heads-up if you decide to pull the plug on them."

Yianni smacked Stavros on the shoulder. "You've got my word on that too."

Stavros smacked him back. "Great. You should leave now. I'll hang here with Ioanna." He smiled. "After all, I've gotta maintain my cover story."

Yianni laughed. "No comment. Stay in touch." He cracked open the door wide enough to make sure no one would see him leaving the office. When he stepped out, he closed the door and headed straight for the stairs leading down to the ground floor. At the second floor he paused to look at a display case filled with creations made of twenty-two-carat gold and precious stones. He wasn't big on jewelry, but he'd never seen anything like this.

The exhibition hall held one glittering case after another, each filled with objects, artwork, and jewelry in testament to the extraordinary talent of the museum's founder.

"What the hell," mumbled Yianni to himself. "This is likely the only time I'll ever be here. I might as well take a look."

Five minutes into exploring, he heard the sound of breaking glass on the floor below.

Oops. Someone's got a big mess to clean up.

An instant later he heard a muffled scream from the same floor.

Yianni drew his gun and ran on his toes toward the stairs, hoping to mute the sound of his shoes on the marble floor. The stairs reversed at a landing halfway to the ground floor, continued down between two walls that shielded Yianni's view of what he'd find at the bottom, and ended, still between the walls, five meters directly across from the elevator door.

He heard three male voices softly arguing about where they should go next. One wanted to stay on that floor, the others said the truly valuable stuff was upstairs.

He heard no other voices. The last thing he wanted to do was blindly jump into the middle of a potential armed robbery, with unknown hostages at risk. He reached for his phone to call for backup, but his plans changed when the elevator door across from him opened, and out stepped Stavros onto the wide-open main floor.

"What the fuck…" said Stavros, looking at Yianni crouched hidden at the bottom of the staircase, gun drawn.

Yianni waved his gun across his chest in the direction of the front of the building.

"Put up your hands," yelled a brusque voice from across the room.

Stavros turned toward the voice, "What are you shit heads doing?" He looked at Ioanna on the floor. "What have you done to my girlfriend?"

"Not nearly as much as we're going to do to you if you don't put your hands up and shut up."

Stavros put up his hands and ran toward Ioanna. He dropped to a crouch and felt for a pulse. "She needs a doctor."

"You're going to need a morgue if you don't get away from her."

"What did you hit her with?"

"With this," said a voice behind Stavros.

Yianni heard the crack. He jumped out from the stairs, training his gun back and forth between a man holding a gun at his side and another holding a hammer over Stavros's body.

"Police! Drop your weapons!"

The man with the hammer didn't, and Yianni shot him.

The man with the gun swung it up toward Yianni.

Yianni shot him too.

A third man made a run for the front door.

Yianni shot him. Twice.

Yianni quickly scanned the room for other threats, then picked up the gun of the second man he'd shot, and searched all three for additional weapons, ignoring their cries of pain as he did. He found a pistol on the guy with the hammer, and a gravity knife on the one who'd bolted for the door.

He hurried back to kneel beside the unconscious Stavros. Blood streamed down the back of his head. Yianni reached for the scarf draped about Ioanna's throat. With one hand he pressed the scarf tightly up against Stavros's wound, and with the other slowly and deliberately aimed his pistol in the direction of the men he'd shot.

"I took out your shoulders and your knees. Are there any more of you around here or expected? Don't lie, because if someone else shows up, my first bullets are between your eyes."

They growled that it was just the three of them.

Glaring at the men, he pointed his gun at each of them. "I dare any of you to make a move." He placed his gun on the floor, reached into his pocket, pulled out his phone, and pressed a speed dial button. He identified himself to the dispatcher, gave his location, and requested immediate backup and medical help for an officer and civilian in critical condition, and three wounded bad guys in custody.

He shoved the phone back into his pocket and took hold of Stavros's hand, all the while keeping pressure on the wound and his eyes on the bad guys. "Hang in there, buddy. Help is on the way." Yianni wasn't sure Stavros could hear him, but that didn't matter. He told him the sorts of things he'd want to hear were he in Stavros's position.

Yianni reached over and felt for Ioanna's pulse. Weak but steady. "Stay with me, Ioanna. It's all going to be fine. Help is almost here."

Yianni kept up his reassuring chatter until the ambulances arrived and the EMTs took charge. He'd been spouting whatever positive thoughts came into his mind that he hoped might keep Stavros and Ioanna battling to survive. But his performance also served another purpose. It distracted him from a gnawing, growing sense of guilt that, in not coming out from the stairs sooner, he'd failed in his promise to have Stavros's back.

As Yianni watched the EMTs struggle to work their magic on the two, he swept away a tear. Then said a prayer.

———

Andreas hung up the house phone, slunk back into the sofa, shut his eyes, and crossed himself.

Across the room, in the doorway to the kitchen, Lila stood watching her husband. "I'm afraid to ask what that call was about."

Andreas shook his head from side to side. "Short, unpredictable, and merciless. That's life. You're here one moment all bright, cheery, and full of life, and the next instant…"

Lila made a beeline to the sofa and dropped down next to Andreas.

She took his hands in hers, "Who died?"

Andreas paused, wondering how much to say. "A truly fine young man named Stavros. He worked undercover on a very dangerous assignment." Andreas drew in and let out a deep breath. "The kind of an assignment where what happened to him is always a risk." He paused. "But that's not what happened this time. He just happened to be in the wrong place at the wrong time. He stumbled upon three hyped-up scumbag junkies trying to pull off an armed robbery at a jewelry museum. They'd knocked out his girlfriend who managed the place, and when Stavros went over to care for her, they killed him."

"How awful! What's her name?"

"Ioanna."

"From ILJM?"

Andreas nodded.

"Oh my God, I know her. How is she?"

"She's in the hospital, but doctors say she'll recover. Both were hit in the head with a hammer, but the killer hit Stavros way harder than he did the girlfriend."

"Who called you?"

"Yianni. He was there when it happened and is blaming himself."

"Why's he doing that?"

Andreas squeezed Lila's hand. "Cops tend to do that when something bad happens to a cop you're working with, no matter how freakish or unanticipated the event. We see ourselves as somehow responsible for the most unimaginable things, and the guilt, misplaced as it is, can be overwhelming." Andreas let himself breathe deeply. "I told Yianni to take a couple of days off and to speak to GADA's psychologist."

"Will he?"

Andreas shrugged. "I hope so but wouldn't bet on it. He's all pumped up to chase down the only potential lead we have left in the case Stavros was working on. It's part of that *responsibility* thing. As for seeing a shrink, Yianni comes from a long line of macho Greeks who don't put much stock in that sort of thing."

"I'll speak to Toni. It's the kind of thing a girlfriend can help him with. Especially someone as tough as Toni."

Andreas smiled. "Yes. I'm familiar with the breed."

Lila poked him in the arm. "I fully relate to what you were saying about guilty feelings arising from events over which you had no control or responsibility. When you hung up, I thought for sure someone we knew had died, but when I realized the poor man was a stranger to me, I felt a sense of relief." She squeezed his hand. "I'm ashamed of myself."

Andreas kissed her on the cheek. "It's human nature to sense relief when you learn someone you care about survived a disaster. But for the empathetic among us, relief comes mixed with guilt over those who didn't survive."

Andreas's mobile rang. He picked it up off the coffee table in front of them and looked at the number. "I don't recognize it." He paused. "I think it's from Ikaria."

"Maybe it's Maggie?"

"But it's not her number."

"Just answer it."

"It's not like her to call me in the evening." Andreas stared at the phone, letting it go into voicemail.

"Why didn't you take the call? If it is Maggie, it might be important."

Andreas bit at his lip. "I'm certain the conversation we're having is more important. Besides, I'll call back later."

"You seem worried."

Andreas sighed. "Perhaps I am. I'm still shell-shocked from my conversation with Yianni. I don't want any more surprises tonight."

The phone rang again.

Andreas looked at the number.

"It's the same number, isn't it?"

Andreas nodded. "Yes."

"You really should answer it."

Andreas drew in a deep breath and held it as he brought the phone up to his ear. "Kaldis here."

It wasn't Maggie.

It was Ikaria's chief of police.

———

Maggie had spun full circle, plus one-hundred-eighty degrees, before hitting the ground. She lay flat on her back, eyes shut, wondering whether she was dead or alive. Rain pelted her body, and she took that to mean she was alive. She debated whether to attempt wiggling her toes or moving her fingers, afraid of what it would mean if she couldn't. Thirty seconds went by before she took the risk. The toes wiggled, and so she tried her fingers. Success again.

Feeling braver, she tried to sit up. That's when she felt pains in her right-side shoulder, rib cage, and butt cheek. Not sharp pains, more as if she'd been kicked by a mule. A tiny mule, but big enough to have left her with a memory of the experience. She looked down to see what she'd hit.

Orange basketballs, green soccer balls, and oddly shaped tan-yellow bells surrounded her. She couldn't see clearly and panicked at the thought the fall had affected her vision. That's when she realized she still wore her helmet, the deluging rain blurring her visor. She flipped it up, looked around, paused, and began to laugh. She laughed so hard it hurt her side, but she couldn't stop. Pent-up anxieties in need of release and traumas seeking a path toward healing found a way for their processes to begin in a spontaneous fit of nervous laughter. All triggered by a simple, silly, but very real observation: her life had been saved by a pumpkin patch.

Had she gone off the road thirty meters before or after where she did, she'd have tumbled down the mountain to certain death. But she'd been run off the road beside a small plateau, three meters or so below the roadway. It had been turned into a terraced garden by stone retaining walls built to hold back the soil from washing down the mountainside. She'd landed in a part of the garden filled with pumpkins and winter squash, a far more cushioned experience than hitting a field of rocks and boulders.

Once Maggie gained control over her laughter, she drew in and let out a string of deep breaths, followed by a prayer of thanks to God for the rain-softened, rock-free turf on which she'd landed.

As she struggled to her feet, trying to adjust to her pains as she did, a thought ran through her mind that nearly launched her on a new laughing fit. Perhaps she should ask the Lord why her rescue couldn't have taken place in a field of softer produce, like spinach.

Instead, she confined herself to a giggle.

She slowly got to her feet and made her way back to the bike, It lay on the plateau just below the edge of the road, its engine still running. She thought of taking a shot at maneuvering it back up onto the road.

Then what? She leaned down to turn off the engine. Assuming she could somehow muster the strength to get it back up on the road, there was no way she could trust her body to control the bike all the way home. Certainly not in this weather.

"Be sensible," she said to herself, reaching for her mobile.

She dialed her cousin Spiro's number. Nothing happened. She looked at the phone. "Great, no cellphone service."

The urge to laugh had passed. She made her way back up to the road and waited for someone to come by. She'd flag a driver down and get a ride to where she could call her cousin.

She felt like the proverbial drowned rat, this one hoping to be picked up by anyone, even a hungry cat.

Headlights came at her on her side of the road. Despite the pain, she waved at the headlights with both arms long before the driver could likely see her through a rainy and likely foggy windshield. No matter, Maggie would make sure that the driver saw her.

Passing her by without stopping to help would be disappointing. But being run over twice in the same spot on the same evening would be a terminal downer.

———

Andreas had no active cases working on Ikaria, so a call from its police chief likely meant something new was afoot. Andreas wanted the chief to hurry up and get to the point of his call, but the two men had not spoken in years, and being a naturally garrulous fellow, the police chief took a few minutes before getting there.

"I originally planned on calling our mutual friend Tassos about the accident—"

Andreas's heart nearly leaped out of his chest. "What accident?"

He sounded puzzled. "Earlier tonight a motorbike went off a mountain road in the middle of a horrendous rainstorm, and—"

"Was Maggie involved?" barked Andreas into the phone.

Lila's hand shot up to her face.

"Yes. I thought—"

"*Damn it!*" shouted Andreas. "Just tell me how she is."

"She's fine."

Andreas turned to Lila. "She's fine."

Lila crossed herself.

"You just scared the shit out of me," he told the chief.

"Me too," said Lila in the background.

"I thought you knew."

"How would I possibly I know?"

"Because Maggie promised me she'd tell you."

Andreas shut his eyes as he drew in and let out a deep breath. "Okay, I'm sorry I raised my voice. I'm just a little touchy. It's been a bad day at the office."

"No problem. I've had my share of those."

"If you don't mind, I'm going to put you on speaker so my wife can hear straight from you what happened, and that Maggie's okay."

"Sure." He described in detail how Maggie's motorbike had likely been accidentally forced off the road by a driver who couldn't see well in the rain, and how she miraculously ended up only bruised, not broken.

"She managed to get herself back up onto the road to signal for help. A husband and wife stopped to pick her up, and when Maggie told them what happened, they offered to take her to the hospital. She refused, saying she was fine, and they should drop her off at the nearest village so she could call her cousin to pick her up."

"Sounds like Maggie," said Andreas.

"The wife insisted that Maggie at least let them drive her home, so she could get out of her soaked clothes before catching her death of cold."

"Sounds like a traditional caring Greek wife," said Lila with a smile.

The police chief laughed. "Yes, I have one of those. Anyway, Maggie agreed, and they dropped her off where she told them to stop, but the husband insisted on walking her home. By the time he returned to the car, his wife had called us to report the accident and tell us the injured driver refused to go to the hospital."

"I like that wife more and more," smiled Lila.

"She gave Maggie's name as the accident victim, and the

dispatcher recognized it from when I'd sent a car with Tassos to pick her up at the airport. The dispatcher called to tell me she'd been in a potentially serious accident but had refused medical attention. I went straight to her house to check on her condition."

"She must have been happy to see you," said Andreas.

He laughed. "Yeah, I was as welcome as the tax collector. She went ballistic, told me not to dare tell Tassos what happened. She knew he'd worry and feared how that might affect his heart. I said I had to tell someone who could convince her to see a doctor. She promised to see a doctor if I promised not to tell Tassos.

"I said that's not good enough. I had to be sure that someone who knew her well was aware of her accident, just in case complications showed up later. That's when she promised to tell you."

"Since she never told me, I guess you were right not to believe her."

"Oh, I believed her. It's just that as I was driving home it hit me that she'd never said *when* she'd tell you. So, I decided to wait a bit and then call you, just to make sure you knew. After all, as I said, I have a Greek wife, and I know how they don't like to have their loved ones worrying over them."

"Thank you," Andreas and Lila said at the same time.

"Of course," said the chief. "Now, I need a promise from each of you."

"What is it?" said Andreas.

"Please don't ever tell Tassos that I kept this information from him. Life's too short to be on his you-know-what list."

"No problem on this end," said Andreas.

"I do have one question," said Lila.

"Shoot."

"Why was Maggie out and about on a motorbike, on a mountain road, in the middle of a torrential storm?"

"Good question," added Andreas.

"And one for which I have no answer. Because I never thought to ask it."

"Perhaps someone should?" said Lila.

"Not I," said the police chief. "The answer is likely innocent, but if it's not, I'm not about to stick my nose into Tassos's girlfriend's private affairs. To repeat, life is too short to risk his wrath."

"I'm sure it's an innocent explanation," said Lila. "I'm just naturally curious."

"Another trait of the Greek wife," smiled Andreas.

"On that note, I think I'll say goodbye," said the chief.

"Thanks for the call, and again, sorry for the way I reacted."

"No problem. Bye."

Andreas hung up, and looked at Lila. "Quite a day."

Lila nodded. "For sure." She paused. "Why *do* you think Maggie was riding a motorbike in the middle of a storm?"

"No idea, but if the time ever comes that she raises the accident with me, I'll let you know so that you can grill her to your heart's content. Until then, I'm all-in with the chief on his life's-too-short theory to butt in on Maggie's private life."

"Well, then," said Lila pushing herself up from the sofa and reaching down to pull her husband up and off as well, "Let's not waste the little time we have. Come. Allow me to show you something else Greek wives are renowned for."

"God bless Hellas."

Chapter Seven

Maggie had a difficult time falling asleep. As much as she tried to rid her mind of the accident, she couldn't shake loose how close she'd come to dying or spending the rest of her life confined to a wheelchair.

We take living for granted, not realizing how precious life is to protect until we almost lose it. She wondered if the elderly felt that way, too, or did there come a moment when age brought on a different perspective? Not accepting death as obviously inevitable, but a vision of how to retool one's life for the time yet to come.

Maggie fell asleep to thoughts of how to reshape her own life, and awoke to banging clatter at her front door.

"*Kiria* Maggie, are you there? Are you okay?"

"Who is it?" she shouted from her bed.

"It's Dimitri. I picked you up at the airport with Mr. Tassos. Sorry for all the noise, but I've been knocking on the door and getting no answer."

Maggie looked at the clock next to the bed. She couldn't believe it was after nine. "What do you want?"

"The chief told me to give you a ride to the hospital."

Maggie frowned. "That's very nice of you and the chief, but I can't go right now. I have to help my cousin pick up his motorbike from where I left it and make arrangements for it to be fixed."

"Chief said to tell you it's already been picked up and delivered to a repair shop. They'll bill you."

"Well, then I'll get my cousin to take me to the hospital."

"Chief said if that's how you want to do it, I'm to hang around and give you a police escort. But my orders are I don't leave until you're cleared by the hospital."

Maggie fumed. She'd been outfoxed. But for good reasons. People cared for her. "Okay, give me twenty minutes to be ready."

"Take your time. I've got all day."

I don't, thought Maggie. Hours spent at a hospital did not fit in her plans.

She turned on her side to get out of bed and winced. The pain was worse, and she hurt in more places than when she'd gone to bed. A much different story from those falls she took in her younger days, when she woke feeling better the next day.

Maybe that's why everyone's urging you to see a doctor...

Enough grumbling. Get your butt out of bed and be done with it.

———

Yianni went to the hospital straight from the museum and did not leave until dawn. He was there when Ioanna's parents arrived, frightened and anxious, but thankful she'd survived. He was there when Stavros's parents arrived, shaking and crying, to claim their son's body.

He'd spent much of the night fidgeting in an uncomfortable plastic chair and talking with Toni on his mobile. Yianni knew he'd been blessed to have her in his life, and wished she'd come live with him in Athens. Or perhaps he should live with her on Mykonos. With life as short and unpredictable as last night's events had brought home to him, it seemed senseless to allow their jobs to keep them apart.

But that was a subject for another day. It was too serious to raise in the midst of a conversation unpacking the tragic events he'd been through. Toni helped steer him to a better place, one where guilt no longer dominated his thinking, and getting drunk was recognized as but an empty ploy to avoid confronting pain that must be processed in order to move on.

By the time Yianni left the hospital, he'd come up with a far more appropriate tribute to Stavros's memory: He'd find a way to bring meaning and a sense of positive closure to Stavros's unfinished assignment.

But where to start? No way he could step into Stavros's undercover role, or expect to turn any of the crew of bad guys Stavros worked with into informants. Stavros's crew members were far more afraid of their fates should they cooperate with the police than of anything the police could threaten if they did not.

As Yianni saw it, his best potential way back into the loop was through the two drug enforcement agents in the photos. If dirty, they had a lot more to lose, and likely a lot more to tell.

Okay, he told himself. He had his place to start. Identify the men. He'd had no luck overnight with matching them to their agency vehicle's license plates. He'd have to find another way.

But first a shower, a bit of sleep, and a change of clothes.

———

Like many island hospitals, the Ikaria Prefectural General Hospital in Agios Kirykos was equipped to handle most emergencies, while relying upon evacuation to larger, off-island facilities for the more serious cases. When Maggie and Dimitri walked into the hospital's emergency care area, the place was packed with injured and ill people of all ages seeking healing. She stared at the long line of people waiting to speak with a receptionist separated from the rest of the room by a plexiglass partition.

Maggie sighed. *I'll be here forever.* She took her place at the back of the line.

Dimitri headed straight for the receptionist and spoke to her for a few seconds before waving for Maggie to join him. She could feel the glares of those she passed on her way to the head of the line.

"*Kiria* Maggie?" asked the receptionist.

"Yes."

The receptionist nodded to Dimitri.

"Come, follow me," he said.

Maggie dared not look back at the line, for by now the glares must be daggers.

She quietly followed Dimitri along a wide, pale yellow hallway. He stopped at a door marked EXAMINATION ROOM and knocked twice.

From inside a voice said, "Come in."

"I'm sure you can take it from here," said Dimitri. "I'll wait for you back in reception."

Again, the voice said, "Come in."

Maggie opened the door. A doctor somewhat younger than she and a younger nurse stood waiting for her.

"You must be she who your many friends call Maggie," said the doctor with a smile.

"Yes, that's me."

"I understand you had an accident."

Maggie's heart raced. "I appreciate all this special attention, but frankly, it's making me anxious. Is there something I don't know about that should have me worried?"

"Since I haven't examined you yet, I can't speak to your condition, but I think I can allay your fears over the reason for all the attention you're getting. Our police chief called me to ask that, as a personal favor to him, he'd appreciate my taking special care of his dear friend Maggie." He shrugged, "So, what choice did I have but to do as he asked? After all, I don't want my car towed every time I park where I shouldn't."

Maggie heaved a sigh of relief, but the thought of having jumped the line over so many people in greater need embarrassed her to the point of blushing—more so than at any point during her ensuing, extraordinarily thorough head-to-toe examination.

"You're one lucky lady," said the doctor. "Aside from contusions and a few scrapes, you seem fine. Nothing appears broken or torn, and assuming the lab tests don't show anything unexpected, you should heal up nicely."

"Thank God. Would you mind telling that to the young officer who brought me here? As much as I appreciate all this attention, I really would like to leave."

"I fully understand, but not quite yet. You took a brutal fall. We should do a CAT scan and MRI to make sure you're okay."

Maggie sighed. "How long will those take?"

"Sadly, we don't have those capabilities here at this time. They'll have to be done in Athens."

Maggie grimaced. "Sorry, no can do. What are other options?"

"I recommend you go for those tests, but at a bare minimum we need X-rays."

"How long will they take?"

"Not long."

Considering the Greeks' reputation for a rather flexible attitude toward time, an estimate of "not long" had Maggie bidding farewell to her plans for the rest of the day. She saw a glimmer of hope when ten minutes later she was taken to the X-ray unit, but that faded as she waited an hour for her turn. Something about the technician being unavailable…

With nothing she could do to hurry things along and everyone treating her so warmly, she saw no point to engaging in the sort of aggressive complaining that was so often necessary to get institutional attention in Athens. Instead, she sat quietly, waiting to be called, attaining a state of peaceful acceptance that the rest of her day was shot.

She'd drifted off into a dozing sleep, when an idea popped into her head that might salvage her day.

As soon as she'd finished with her X-rays, Maggie went straight to the reception area. Dimitri stood leaning up against the plexiglass, chatting with the receptionist.

"Where's everyone gone? Reception's empty,"

"It's our slow time," said the receptionist.

"Are you done, *kiria*?" Dimitri asked.

"Not yet." Maggie asked the receptionist, "Do you happen to know a priest named Giorgos?"

"I know several."

"This one works primarily with the very old, so my guess is he spends a lot of time in the hospital."

"Oh, you must mean Papa George. He uses George so he won't be confused with other priests named Giorgos."

"Do you happen to know the next time Papa George will be here?"

"No. It depends on whether a member of his flock—that's what he calls them—is admitted here. He's friends with all the doctors, and when a patient of theirs admitted here happens to be a member of his flock, they let him know."

Maggie shook her head. "Too bad. I believe he included my *yaya* in his flock. I wanted to thank him."

"Well, then why wait until the next time he's here? He's here today."

Maggie forgot how literal and precise even the smartest of country folk could be. Ask a question and get an answer to that question. No more, no less.

"Do you think it's possible to see him today?"

"Papa George is always willing to meet new people. No matter how busy he might be. I'll tell him you wish to see him. What was your *yaya*'s name?"

Maggie told her, and the receptionist placed her call.

"May I ask what we're waiting for?" asked Dimitri.

"I'm waiting for the doctor to give me my test results. In the meantime I thought I'd speak to this priest."

"No problem, just curious."

Maggie went to sit in a chair on the far side of the room, while Dimitri went back to his conversation with the receptionist.

Five minutes passed with no sign of the priest. Maggie remained patient, reminding herself that he'd come here to minister to his flock, not to drop everything to chat with her.

Hmm, maybe this retooling idea actually works.

Two minutes later a priest came striding down the hallway toward the reception, announcing in a confident, cheery voice as he entered, "So, where's this lovely lady who calls one of my favorite people of all time *yaya*?"

Only somewhat taller than Maggie, though likely a couple of decades younger, Papa George knew how to make a grand first impression. A full head of tousled black hair, a neatly trimmed jet-black beard, and stark blue eyes conveyed a leading-man presence. A tailored black cassock with a classic Montblanc 149 fountain pen protruding discreetly from an exterior breast pocket, and a pair of neatly polished black Gucci loafers lent him intrigue. He was not the sort of priest you typically found on Ikaria. Or anywhere else, for that matter.

The politics of the Church could be brutal, and this young man had obviously charted what he saw as his best course for advancing in the ranks.

Maggie waved to the priest from across the room. "I'm over here, Papa."

He smiled at the receptionist and Dimitri as he kept walking straight for Maggie. She began to stand.

"No need to rise, my child. I'll sit beside you."

He dropped into a chair and flashed Maggie his leading-man smile. "So, you're Yaya's granddaughter. I should have recognized you from the photos I've seen of her as a young woman. Startling resemblance."

"Thank you. That's a great compliment."

"It was meant to be." He smiled again.

Maggie nodded. "I understand you spent a lot of time with her during her final days."

"It is what I see as my calling. To tend to those blessed by the Lord to have lived more than ninety years among us."

"It must be difficult for you, what with how few years they have left to live. So soon after you get to know them, so many pass away."

"Yes, that part is sad, but it's more than compensated for by all that I learn as they reflect on their lives. Especially when they sense they're in their final days and talk openly about what's been most meaningful to them in their time on earth."

Maggie's eyes welled up in tears. "I understand what you're saying. But it still takes a special person to do what you do."

"Now it's my turn to acknowledge a compliment."

"And my turn to say it was intended."

Both smiled.

Maggie paused. "Papa, may I ask how you came to know my *yaya*?"

"Certainly. I moved to Ikaria from Athens two years ago, having given up my past life to pursue God's work."

Maggie interrupted. "So, you're new to the priesthood?"

"Yes. I'd spent a number of years in the military and then worked as a salesman in the fine jewelry and accessories business." He tapped at his pen. "This was a gift from my former employer on my ordination."

"Training for battle and knowing how to sell the goods sound like perfect training for the priesthood."

He laughed. "Well, permit me to demur from answering that and get back to how I met your *yaya*."

Maggie nodded.

"I keep a list of every soul on Ikaria who's attained nonagenarian status. I seek them out at their local churches to inquire whether I might be of some assistance or comfort to them and their families. If they agree, I make a point of visiting them regularly at their homes, and if they're blessed to be centenarians, I see them every week, sometimes several times a week, depending on their level of need. At times, my commitment to them brings me here. Sadly, today I have several to visit before I leave." He leaned back in the chair. "When I introduced myself to your *yaya* at her village church, she invited me to stop by her home whenever I felt the need." With twinkle in his eye he added, "Whenever I visited her, I often felt she was ministering to me, more than the other way around."

Maggie smiled. "That sounds like Yaya."

"I'd stop by to see her whenever I was in the neighborhood, usually a couple of times a week. She truly was one of my favorites." He bit at his lip. "A real joy to be with."

Maggie wiped away a tear.

"I saw her several times during her final weeks," he said quietly. "Her passing came as a total surprise."

"To me too." Maggie hesitated. "Do you happen to know whether she'd been to the hospital during those weeks?"

"Not that I know of."

"What about seeing a doctor?"

"Not that I'm aware of." He cocked his head toward Maggie. "May I inquire why you ask?"

Here we go. "After Yaya died, I noticed bruise marks on her arm, and no one can explain where they came from. The best guess is they're from some sort of IV."

"IV?"

"An intravenous needle, of the sort used for infusions, transfusions…whatever."

"I never noticed any bruises, though whenever I saw her, she wore long sleeves." He smiled. "Always proper, your *yaya*."

Maggie shrugged. "I guess it's just my suspicious nature. But at least I come by it honestly."

"How's that?"

"I've worked with the police my entire career, and now I'm with the most suspicious cops of all. GADA's Special Crimes Unit."

Papa George nodded. "Sounds interesting."

Maggie saw her doctor walk into the reception area and wave to her. "If you'll excuse me for a minute, my doctor wants to speak with me. I'll be right back."

"No problem at all. Do what you have to do."

Maggie pushed herself up from the chair and hurried toward the doctor. "So, what's the verdict?"

"The X-rays are all good news. I still recommend you have the other tests, but since I assume you won't listen to me, just take it easy for a few days to give all the places where you're hurting time to heal."

Maggie instinctively hugged him. "I don't know how to thank you enough."

"The hug was more than sufficient," he said with a wry smile. "But I do have a suggestion you might consider following."

"What's that?"

"Light a candle in church for your good fortune at being delivered from what could have been...well...I think you know without me elaborating."

"Believe me, Doctor, I do and I'll be lighting many candles. In fact, I'm going to ask Papa George to say a special prayer of thanks on my behalf."

She turned her head toward the seating area. "Where is he?"

The doctor shook his head. "Papa George never sits still for long. He's always doing something for someone."

"I guess he didn't understand that I wanted him to wait."

Maggie thanked the doctor and the receptionist and told Dimitri she was ready to leave.

As they walked to the car, a beep sounded on Dimitri's mobile. "It's a message from my chief. He said to tell you he's thrilled that everything turned out so well."

So much for doctor-patient confidentiality.

"And he told me to tell you not to forget to update Andreas on your status."

"Please tell him message received, and that I can't thank him enough for all he's done for me."

With all the concern the police chief kept voicing for Maggie to keep Andreas informed about her health, she guessed the two had already spoken. His not-so-subtle reminders to her amounted to the sort of inside jokes little boys think they're playing on unsuspecting little girls. None of that bothered Maggie, though, because truth be told, he had done the right thing by telling Andreas.

Between all the good news on the medical front, and Andreas likely already in the loop, Maggie felt the pressure lessening to tell him about the accident. On the other hand, if Andreas did not know, even Maggie's clean bill of health would not deter him from hounding her to return to Athens at once to take advantage of its far better medical care.

Maggie decided to stick to her original plan and wait to tell Andreas in person, when he'd see for himself that all was fine. She'd make him laugh, by turning the accident into a funny story of how, one dark and stormy night, a pumpkin patch had saved her life as she raced a motorbike along mountain roads, playing amateur detective.

Maggie's eyes fixed on a bruise on the back of her hand, one that she'd not noticed before. Her thoughts bounced back to Yaya and the bruising on her arm.

Maggie shut her eyes and shrugged. *Amateur being the operative word. And I am still playing.*

———

On the drive back from the hospital to Yaya's cottage, Maggie pressed Dimitri for everything he knew about Papa George. It wasn't much, because they'd barely exchanged more than an occasional hello, and Dimitri couldn't recall seeing him anywhere on the island except at the hospital visiting a patient or paying his respects at a funeral.

By the time Dimitri dropped Maggie off at the path to Yaya's house, she'd compiled a list of questions in her mind to ask Papa George.

Maggie wandered through the groves of ripening fruit, taking in the end-of-summer scents of what had blossomed in the spring, plus of course, grapes in the vineyard that yielded up the deep-red wine every Ikariot treasured. Yaya had loved this time of year, when the light turned softer and the weather cooler.

Once back at the cottage, she'd call Papa George with her

questions. For that, though, she'd need his phone number. The *savanotria* she'd spoken to shortly before her accident had promised to text it to her, but hadn't yet. Certainly, the hospital would have it.

But, first, she had to call Tassos. Already today, he'd sent her a zillion text messages. She'd barely had the chance to respond to a tenth of them, and in many he apologized for their sheer number, but that he thought a message less intrusive than a call. What he didn't know was that the incessant message notifications—even with pinging turned off—were driving her crazy. Thankfully, nothing in any of his messages suggested he knew about her accident. The police chief had apparently kept his word on that score.

Maggie smiled, for she realized all of Tassos's texting was because he missed her. She'd call him, reassure him that she felt the same way, and gently suggest, STOP WITH THE MESSAGES ALREADY. YOU'RE DRIVING ME NUTS. Yes, that sort of subtlety was the only way to get her message across to her loving huggy-bear of a boyfriend.

After speaking to Tassos, she'd take a nap, and then track down Papa George. At the moment, he seemed the likeliest candidate for offering answers, or at least shedding light on what troubled her.

One way or another she'd get her answers.

————

Maggie woke from her nap to the sound of bleating goats. She picked up her mobile and noticed she'd missed a call. It couldn't be Tassos. They'd spoken for so long before she fell off into her nap that she couldn't imagine what more was left to say.

She looked at the number but didn't recognize it. Another robocall, perhaps. She wasn't in the mood to waste time on idle chatter. Still, she sat up on the edge of the bed and called the number to get whatever it was about out of the way.

"Hello, *Kiria* Maggie. Thank you for returning my call."

She paused, trying to recognize the voice. "Papa George?"

"I'm sorry to bother you, but I called to apologize for how abruptly I left you today at the hospital. When you got up to talk to your doctor, I looked at my watch and saw how late it was. I'd promised one of my flock in the hospital that I'd bring her some of her favorite pastries and realized the bakery was about to close for the afternoon. I ran off to get there before it did. I hoped I'd be back before you left, but I missed you. Sorry about that."

"Did you get the pastries?"

"Just made it."

"Good, that's all that matters." Maggie cleared her throat. "May I speak frankly?"

"Certainly."

"There is one thing that bothers me, and only you can resolve it for me."

"If I can, I will." He paused. "What is it?"

"From our conversation at the hospital, I understand how dedicated you were to my *yaya*, especially in her final days. And I truly do appreciate your ministering to her."

"Thank you."

"But I can't help wondering why, with all your strong feelings for Yaya, you never came to the house during our vigil over her body."

Not a peep from Papa George.

"Are you there?" said Maggie.

"Yes. I'm trying to decide how best to confess."

Maggie sat up straight. "Confess to what?"

"My Achilles' heel."

"I'm sorry, but I don't understand."

She heard an audible sigh on the other end of the line.

"It depresses me enormously to be in the home of one I've tended to for so long as a living being, only to see that member of my flock laid out in a coffin. When I first embarked on this ministry, I went to every wake, and spent much of the evening into the morning hours consoling the bereaved, but the process took a great toll on me. So much so, that I considered giving up my ministry. I prayed for guidance, and the solution came to me that I've followed ever since. I no longer attend the *xemenoume to leipsano* of my flock, but only their funerals, for respect must be shown. I apologize if my absence from Yaya's wake offended you, but I did attend her funeral."

Maggie exhaled. "I understand, Papa. Thank you for the explanation."

"You're quite welcome. Do you have any other questions?"

"A couple, but I'm not sure you'll consider them appropriate."

"Ask away."

"I'm amazed at how the other priests on the island don't object to you so freely interacting with their parishioners. In my experience most priests do not take kindly to that."

Maggie heard a chuckle.

"You're right about that, but in my case I don't present a threat to their relationship with their parishioners. To the contrary, they view me as a benefit."

"I don't understand."

"As I'm sure you know, priests in Greece are paid by the state, and augment their incomes by receiving honoraria for performing weddings, baptisms, funerals, and other such services for their parishioners. I do not accept any honoraria for what I do for my flock or their families, but instead tell them to be generous to their local churches and priests. I seek no payment for what I do."

"You receive nothing beyond your state salary?"

Papa George laughed. "So, you noticed the shoes. On occasion, I'm offered and accept a personal gift, but never money. My fellow priests are okay with that."

Maggie paused. "Just one more question. Out of idle curiosity, how many are in your flock at present?"

"As many as may need my assistance. But if you're asking how many I strive to visit several times a week, I try to keep that number to the six oldest. They seem to be in the greatest need. With your *yaya's* passing, it's five at the moment."

"Why six?"

Maggie heard a light laugh.

"The Lord created the world in six days and on the seventh day rested. I thought that dedicating a total of approximately one day's worth of time to each member of my flock made six the appropriate number, leaving me one day of rest to myself."

"Interesting thinking."

"Thank you. As I said, your *yaya* was one of my favorites. I want you to truly feel free to call me at any time with any other questions or concerns you might have."

"I appreciate that."

"You're very welcome, Maggie. God bless and goodbye."

"Same to you, Papa." Maggie put on her robe and stepped to the front door. She pulled it open and stared out across the sloping hillside down to the sea.

One thing's for sure, she thought, *that's one smooth and savvy priest.*

Chapter Eight

Several of Yianni's buddies from his days as a Greek Navy SEAL had been attracted to drug enforcement police work when they left the military. He admired them all, especially those who chose to work undercover. That sort faced the unique risks of being discovered by their targets, caught up in internecine criminal battles, arrested by law-enforcement unaware of their identity, and tempted by the vast amounts of drugs and money that were often available.

For what Yianni had in mind, he sought out his friend Marco. A highly decorated undercover agent, Marco ended up on the administrative side of the Narcotics and Arms Division of Greece's Financial and Economic Crimes Unit, better known as SDOE, after saving the lives of two fellow agents at the cost of a crippling leg injury. He'd given up the streets for a cubicle, and now oversaw many of SDOE's most secure data operations.

Yianni hadn't seen Marco in two years, and when he called him to meet ASAP, Marco's only question was, "Is this an on- or off-the-record meeting?"

When Yianni answered, "A bit of both," Marco suggested they meet near SDOE's Pireos Avenue and Alkifronos Street headquarters southwest of Athens. He picked a *kafenion* on the first floor of a nearby mega mall.

Yianni arrived a few minutes early, hoping to find an inconspicuous table in an otherwise heavily trafficked space. Instead, he found a virtual fishbowl of a meeting site, with no place to hide.

The moment Marco walked into the *kafenion*, Yianni jumped up to hug him.

"It's been way too long since we've seen each other," said Marco.

"Agreed. But I have to say you look terrific."

"Cut the BS, Yianni. We've known each other far too long for that sort of jive."

"No, I'm being honest." He paused, wondering whether or not he should say more.

"I know what you're thinking. 'Should I mention his leg?'"

"Sorry if I'm that obvious, but you *are* walking far better than when I last saw you."

"I'd certainly hope so," said Marco, with an impish grin. "It's taken three surgeries and a hell of a lot of rehab to get me to this point. If you hadn't noticed, I'd have been pissed."

Yianni laughed. "Speaking of being noticed, why in the world did you pick this place? We're practically the only customers in it. If I didn't know better, I'd say you wanted the world to know we're meeting."

"I do." Marco led them away from the table Yianni had chosen to the most conspicuous one in the place. "I want no one who happens to see us together to think there is anything I'm trying to hide. We're just old Navy buddies getting together for a coffee, and that's all there is to it."

"I guess that's one way to play it."

"These days, with the EU breathing down our necks for even a hint of corruption among us administrative types at SDOE, if you want to keep your job, forget about being as chaste as Caesar's wife, you'd best be as she was when a virgin."

"You'll be pleased to know then, that my reason for asking to see you shall not compromise your reputation in any way. Indeed, it may enhance it."

"Okay, you've got my attention."

"Here's my problem. In the middle of a serious undercover operation, two guys popped up who we have reason to believe are drug enforcement agents. We have photographs of them in a vehicle with Greek government plates."

"Do you think they're dirty?"

"On that point all we have is the conjecture of a lone bad guy. It could be they're running their own investigation, and the last thing we want to do is risk getting our wires crossed with theirs."

"Yeah, people have been known to get hurt real bad when that happens." Marco patted his injured leg.

A waiter arrived at the table with two Greek coffees, two glasses of water, and a plate of assorted cookies.

Yianni looked at the waiter, then at Marco. "We didn't order anything."

Marco smiled. "I come here a lot. They know what I like, and just doubled my order. If you prefer something else, just ask. At this hour they don't have much more to do in the kitchen than take care of us."

Yianni took a sip of coffee. "I'm trying to identify the two guys so we can get a better fix on them. We can't do it through official channels, because if they are dirty, and someone in those channels is also involved, us nosing about could tip them off that we're on to them."

Marco lowered his voice, "In other words, you're asking me to use my privileged status, as one of the few people in government with authority to access files on virtually anyone in Greece, to identify two government agents just because some bad guy said something that has you thinking they *might* be dirty?"

Yianni picked up a cookie. "In a word," he took a bite, "yes."

Marco sighed. "Show me the photos."

Yianni pulled a packet out of his coat pocket and slid it across the table.

Marco began looking through the photos but stopped at the second picture. "You must be kidding me. These are the two guys you're after?"

"Why do I sense there's no need for me to answer that question?"

Marco pressed his index finger hard against one pictured face, then the other. "These two bastards are perhaps the most corrupt drug enforcement guys in Greece."

"You make it sound like it's common knowledge."

"It is to anyone with access to the same classified files as I have."

"If the EU is all about rooting out corruption, why hasn't anyone done something about them? Like bring them to the attention of my unit?"

"You're the big shot Special Crimes detective. You tell me."

"I take it you're suggesting they're protected."

"That sort of information isn't in my files." Marco paused. "Just do us all some good and get rid of these guys. They're the proverbial rotten apples in our barrel."

"What are their names and where I can find them?"

Marco told Yianni their names. "But their nicknames are Tom and Jerry."

"After the American ice cream?"

"No, that's Ben and Jerry. Tom and Jerry are American cartoon characters." Marco paused. "I take it you don't have kids."

Yianni smiled. "No, but I'd like to have some with my girlfriend." He froze. "Jesus, Marco. That's the first time I've even thought that, let alone said it aloud."

Marco leaned across the table, patted him on the shoulder, and smiled. "That's great news. But may I suggest you tell it to her rather than me?"

Yianni shook his head to clear his thoughts. "So why the nicknames?"

"Cartoon Tom and Jerry are American favorites, and the same holds true for our real-life Greek versions. They're Greece's official liaison to American DEA operations run out of the U.S. embassy. Americans love them for what they see as their cowboy ways, and that gives them a lot of power, independence, and discretion. Personally, I think the nicknames suit them because of their resemblance to the cartoon cat and mouse." Marco leaned in across the table. "But don't be misled. Our Tom and Jerry version are *not* cartoon characters. People who cross them tend to disappear."

"Then why are they still breathing? If they're known to go after other cops, I'd think they'd be the ones to disappear."

Marco gestured no. "That's precisely why they've never gone after other cops, at least as far as I've heard. But I wouldn't put it past them if they felt cornered."

"So, where do I find this pair of characters?"

"They hang out in a nightclub not far from here. Word is, in exchange for protecting the drug-dealing going on inside, they have an off-the-books interest in the place. Local cops stopped trying to make busts there long ago. Every time they tried, Tom or Jerry would step in and claim it's a protected venue used for gathering vital information for the arrest and conviction of big fish in the drug trade."

"And the local cops and prosecutor bought that BS?"

"Their superiors did, which is end of story for rank and file who want to keep their jobs."

"Sounds to me that there's more than Tom and Jerry who are dirty."

"Could be, but they're clever at how they run their hustle. Every once in a while, they pull off a major drug bust with information allegedly obtained through their club. That generates a lot of splashy media coverage and makes their superiors and the Americans look terrific." Marco smirked. "What no one seems to notice, or doesn't care to notice, about their busts, is they're always competitors of whoever is paying Tom and Jerry at the moment."

"Quite a racket they've got going."

"It's even earned them promotions." Marco feigned to spit on the photos. "That alone is enough to piss off honest cops. But for guys working undercover, it's a hell of a lot more personal than that. They fear someday they'll run into them on an operation, be recognized, and set up to get whacked in a way that can't be traced back to them."

"Do these guys have anything to do with the docks in Piraeus?"

"I'd be surprised if they didn't. After all, it's the primary port for all maritime commerce into and out of Greece, legal and illegal."

Yianni leaned back in his chair and rolled his head from side to side, stretching out his neck. "You've given me a lot to think about, my friend."

Marco waggled a finger at Yianni. "And hopefully a lot of reasons to be careful. After all, now you have a woman in your life to consider. It's no longer just you and your show-no-fear, big-dog bravado to consider."

The image of Stavros lying on the museum floor next to his unconscious girlfriend flashed through Yianni's mind. "Believe me, I get it."

Marco slid the packet of photos back to Yianni and called for the check. After the customary fight among Greek men over who would pay the check—a battle Yianni lost to the *kafenion's* regular customer—they promised to stay in touch more often. They also agreed to leave separately.

Marco left first, leaving Yianni to contemplate his next move. He picked up the packet of photos and slowly thumbed through them. As he saw it, he had but a single hope for picking up the severed thread of Stavros's investigation.

It was time for the big dog to chase the cat and mouse.

———

Maggie spent the rest of the daylight hours wandering about Yaya's orchards, gullies, and rock formations, seeking out places she'd kept secret as a child, or shared with lovers as a young woman. So much of her life had been shaped by moments on this property: her first broken arm, sustained by falling from a rock formation she'd been told never to climb; her first encounter with an angry hog that she'd been warned not to pester; and her loss of virginity to a boy she'd been advised to avoid.

She shook her head and smiled. *Stubbornness is still my downfall.*

At sunset, she joined Spiro and his family for dinner in the big house. She'd offered to help with the cooking, but Spiro's wife, Sonia, would not hear of it.

"I invited you to eat in our home. You are our guest tonight. I do the cooking, you do the eating."

"I'll take that as a yes to my doing the dishes."

Sonia shooed Maggie out of the kitchen with a smile and a wave of her hand.

Their teenage son and daughter sat crowded together in front of a television, watching a competition among nervous amateur singers straining for the praise of three vaguely familiar minor celebrities. Maggie could not begin to understand how the show held their interest.

Spiro sat by a window in a frayed upholstered chair, staring out at what remained of the sunset, and scratching the ears of his Labrador-sized mutt of many breeds.

"Come sit." Spiro pointed at a straight-backed wooden chair beside his. "How did your afternoon go?"

"A lot better than yesterday's."

Spiro laughed. "Thank God you weren't hurt."

"I'm just sorry about the motorbike."

"That can be replaced. You can't."

She gave him a look. "Remember, I'm paying whatever it costs to repair it."

Spiro nodded. "I think my insurance will cover it."

"Even if I was driving?"

"Let that little detail be my worry."

Maggie rolled her eyes.

"These are hard times, Cousin. We do what we must to survive."

Maggie grinned. "Sounds like a traditional Ikarian motto."

Spiro's face grew grim. "I'm serious. Just when tourism was looking up for the island, we got knocked down by the pandemic much harder than we could've imagined. The bottom has fallen out on us."

Maggie patted her cousin's knee. "Don't lose hope. Things are coming back. It'll just take some time."

"I know things will get better, but all I can do is pray that it happens in time." Spiro shook his head. "Frankly, I don't think we'll make it. We may have to sell the property. Or at least some of it." He pointed toward the orchard. "The builder who put up those new homes called me today. He wants to buy our property."

Maggie snickered. "At least he waited until Yaya was buried."

Spiro shrugged. "For him it's business." He sighed. "For us, it's family history. But if we can't afford to pay the taxes or earn a living off it, what other choice do we have?"

"One thing's for sure, we're not going to be making any

decisions today, and once I get back to Athens next week, I'll see if I can get some advice from people who know about this sort of thing."

"Some of our cousins will want to sell."

"I'm sure. There always are cousins who want to sell."

"I can't blame them. I have the benefit of living here, but they get nothing out of it."

"Don't be so hard on yourself. You, Sonia, and the kids not only keep this place up, you pay its taxes and utilities."

"That's the point I'm making, I can't do it for much longer. The hotel where I managed to get a part-time maintenance job is closing until next season, and there's no more work to be found." He pointed to the kitchen. "Sonia's job cleaning rooms at another hotel is about to end too."

Maggie leaned back in her chair. "As I said. Before you do anything, let me speak to friends in Athens."

"A lot of people on this island are desperate. They may not look or act like it, but they are."

"Believe me, I know."

Spiro smiled. "Thank God we have you to make us feel better. You give us hope, Cousin."

An image rose in her mind. "That's more in Papa George's bailiwick, isn't it?" she asked.

"Papa George?"

"The priest who spent time with Yaya in her final weeks."

"Oh, that guy. You know I'm not a big fan of priests, so many of them seem to hover around the old with property hoping to score something for themselves or the Church in the will."

Maggie's eyes widened. "Are you saying that's what he was doing?"

"No, not at all. I thought that at first, but Yaya assured me he never mentioned anything like that. He spoke more in terms of what she could do through her spirit and good heart to make life better for those not as blessed as she to be living such a long and healthy life."

Maggie smiled. "He seems to know the right thing to say for any occasion."

"I really don't know the man. I heard all of that from Yaya."

"You mean you never met him?"

"Only a couple times, when I hadn't left for work by the time he showed up. But we never said much more to each other than hello. He made a point of coming by after we were at work. Yaya said he purposely followed that schedule as a means for comforting us with the knowledge that someone was with her when we couldn't be."

"Sounds like the perfect priest."

Spiro shrugged. "Once you achieve perfection, you can only get worse."

Maggie nodded. "I'll keep that in mind."

"All I can say about him is that Yaya seemed to like him. She said he helped to get her through some things."

"What sorts of things?"

Spiro stopped scratching his dog's ears, patted him twice, and leaned back in his chair. "She didn't and wouldn't say."

"Medical things?"

He gestured no. "I don't think so."

"Who took her to her doctor visits?"

"I did or I'd get one of our cousins to take her."

"Papa George never took her?"

"He had no reason to. She saw no doctors during the weeks he visited her."

"What about trips to the hospital?"

"None." He cocked his head. "Why are you asking about this?"

Maggie paused, wondering if she should say more. "Because

I can't figure out why she had IV bruises on her arm if she hadn't been to a hospital or seen a doctor."

"What? I never noticed any bruises."

"Dinner's ready," came in a rousing shout from the kitchen. "Turn off the television, stop the chatter, wash your hands, and come sit at the table." Sonia came rushing in with a casserole pot brimming with colors, and placed it in middle of a table filled with newly baked bread, fresh goat cheese, olives, oranges, grapefruit, and dark red wine.

Maggie gasped. "I don't believe you made *soufiko*." She leaned in to take a whiff from the pot. "It's my favorite dish in the whole world."

"Of course it is," said Sophia, "You are Ikarian, and it is our soul food."

"Made fresh from wild herbs and whatever she found ripe today in our garden," said Spiro.

"And lots and lots of olive oil," added Sonia.

"But of course," smiled Spiro, patting his wife on her butt.

"Children, get in here!" shouted Sonia. "It's time to be with your family."

Her shout brought the children racing into the room, each giving a quick hug and kiss to their parents, and then the same to Maggie.

The matter of Yaya's bruises did not come up again, and Maggie spent the rest of the evening with her family, reflecting on how blessed she was to have had Yaya in her life. She'd given Maggie strong values, a steel will, and an irreverent sense of humor. But Yaya had also left her with cousins like Spiro and Sonia. Hardworking, honest, practical folk who put family first. Yes, they had their troubles, differences, and share of wacky relatives—what families didn't? But when push came to shove, being there for one another in times of need stood above all else as the primary principle for a life well-lived.

Yaya had embodied all of that. And she'd taken great care to instill it in every member of her family.

Maggie's smile abruptly faded away as the many things she'd learned about Yaya's final days slowly crystallized into a single question: Why did the family's matriarch, who'd spent her lifetime instilling in her descendants the overriding value of trusting family in times of need, at the end of her days, decide to reject that and turn to a perfect stranger *to get her through some things*?

Maggie couldn't stop wondering what those *things* might be, and as she made her way back to Yaya's cottage, a new question popped into her mind: *Do I really want to know?*

Yaya had secrets. Everyone did. Whatever they were, they had passed on with her, and it should remain that way. But what of secrets she chose to share with Papa George? The secrets themselves were not as important to Maggie as the explanation for why Yaya chose to share those secrets only with him.

And beginning tomorrow, I'm going to find out why.

———

From the outside, The Buzz Club looked like the first-place finisher in an ugly design contest for wannabe architects. It brought together in one structure the worst elements of the 1980s' fragmentation style of architecture. Utterly lacking in harmony, continuity, or symmetry, and trimmed in bizarre combinations of black, pink, and turquoise shapes, the two-story building stood out like the proverbial sore thumb on an otherwise nondescript commercial block. In other words, it was precisely the sort of attention-grabbing venue its owners wanted.

But Yianni wasn't interested in any of that. He headed straight for the club entrance. The bouncer at the door paid him no attention, and Yianni walked right past. Inside, the place wasn't much different from other Athens late-night clubs, dark and smoky, with a big bar, loud music, and randomly flashing lights. The Buzz Club's bar stood horseshoe-shaped in the middle of a large, two-story open space, with music videos streaming through giant monitors and a state-of-the-art acoustics system mounted high above the floor. Tiny tables randomly occupied narrow swaths of open floor space, while wine-colored faux-leather banquettes lined the walls. A narrow, second-floor balcony ringed the space, offering VIP guests a place to feel special and deejays room to do their thing.

It was not yet midnight, so the place wasn't busy, which likely explained why the guy at the door didn't seem to mind who walked in. Yianni sat on a stool at the curve of the bar, positioned to watch the front door. He ordered a beer and looked around for Tom and Jerry.

From his bit of Internet research on their cartoon namesakes, Yianni figured the big guy with short gray hair in the photos was Tom, and the brown-haired, mousy-looking character was Jerry. He wondered if their similarities to the fictional characters went beyond that. Cartoon Tom was said to be the muscle—large, energetic, and determined, bordering on manic. The much smaller Jerry was the brains of the duo, always remaining calm under pressure, yet surprisingly tough when required to be.

Yianni scanned the room, but no one matching the photographs was anywhere to be seen. Still, it was early. The place probably wouldn't get jumping until two. He wasn't up for late nights in the middle of the workweek unless it was with Toni at one of her piano bar gigs. That got him thinking about his conversation with his Navy buddy about having children with her, and his buddy's suggestion that he take that up with her. That meant a frank discussion about making changes to the independent lives each now led—his as a 24/7 cop, and hers as a quick-witted American piano player performing late into the night at an iconic gender-bending Mykonos bar, and serving by day as the island's preeminent finder of stolen goods for tourists and locals who'd been preyed upon by opportunistic thieves.

Yianni shook his head to clear his thoughts. This was not the time or place to address that. Besides, Andreas had told him to take some time off. Perhaps he'd do that tomorrow and surprise Toni on Mykonos. At this moment, though, he had to focus on the reason he was here.

Yeah, why am I here?

Just to get a look at the duo in the flesh made no sense. Striking up a conversation with them made even less sense. No way he could learn anything by introducing himself as a fellow cop. And lest he try striking up a conversation by passing himself off as something else, cops, especially dirty ones, were inherently suspicious of that sort of gambit by a civilian.

His only reason for being there was the blind hope that the Fates might toss him a bone, that something he saw or heard in the club would give him a lead. The chances of that happening were rapidly falling to between slim and none.

He looked at his beer bottle. The smart move was to drink it and leave. Yianni compromised by finishing it off and ordering one more. He'd leave after that one.

Halfway through his second beer, Tom and Jerry sauntered in, wearing designer jeans, Gucci loafers, and Versace silk shirts. Yianni's less-than-high-end jeans, tennis shoes, and Grateful Dead T-shirt suddenly seemed painfully inadequate. Then again, he had to live on what the government paid him as a cop.

The duo headed for an empty banquette along the rear wall. It afforded an unobstructed view of the front door and the bar. Customers greeted the two as if they were rock stars, waving at them, hugging them, and kissing them—all while the theme from *Rocky* played through the speakers.

Tom looked just as Yianni expected, a head taller than Yianni, but with a similar, bull-like build. Jerry appeared wiry, not weak, and only small in stature when compared to Tom.

The instant they sat down, Yianni looked away, and did not look back in their direction for several minutes. When he did look, it was casually, as if scanning the room for a potential companion for the night. He knew Tom and Jerry were also scanning the room, focusing on faces they didn't recognize to assess potential threats. At least that's what Yianni would be doing were the roles reversed.

Yianni went back to wondering why he was there. He didn't see himself accomplishing a thing sitting at the bar, hoping to catch glimpses of Tom and Jerry holding court for drugged-out clubbies stopping by to fawn over them. This public spectacle would not be where he'd expect Tom and Jerry to be conducting their serious dirty business, in any case.

The two took it all in as if they were royalty, never getting up to greet any of their well-wishers. They simply tossed them all a nod and a glad-hander's smile.

I can't take any more of this, thought Yianni. *I'm out of here.*

He lifted his beer to finish it off just as an expensively well-dressed young Asian couple approached Tom and Jerry. The duo immediately jumped up, bowed, and waved for the couple to join them. Yianni casually put down his beer, raised his mobile up from the bar just enough to stand it on its side, focused in on the banquette, and ran through half a dozen, silent multiple exposures in hopes that some of the randomly flashing strobes would yield a clear picture of Tom and Jerry's VIP visitors.

Yianni sensed the pair was uncomfortable with their new guests. Tom kept looking around the room as if checking to see who might be watching them, while Jerry kept a stone-faced concentration on the male VIP, repeatedly nodding at whatever he said.

This could be the break Yianni was hoping for, but he had no idea what it might be, or how to even begin figuring that out. He couldn't take his eyes off Jerry's unblinking focus on his guest. And when he brought himself to glance in Tom's direction, they locked eyes for an instant before Yianni quickly turned away to finish his beer.

Shit. He's made me.

Yianni put the bottle down on the counter, left some money for the bartender, and slowly headed for the front door. He resisted the temptation to look back at the banquette. He knew Tom was waiting for him to make that move. It would be the tell that eliminated any doubt about whether Yianni was interested in more than his beer.

Once outside, Yianni made his way past the line of people waiting to get in and headed for his car. He'd parked with a view of the entrance in order to get a sense of the crowd before going inside. That's how he'd come to settle on his T-shirt, rather than the other shirts he'd brought with him. Now he had a better use for his prime parking space. He'd sit and wait for the Asian couple to leave. Then tail them.

He fluttered his lips. No telling when they'll come out. *Too bad,* he told himself. *Wait it out.* This could be the break he needed. He looked at his watch. Nearly two. Toni would be finishing her gig at the piano bar. Maybe he'd call her. No, again, this wasn't the time or place for that.

Yianni adjusted his position on the seat. The beers were beginning to have their legendary effect. He needed a men's room. No way he could use the one in The Buzz Club, even assuming the bouncer would let him back in. Should Tom spot him, his cover would be blown for sure. But nor could he go hunting for another WC and risk missing the couple coming out of the club.

Options were limited, but bushes were near. It wouldn't be the first time. Or the last.

This was going to be a long night.

———

It was a little past three when the couple came out of the club. Two men accompanied them, neither of them Tom or Jerry. They looked like bodyguards. One man waved in Yianni's direction. Yianni froze. How could they have spotted him? Headlights lit up across the street a half block behind him, and a black SUV started moving toward him. Yianni slunk down in his seat.

The SUV drove straight past his car and stopped in front of the club. One of the bodyguards opened the passenger door to allow his colleague to crawl into the third row of seats. The couple followed him, sliding into the middle row. The bodyguard closed the door behind them and jumped in next to the driver, nodding for him to get moving.

Once the SUV pulled away from the club, Yianni counted to five before starting his engine, and to another five before turning on the headlights and following the SUV. This would be a tricky tail.

The guy in the third row was there to keep an eye on anything coming up on them from behind. If Yianni got too close, he'd be noticed. On the other hand, even at this hour, if he stayed too far back, crazy Athens traffic would quickly swallow up whatever space he left between his car and the SUV. He'd lose it at the first traffic light that shone green for the SUV, but turned red for a vehicle between the SUV and Yianni.

If only he'd known that the SUV had been waiting for the Asian couple. He could have taken down its license number, run it by GADA, and by now had a name for its owner. Not that the likely name of a shell corporation would prove helpful to his investigation, at least he'd feel the evening hadn't been a total loss.

Now he had to find a way to get close enough to the SUV to catch its plate number before he lost it in traffic, but not in a way that would get him noticed.

Yianni lost sight of the SUV when it turned right at the first intersection. He sped up. It would be a real downer losing them on the first turn.

By the time he reached the intersection and made the turn, the SUV was nowhere to be seen.

Yianni cursed himself as he rushed toward the next intersecting street. He looked left. No traffic that way. He looked right. Down at the intersection with Pireos Avenue, a black SUV sat at a traffic light, its left turn signal blinking.

Yianni didn't turn, but raced straight ahead through the next two intersections, dodging pallets of building supplies haphazardly stacked out onto the street, before making a screeching right at a dead-ending third intersection, then barreling on toward Pireos Avenue. Two cars sat by the traffic signal at Pireos, waiting for the light to turn green.

Yianni swung out into the lane and shot across the intersection, barely missing being T-boned by an oncoming bus to his left, and narrowly avoiding doing the same to a motorcycle on his right as his hard left turn sent his car skidding into the avenue's Athens-bound lanes.

Yianni didn't want to think about the string of curses his dear mother and the Virgin Mother were incurring at that moment from the wrath of one badly shaken bus driver and an undoubtedly self-soiled motorcyclist.

Thankfully, it was a no-harm, no-foul ending. At least so far.

Assuming he'd guessed right, the SUV was headed toward Athens. He figured if he got ahead of it and stayed ahead until letting it pass, those in the SUV watching for tails would be less likely to think they were being followed by a vehicle they'd passed.

He adjusted his mirrors, moved over to the right lane, and slowed down. Two minutes later he spotted the SUV coming up on the left. He sped up to stay several car lengths in front of it but stayed in the right lane, hoping to get its license plate.

He concentrated so hard on keeping the SUV in his mirrors that he didn't see the bus stopped dead in his lane until he was almost upon it. There was no time to brake, only swerve, which he did, directly into the path of the SUV, nearly forcing it onto the median.

So much for being inconspicuous. Once he was back in his lane, the SUV passed him slowly, as if the driver were checking out the *malaka* who'd almost driven them into oncoming traffic. Yianni did not look up but kept rubbing his left hand against the side of his face as if calming his nerves, while actually working to conceal his face.

As the SUV moved ahead, Yianni caught a glimpse of its license plate. A Greek tag, Athens issue, with a number easy to remember. He picked up his phone and called GADA's dispatcher.

He identified himself and requested vehicle plate information in connection with an ongoing pursuit. That sort of call received priority, because traffic stops and domestic violence calls represented the most dangerous encounters for police. Within a minute, the dispatcher was back with the registered owner's name.

The instant Yianni heard it, a broad smile spread across his face. He no longer worried about losing sight of the SUV, because he knew precisely where it was headed. He also knew what back streets would get him there well ahead of the SUV.

They were headed to the heart of Athens, next to Syntagma

Square, close by the National Gardens, and across from Parliament. There he'd find the registered owner of the SUV—Athens's most famous and pricey old-line hotel.

The night wasn't turning out so bad after all.

Chapter Nine

Andreas woke to a pinging coming from across the bedroom.

"Is that your phone?" said Lila, pulling a pillow over her head. "I don't want to know what time it is."

"My phone's silenced." He swung his legs out of bed. "It's my beeper. I set it so only Yianni and Maggie can get through to me at this hour."

She pulled the pillow from her face. "What time is it?"

"Close to four thirty."

Lila sat up in bed. "It must be important."

"Go back to sleep. I'll return the call from your study."

"As if I could sleep not knowing whether everything's okay."

Andreas yawned as he lumbered over to the beeper on his dresser. "It's Yianni." He picked up the beeper and his mobile next to it, and headed for the open doorway into Lila's study.

Andreas had tried to sound nonchalant in front of his wife, but middle-of-the-night calls rarely brought good news. He closed the study door, dropped into a chair next to it, and drew in and let out a deep breath. Then he called.

On the first ring he heard, "Chief?"

"I assume the world's coming to an immediate and dramatic end if you're beeping me at this hour."

"Not yet, but it sure as hell seems headed that way." Yianni told him what he'd learned from Marco about Tom and Jerry, of his evening at The Buzz Club, and of his efforts to follow the Asian couple in their chauffeured SUV.

"When I heard the SUV was registered to the hotel, I figured it was part of a limo service provided to guests. That's when I took the gamble that they were headed there, and raced to beat them back to the hotel."

"I take that to mean you won your bet."

"They arrived ten minutes after I got there. I ditched the T-shirt for a blue dress shirt and sports jacket and sat in the lobby with a couple of non-hotel limo drivers waiting for early morning calls to the airport. The couple and their muscle took no notice of us."

"That's all very nice to hear, but it leaves me with one question. Why the hell are you calling me now, as opposed to, say...some reasonable hour?"

"My instincts are screaming there's something seriously wrong about this couple. And not because of their hired muscle. A lot of good guys, not just bad guys, need that sort of protection these days. But Tom and Jerry acted nervous as hell around them and treated them as if they were royalty."

"Which leads you to conclude what?"

"If they're legitimate major players, why are they cozying up to notorious dirty cops? And why do those same dirty cops seem so afraid of them?"

"I take it they're not from Greece."

"They look Asian. All I could get from the desk clerk is they're from Hong Kong."

"Nothing else?"

"After the couple and their bodyguards went upstairs, I started up a conversation with the desk clerk. I told him the couple looked like folks I'd once picked up at the airport, and asked if they were from China. He said Hong Kong. That led to a bullshit session over how we agreed China seemed interested in taking over whatever it could in Greece. Yet, whenever I brought the conversation around to where he could have tied a name or occupation to the couple, he avoided going there."

"Sounds like the sort of hotel desk clerk you want in your employ."

"But that's what has me calling you in the middle of the night. Something big is about to go down. I can feel it. But until I know more about the couple, I've no idea what it might be."

"Didn't you tell the desk clerk you were a cop?"

"Too risky. A guy like that might live for tips. If he told the couple a cop was snooping around for information, and they're into something dirty, they could just take off."

"Fine. So let's get back to the part about why you're beeping me at four thirty in the morning."

"I know you and Lila are close to the family that owns the hotel. I thought maybe they'd give you information their desk clerk won't give me."

Andreas looked at the time on his phone. "At five in the morning?"

"Chief, if something really big is about to go down, it could happen any minute now. I don't want to blow whatever slim chance we have at shutting it down. I owe that much to Stavros."

A vision of the slain young undercover cop passed through Andreas's mind. "I trust you realize this could cost me my happy marriage."

"Nah, Lila's an even softer touch than you are."

Andreas smiled. "Okay, I'll ask her how she thinks we should handle this. Where will you be?"

"Sitting here with my newfound limo-driver friends. There's now four of us, and I'm learning a lot of interesting ways to make money off uninformed tourists."

"Enjoy yourself, I'll be back as soon as I have something for you. Or learn there's nothing to be had."

Andreas hung up and stared at the carpet. *Now what?*

He heard Lila's voice filter in through the bedroom door. "You speak too loudly, and though I only heard your side of the conversation, I suspect there is something you have in mind for me to do."

Andreas got up from the chair and pulled open the door. "Eavesdropper."

Lila turned on the light by her side of the bed. "As you well know, eavesdropping is a Greek national pastime. So, what can I do for you, Officer?"

He recounted his conversation with Yianni. "He's hoping we can get whatever information the hotel might have on the couple through your family's relationship with the owners."

"I assume that's when you said, 'at five in the morning?'"

Andreas nodded.

"You've come to the right place, dear husband. Yes, my childhood girlfriend's family owns the hotel, and she's always in her office at the hotel by seven thirty. But I assume you want more immediate service."

Lila reached for her mobile on the nightstand and checked the time. "By now she's wide awake and in the midst of her morning workout with her trainer." She hit a favorites button and put the phone to her ear. "Aren't you lucky you married me?"

Andreas dropped down beside her on the bed. "Ever more so every day, my love," and kissed her on the cheek.

———

Lila's girlfriend agreed to tell her hotel manager on duty to give Yianni whatever information he wanted. She also promised to instruct him to keep it all to himself.

Andreas relayed all of that to Yianni in a text message. That was thirty minutes ago, and he'd not yet heard back. Andreas knew he couldn't fall back to sleep, but Lila did not share that problem, so Andreas crept off to the kitchen and, in a sign of surrender to no more sleep, made himself a cup of coffee.

Coffee mug in one hand and mobile phone in the other, Andreas made his way to his favorite place in the apartment for watching the rose-gold light of sunrise gild the Acropolis. No more inspiring sight existed on earth. At least for a Greek.

Ring.

Andreas answered before the phone rang twice. "How did it go?"

"Remind me to buy Lila flowers. Better yet, do you think she'd mind my dropping her name any time I need cooperation from a reluctant witness?"

"Sounds like it worked out."

"Did it ever. The guy who I thought was a desk clerk turned out to be the night manager. When he realized I was the one he'd been told to assist, he treated me like we were old friends."

"What's the bottom line?"

"If that couple is involved in something illegal, we're talking about a potentially humongous international mess."

Andreas took a sip of coffee. "Just the sort of situation we underpaid public servants dream of to bring excitement to our otherwise boring, stress-free days."

"Go ahead, be sarcastic. I'm too tired to care."

"What did you learn from him?"

"A lot more than I expected. High-end hotels keep extensive files on VIP clients, covering such things as their favorite rooms, flowers, toiletries, food, drink, even the names of their favorite hotel staff."

"That's all very interesting, but what's any of that have to do with what has you so worked up?"

"That's only part of what's in those files. They also contain extensive background information on VIP guests, compiled from newspapers, magazines, and other public sources, including a description of what they're currently up to. It's intended to prevent embarrassing a guest, such as by putting an ex-wife in an adjoining room to an ex-husband, or seating a despised business rival at an adjacent dinner table."

"What did that file have to say about your mysterious couple?"

"Well, for a start, they're brother and sister, Chen Bo Heng, and his sister, Chen Li Ling. They're based in Hong Kong but are the favorite children of a politically powerful, multibillionaire mainland China family. Both of them went to school in the United States. The son went to Harvard for college and business school, and the daughter to Yale, where she obtained degrees in applied biochemistry and philosophy. Both graduated Phi Beta Kappa."

"Sounds like a typical pair of slackers."

"It gets better. After university, they started a pharmaceutical import-export business in Hong Kong. It's now one of the fastest-growing companies in the region."

"How old are these two superachievers?"

"From their passports, he's thirty-five, she's thirty-two."

"Are they married?"

"No record of either ever being married, and a magazine article describes them as married to their business."

Andreas shook his head from side to side. "You were right. It doesn't make sense that the Chen siblings would be hanging out with Tom and Jerry. Or for that matter, how they'd even know each other." Andreas paused. "Then again, it is a nightclub, and they're relatively young. Maybe they're into the action and that's all there is to it. No more, no less."

"But why would Tom and Jerry be nervous around them?"

"You're the one with the instincts on this crew. Do you think the reason is business or personal?"

"No idea, Chief. At least not yet. But that brings me around to what else I saw in the hotel files. It's what the manager called self-protection information. It details rumors, peccadilloes, vices, and scandals. The sorts of things a high-class hotel needs to know about VIP guests that could someday bite the hotel on its ass if it didn't know and wasn't prepared for it."

"This sounds like the sexy stuff."

"Yep, but surprisingly nonjudgmental. On the one hand it describes kooky practices—like wild S&M sessions in the middle of the night—that could lead some adjacent room guests to call for security. On the other hand, it also lists the names and contact information for the VIP's preferred sadomasochistic dominatrix or other kook of choice. The manager said the primary reason for having that kind of information is to protect the hotel from guests notorious for trashing their rooms."

"So they can use it as justification for refusing them a room?"

"Possibly," said Yianni, "but I'm told it's more commonly used for purposes of setting a significant room premium for that sort of VIP. It also assists the hotel in determining the appropriate amount for the letter of credit such a guest will be required to post to cover anticipated damages."

"What nasties did the file have on the Chens?"

"Nothing. Not a word. The brother and sister always share a suite, which is common among families, and they never entertain in their rooms. The worst that could be said about them is they're big-time shoppers. Real fashionistas, who love to stay out late and party."

"All of which is consistent with an innocent visit to The Buzz Club."

"I know, and they do travel a lot. Their passports show them entering the EU a half dozen times over the past year, three of those times, including this one, through Greece. No telling how many more times they've been to Greece, though, because passports only show places of entry and exit from the EU. The hotel lists the Chens as guests at least twice every summer for the past seven years, separated by a month between stays. I'm told they spent the intervening month traveling the islands."

"Doing what?"

"The manager's best guess is shopping and partying."

"Is there anything to suggest they're doing business in Greece?"

"According to a magazine article, they do a lot of business selling Chinese drugs to our Health Ministry."

"What about the other kind of drugs, notably heroin?"

"We know China has been a primary source of fentanyl trafficking, but there's nothing to suggest they're involved in that. They seem to prefer going up against competitors in the legitimate drug market."

"It's a healthier choice, for sure. But it brings us back to why are two seemingly innocent business types hanging out with two dirty drug cops?"

"No idea, but I think I'll give it a last shot before walking away from my initial hunch."

"What sort of last shot?"

"They had the hotel charter a motor yacht for them, and it leaves tomorrow for a one-week cruise."

"Where to?"

"They only gave the first destination, which isn't unusual for island hoppers. I thought I'd catch up with them at their first port and see what turns up."

Andreas chuckled. "Let me guess…that first port is Mykonos."

"Good guess, Chief, but no cigar."

"Santorini? Ios? Paros?"

"No, no, and no. You might as well give up. You'll likely name a hundred islands before hitting this one."

"Okay, so tell me."

"Ikaria."

"Come on, what self-respecting partier or fashionista would pick Ikaria as a destination? They'd be bored to death."

"I'll make it a point *not* to pass that observation along to Maggie when I see her. But I do have to admit that the same thought made me curious about what they're planning to do there."

"At least you'll get to check in on Maggie."

"I might just ask her to serve as my guide. She must be bored to death by now."

"Just make sure not to let her know we heard about her accident. No reason to aggravate her."

"Understood. Hard to imagine, though, that with all the aggravation she puts up with in our office, anything on stress-free Ikaria could get to her. But don't worry. I could use a good dose of boredom, myself. I've had it with bad guys, bloodshed, and bullshit."

"Terrific. Enjoy your escape to calm, tranquility, and Maggie."

"Amen."

———

This time chickens, not goats, roused Maggie from her sleep. She'd not yet become as accustomed to the morning sounds of nature as she had to those of trucks and motorcycles roaring past her Athens apartment. She struggled to fall back to sleep, but her mind had engaged, ending that possibility. Instead, she lay in bed, her eyes wide open, concentrating on the ceiling, on where it met the wall above the front door, on the door, and back again to the ceiling. She couldn't shake the thought that somewhere out there among all that she'd learned thus far, lay a common thread tying everything together.

Mihali, the pharmacist, had given her a list of four names in addition to Yaya who'd passed away within two weeks of one another; all peacefully in their sleep, alone and at home. He'd also described Yaya as not being her normal upbeat self during her final weeks.

Calliope, the *savanotria* who'd prepared Yaya for her funeral, had noticed what she called "botched IV bruises" on Yaya and on two other departed nonagenarians that she'd prepared during the same two weeks, both of whom also appeared on Mihali's list.

Of the four *savanotria* Calliope had listed for Maggie, only Diony worked on the south side of the island. She worked in Therma, close by Agios Kirykos, and up until two weeks ago hadn't been called upon to prepare a centenarian or nonagenarian in six months. In those two weeks she'd attended to one of each, both bearing similar IV bruises to those described by Calliope. But rather than attributing the bruising she saw to botched one-time IV insertions, Diony saw them as bruises caused by multiple vein piercings on different occasions.

The three other *savanotria* all worked on the north side. The one from Perdiki had not tended to someone over ninety in more than a year, nor had she seen or heard of anyone of that age who'd died bearing that sort of bruising.

The *savanotria* in Christos Raches had prepared a centenarian the week before, but the body bore no signs of IV bruising, and she knew of no centenarian or nonagenarian who had.

The Evdilos *savanotria* said that four weeks ago she'd prepared her centenarian friend, Alki, for burial, and noticed IV bruising on her arm, something she'd not seen on other centenarians. She'd also heaped high praise on Papa George as a local priest who'd spent the month preceding her friend's death, converting Alki from a deeply depressed being into a spirited soul who'd found new meaning for her life.

What do these bruised souls have in common? wondered Maggie.

Three centenarians and three nonagenarians, all churchgoers in relatively good health, dying in their own beds, and interred without an autopsy. All but one had died within the same two-week period. The lone exception died four weeks before Yaya and, like Yaya, was a centenarian in Papa George's flock. She wondered how many other of those who died were visited by the priest.

She wouldn't be surprised if several were. After all, with the wondrous praise he received for the attention he showered on the oldest Ikariots, many must be drawn to his ministry.

Maggie shut her eyes, and let her mind run free, hoping for an answer to the seminal question haunting her. No such luck.

She opened her eyes, and swung her feet out of bed, mumbling to herself, "Time to get to work."

She decided to start by speaking to the families on Mihali's list.

Perhaps one of them could help her find an answer to a question she could not shake: Why did Yaya's spirit crash so dramatically on Papa George's watch?

———

"Hi, my name is Maggie Sikestes, and I'm calling you at the suggestion of Mr. Mihali, the pharmacist. Like you, I just lost a loved one. My *yaya* passed away a few days ago, and I'm still in shock. I've all these crazy thoughts running through my mind, and Mr. Mihali thought perhaps talking to you would help me get my head back in the right place. I don't mean to intrude on your privacy—I know you're mourning your loss at least as much as I am mine—so if my call is in any way making you uncomfortable, please tell me, because the last thing I want to do is upset anyone with what's adding to my grief."

Maggie's call to each family on Mihali's list started with that introduction. No one hung up, nor did anyone simply say, "Yes, tell me what's bothering you." Maggie hadn't expected a different reaction. Everyone wanted to know more about who Maggie was, who'd passed away, and how she knew Mihali. Once invested in the conversation, and convinced Maggie was not some hustler preying on the aggrieved, they opened up about their own feelings of loss, and then asked what they could do for her.

Maggie had to be careful how she phrased her questions, because she knew for certain that whatever she said would instantly become a hot topic of gossip and speculation among islanders perpetually on the lookout for something new to talk about in the *kafenion*. From Calliope she already knew that two of the departed showed bruising, so she had no need to raise that subject with their families. Nor did she want to start out with a question to the other families about "bruises." No telling how that might be ground up and exaggerated in the gossip mill.

Instead, she said to each family, "I wasn't able to be with my *yaya* during her final weeks, and I feel deeply guilty about that. However, I understand she was blessed to have been comforted during those final days by a priest she'd met in church. I feel as if I should do something for him to thank him for all that he did for her, but I'm worried I might offend him with such an offer. I was hoping you might be able to give me some guidance on how best to handle it."

The first words out of everyone's mouth was, "Who's the priest?"

Maggie's response was always the same. "Papa George from Evdilos. Why, do you know him?"

Two did not know him. Two did, and they praised him for the peace he'd brought to their deceased loved one.

Maggie raised her second question in a manner that could be vouched for as accurate if anyone sought confirmation. "*Savanotria* Calliope mentioned to me that in preparing my *yaya*, she noticed IV bruise marks on her arm that showed sloppy work by whoever had administered the IV. She suggested I tell the hospital to retrain that person. I don't want to cause a problem for someone over an isolated incident, but if you had a similar experience with bruising on your loved one, I think I should do as Calliope suggested."

None had noticed any bruises.

Maggie thanked each one profusely. When done with her fourth call, she stared out the window and wondered about Yaya's last days. Just as quickly, she stopped herself. This was not the time to go there. She had two other calls to make.

Her first call was to the *savanotria* in Christos Raches, her second went to Diony in Therma. Both answered her questions. The results were in.

Of the four centenarians and five nonagenarians who'd passed away over the past month, three in each age group bore IV bruises on their arms, and *all six* of those were members of Papa George's flock.

Of the other three, none had anything to do with him.

Now was the time for Maggie to think of Yaya's last days... *and get answers.*

———

Maggie bounced between confronting Papa George face-to-face and telling Andreas of her suspicions. The former would undoubtedly lead to a cathartic rant, the latter to potential prosecutions for whatever cost Yaya and so many others their lives.

It seemed insane that a man of the cloth could be in any way involved in what would be the greatest serial-killer rampage in the history of modern Greece. How could it be? But from the facts, barring statistically inconceivable coincidences... Maggie left the question hanging, unanswered. She knew enough about herself to realize her judgment was under siege from her anger. Calling out Papa George would achieve nothing good, and if by chance he was involved, doing so without police backup could prove fatal.

He claimed to favor the six oldest in his flock with multiple weekly visits. With so many perishing in the last month alone, whether complicit or not in their deaths, he'd likely been busy lining up replacements, all of whom could now be in mortal danger. She had to do *something*, and immediately.

She thought to call Tassos, but he'd come charging onto Ikaria like the proverbial bull in a china shop. Papa George's reputation would be finished, whether arrested, convicted, or not. There still remained doubt in Maggie's mind, but whether of the reasonable kind, she could not say.

She decided to call Andreas. He'd know what to do. Or if not, at least be measured in his response. She couldn't imagine a dicier situation than accusing a priest of participating in the serial murder of more than half a dozen Ikarian centenarians and nonagenarians in his care.

"Good morning, Chief Inspector Kaldis's office."

"Morning, Mister Happiness, it's Maggie. How goes it?"

"It's hard to fill your chair, but I'm trying my best."

"I'll take that in the spirit in which I assume it was intended, and not how it came out."

The temporary secretary laughed. "We all miss you, my love."

"I miss you too."

"Speaking of missing, you just missed the chief. He left for a meeting at the Ministry. I guess you could call him on his mobile."

"I don't want to bother him if he's in the middle of some meeting at that snake pit. Just tell him I called when you hear from him."

"Perhaps it's something Yianni can help you with."

"Thanks for the suggestion, but it's really a matter for Andreas. Besides, no need to bother Yianni."

"I doubt it will be a bother, as he's headed your way."

Maggie's voice tightened. "What do you mean?"

"Yianni's on his way to Venizelos to catch the next plane to Ikaria."

"Why is he coming here?"

"No idea, but I thought you knew. First thing this morning, he had me book him a ticket and a rental car."

"What time does the plane land on Ikaria?"

"Around two."

"Thanks." Maggie paused. "Forget about passing along my message to Andreas. I'll follow your suggestion and take it up with Yianni. It will be easier in person."

"For Yianni?"

"No. For me."

Chapter Ten

Maggie stood outside the entrance to the air terminal. She almost didn't recognize the scruffy-looking guy in sunglasses, jeans, and zipped-up windbreaker walking toward her with a knapsack slung over one shoulder. But his walk gave him away. A mix of John Wayne and The Hulk.

"What are you doing here?" said a surprised Yianni.

"That's supposed to be my line. After all, I was here first. By the way, you look exhausted."

"Long story. And you look a bit gimpy yourself."

Maggie forced a smile. "Long story."

"No, seriously, how did you know I'd be here?"

"I called the office and heard you were on your way, so I thought I'd surprise you."

"What a crazy coincidence. I wanted to call you because I could use your help, but I didn't want to intrude."

Maggie stared at him and shook her head. "Talk about coincidences. Have I got a story for you. But before I get into my situation, what do you need from me?"

"I'm following a couple on a chartered motor yacht that's supposed to arrive this afternoon. Since I've never been to Ikaria and have no idea where they plan to go once they land, I sense things could get pretty tricky real fast if I have to chase them around the island."

"Why don't you ask the local police for assistance? They're very helpful."

Yianni gestured no. "Can't risk it. It's a highly confidential matter, one that would send the media on a feeding frenzy if they got wind of our unit's interest in the people I'm following."

Maggie rolled her eyes. "I can't believe how much your situation and mine have in common. But let's focus on yours for now. Where's the boat headed?"

"All I know is its name. I'm using a yacht-tracker app to see where they are and their direction of sail. They look to be about an hour away."

"Are they headed toward our north or south coast? Because there's a port to the south at Agios Kirykos and to the north at Evdilos. Then again, if they're not interested in harbor services, or want privacy above all else, there's a lot of other places they could drop anchor."

"Great."

"Let me see the app."

Yianni handed her his phone.

"From its course, I'd say they're aiming for the north side. If I knew a bit more about what they're looking to do here, I might be able to make a better guess at their destination."

Yianni paused for a moment. "Which port has better shopping and nightlife?"

"We're talking Ikaria, Yianni. Not Athens or Mykonos."

"I know, just humor me."

"I'd say Evdilos."

"Fine, let's head there."

"Evdilos and Agios Kirykos are about an hour's drive apart,

so if the boat's an hour away, and we guess wrong, they'll be in port an hour before we get to them."

Yianni smiled. "Sounds like a math problem. But if we head toward Evdilos, in a half hour we should know from the app if we guessed wrong. If we did, we'll turn around and still beat them to Agios Kirykos."

She handed Yianni back his phone. "I didn't do well in math."

He looked around the parking lot. "How did you get here?"

"By taxi. I heard you'd rented a car, and figured you'd give me a ride back to my place, little realizing you'd shanghai me."

"Hongkong you would be more appropriate under the circumstances."

"Huh?"

"Inside joke. You'll get it after you hear the backstory as to why I'm here."

Yianni pointed to a faded blue Hyundai Atos. "Our chariot awaits."

"I see our unit's expense account remains on the slim side these days."

"I specifically requested an inconspicuous car. I don't want to broadcast that I'm from Athens."

"That explains how you're dressed."

"Does it work?"

"Just ditch the knapsack if you're trying to look local. Too preppy."

"Your suggestion is my command. I'll toss it on the back seat."

"A motto to live by." She held out her hand. "Keys, please. I'll drive. I may have been bad in math, but my time estimate is based on being driven by one familiar with taking one's life in one's hands on Ikarian roads."

Yianni flipped her the key. "Enjoy. Besides, I could use a nap."

Maggie got in behind the steering wheel, adjusted the seat

and mirrors, and put on her seat belt. "There will be no napping on this trip. That is, unless you don't mind me joining you in a snooze." She turned on the engine and headed for the exit. "Do us both a favor and keep me awake. You can do that by filling me in on this *confidential* matter that brought you here."

Yianni rotated his head to relax his neck. "It's tied in to that undercover operation we're running on the extent of foreign involvement in domestic drug trafficking." He told her about Stavros alerting him that Greek drug enforcement agents might be providing protection for traffickers, how Yianni obtained photographs of the potentially dirty cops from surveillance cameras, and his meeting with Stavros at the museum. He paused.

"Don't stop now, dear. The story's just getting interesting."

"I was distracted by the scenery. The place is so rocky and yet so green and lush."

"Wait until you see the view up ahead. I was just through here the other day on a motorbike. It's a lot more comfortable in a car."

Yianni stared down the sheer drop on his side of the road. "Maybe from where you're sitting, but not for a passenger hanging on out here on the edge."

Maggie smiled, "We haven't even reached the roller-coaster parts. These are just baby hills. Don't be such a complainer."

"To put my feelings at the moment in musical terms, I can handle the rock, but let's just avoid the roll."

Maggie moaned, "Please no more attempts at humor. Just get back to what happened at the museum."

Yianni swallowed, and continued in a subdued voice, stopping at the point where the ambulances drove off with Stavros and his girlfriend.

Maggie bit at her lip. "I'm afraid to ask."

Yianni sighed. "Ioanna is fine. Stavros didn't make it."

Maggie froze for an instant, then pounded the heel of her hand on the steering wheel. "Damn, damn, damn." She rubbed a tear off her cheek. "Such a nice kid. His young life over in an instant. And it didn't have anything to do with what he was working on. Just random violence for no rational reason." She shook her head. "Go on, I'm sorry."

"We all are."

Yianni described how he'd managed to identify the two in the photos through a friend, how that same friend steered him to Tom and Jerry at The Buzz Club, the arrival of the mysterious Asian couple, and the journey back to the hotel where he learned all that they now knew about the Chen siblings of Hong Kong—currently set on a course for Evdilos.

"How much longer until we're at the port?" he asked.

"About twenty minutes."

"According to the tracker app, that should put us there a little before the yacht arrives. It'll take a while to anchor or tie up at the pier, so that should give you more than enough time to tell me your story if you start now."

"In light of what happened to young Stavros and his girlfriend, my story about a mystery surrounding ninety- and hundred-year-old folks passing away under bizarrely similar circumstances doesn't seem quite as compelling as I thought. Let's do it later."

"Whatever you say."

"Sit back, relax, and enjoy the scenery. Even take a nap if you'd like. I'm wide awake now."

Yianni stared out the passenger side window across a sloping rocky hillside running down to the sea. "Why do bad things happen to good people like Stavros, while the truly terrible seem to get away with murder?"

Maggie glanced over at Yianni. "I've been thinking along the same lines these past few days. It has me wondering why God doesn't intervene rather than allow the innocent to perish."

"I once thought God had delegated that responsibility to cops and priests. That was before I had to deal with dirty cops like the ones who led me here."

Maggie shrugged. "Who knows? The Lord works in mysterious ways. If it weren't for those dirty cops, you'd never have found out about the Chens."

"That's an interesting way of looking at things. Certainly one that makes me feel better about my role as a cop in God's grand scheme of things."

"I wish I felt the same way about priests," added Maggie.

Yianni jerked his head around to face Maggie. "You're about the most churchgoing person I know. What gives with that attitude about priests?"

Maggie exhaled. "It's all part of that thing I don't want to talk about now."

"Well, it's bothering the hell out of you, so why don't you just tell me what's up?"

"You'll think I'm crazy."

"I already do, so you have nothing to lose."

Maggie shot him a glare. "Show me more respect or I'll make you get out and walk."

"It's my rental. So, start talking."

She did.

———

The classic port town of Evdilos came into its modern form after the eradication of pirates in the 1830s. It grew amphitheatrically up the hillside above its natural horseshoe bay, taking care to preserve the beauty of the village as it did. Today, it was a modern port that kept within the aesthetically sensitive nature of its community, as reflected in well-cared-for flowers, gardens, and homes. Old mansions and newer structures of neoclassical and more modern design, all white and topped in terra-cotta roof tiles, lay along the village's narrow roads and alleys, at times nestled so close to one another that they seemed blended into a single home. Needless to say, the village had become a popular tourist destination.

Maggie finished laying out all the facts she knew and all the suspicions she carried as they arrived in the Evdilos harbor area. Yianni hadn't said a word or taken his eyes off Maggie the entire time she'd told her story.

"I'll park on the east side of the port. We can hide among the cars there and still have a view of the harbor."

The shoreline road into the port continued west beyond the parking area, across the harbor, and out onto a long concrete pier that served as the harbor's western edge and docking facility for ferry boats and other large vessels.

Maggie parked, turned off the engine, and looked at Yianni. "So, what do you have to say about my problem?"

Yianni grimaced. "I can see why you thought I might think you're crazy. That's an amazing, some might say unbelievable, story. If I didn't know you as well as I do, I might think you were some sort of nut who had it in for the Church."

"But you do know me."

Yianni nodded. "It's hard to believe that a priest would be involved in the murder of anyone, let alone serial killings of ninety- and one-hundred-year-old men and women he's vowed to care for." Yianni shook his head. "You have to admit it seems inconceivable."

"Tell me about it." Maggie shook her head from side to side. "But the facts are all there. Three dead centenarians, three dead nonagenarians, all bearing similar bruise marks, all but one dying within two weeks of one other, all buried without an autopsy, and all members of Papa George's flock."

"Do you have any idea how hard it will be to get the Church to go along with exhuming even one of those bodies for an autopsy, let alone six? And if word of it ever got out to the media…" Yianni made a circle in the air with his right hand. "I'd rather be dealing with an international incident involving my Chen siblings than a church serial killer."

"I know."

"And you said the priest has reasonable explanations for everything?"

"He's a very smooth former fine jewelry salesman and military man."

"That's not grounds for accusing someone of murder."

Maggie glared. "Stop mansplaining to me. I'm old enough to be your mother."

Yianni exhaled but said nothing.

"Sorry, I didn't mean to bark at you. It's just so frustrating when you know someone is dirty but can't prove it."

"Now it's my turn to say, 'Tell me about it.'" Yianni sat up his seat and pointed toward the mouth of the harbor. "There's our boat. It looks like it's headed this way."

They watched the boat maneuver into position to bring its stern up against a pier not far from their car.

"That's a beautiful boat," said Maggie. "Pricey too, I'd bet."

"I'm sure. It's an Italian-made Uniesse 56SS."

An Asian man jumped from the diving platform to the pier. He held a line that he wrapped around a shore-mounted cleat to help stabilize the boat as it hovered close to shore.

"That's the Chen brother," said Yianni.

Another man hurried out of a harbor-front taverna and headed for the boat.

"Damn, I didn't plan for this." Yianni reached for his knapsack and pulled out a camera, hustling to take as many photos of the hurrying man as he could. "If they plan on taking him with them on the boat, I'm screwed. It'll be a miracle if I can identify him, let alone get a grip on why they're here or what they might be up to."

Maggie watched the man adeptly jump onto the boat, followed by the Chen brother. From across the parking lot, she could hear the engine roar as the yacht moved away from the pier, aiming for the mouth of the harbor.

Yianni pounded his fist on the dash. "Damn, damn, damn."

Maggie stared straight ahead at the departing boat.

Yianni pounded a few more times, cursed a bit longer, and turned to look at Maggie. "My luck sucks."

Maggie kept staring at the boat.

"Are you okay?"

She said nothing.

"Maggie, what's wrong?"

"You just met Papa George."

———

"It's Maggie and Yianni on line one, Chief."

"Thanks," said Andreas, putting down the report he'd been reading and picking up his office phone.

"My two favorite people, together again. I hope you're sharing some quality time."

Yianni's rushed voice came through in a speakerphone tone. "Maggie and I are sitting in a parking lot at Evdilos harbor wondering what the hell just happened to us."

Andreas stiffened. "Are you all right?"

"Physically, yes," said Maggie, "though any minute my nerves might have me throwing up."

"Will somebody please tell me what's going on?"

"It's a long and seemingly unbelievable story," said Yianni, "but it's very real, and I have no idea where we go from here."

"Okay, you've got my undivided attention. Just start at the beginning and work your way to the end."

"You already know my story. All I have to add is we watched the Chen yacht arrive in the harbor, pause just long enough to pick up a male passenger, and sail off for parts unknown."

"Any ID on the passenger?"

"Maggie knows him."

"Then what's the problem? They've established contact and given you a lead. Sounds good to me."

"I'm not sure you'll feel that way after you hear what Maggie has to say."

"Okay, Maggie, your turn."

It took twenty minutes for Maggie to tell her story, concluding with witnessing Papa George—not dressed as a priest—join up with the Chens on their boat.

Andreas paused before responding, "It gives me chills just thinking what all this might mean."

"We don't know where to go from here. Maggie wants to confront the priest. Shake him for all that he knows."

"From how you described him, Maggie, he may not be the shakable kind. Besides, he could turn out to be the real bad guy in this epic. Alerting him before we have enough to arrest him would likely see him vanish."

"I admit I'm personally involved in this, Chief," said Maggie, "but I'm convinced this guy's involved in the death of at least six people, *including* my *yaya*."

"From what you've told me, I tend to agree, but we still need evidence."

"We need autopsies," she grumbled.

"True, but before letting all hell break loose, I think we need a better grip on a few points."

"Hell's already broken loose," Maggie pointed out.

"Let me put it this way. Have you confirmed that he really is a priest and not an impersonator?"

"No," snapped Maggie. "But I have a friend who'll be able to answer that question. I'll give her a call, though it's hard to imagine how he could have gotten away with being a phony for so long."

"Fine, so assuming he's legit, give me a *why* for your priest being involved in these deaths."

"He's a psychopath."

"Maggie, let's be realistic here. We need a motive. He's a priest. Calling him names without evidence is only going to stiffen the back of the Church. And if he is a psychopath, we still need proof. Claiming he's one because the deaths can only be explained as the handiwork of a psychopath will be torn apart by his defense lawyer, assuming a prosecutor would even take on the case. Bottom line, we need a *why*."

"Okay," said Yianni. "How do you suggest we find one?"

"Each of the deceased shows multiple IV bruises, likely administered on separate occasions, but no other signs of bruising or violence. That leads me to think the deceased agreed to, or at least did not oppose, the IVs, and voluntarily allowed them to go be administered more than once."

"Then he tricked them!" shouted Maggie.

Andreas responded calmly. "That may be, but how do we prove that he did what you say, and that it constituted a criminal act? I come back to my point. We must find a motive. It may give us an angle on the priest, as well as on the Chens."

"And I come back to, where do we start?" said Yianni.

"Maggie, can you think of anyone you spoke with who might be able to shed some light on how the priest could be connected to the IV bruising?"

"As far as I know, none of the families ever noticed the bruising, and those who've met him have nothing but praise for Papa George."

"Well then, you have a place to start. Do you think you can find someone who doesn't idolize your priest?"

Maggie's voice perked up. "As a matter of fact, I already have one in mind."

"Great, then get on it."

"But what about my investigation, Chief? I'm dead-ended," said Yianni.

"I think the answer to where you go from here turns on what we learn about Papa George. It's hard to imagine why major international business players, with a bent for the high life, would travel to out-of-the-way Ikaria just to say hello to a priest. Papa George's role in whatever's afoot strikes me as key."

"Sounds like you and I have a lead to run down together," said Yianni to Maggie.

"And we better get on it right away."

"Why?"

"Our lead is in his nineties."

———

In the mid-1970s, after his release from Junta detention, Mihali opened a modest pharmacy in Agios Kirykos. A few years later, his only child, a daughter, joined him in the business. A decade later, his granddaughter joined them, but after marrying an Evdilos man, moved to Evdilos to open a pharmacy with him there.

When Mihali's daughter passed away after a long battle with breast cancer, he soldiered on alone for several years, before selling his shop and moving to Evdilos to be closer to his grand-daughter and great-grandchildren. The move also brought him closer to his mates from their revolutionary days who'd settled on the north side of the island.

Maggie had Mihali's mobile number, but she wanted to meet with him face-to-face, and since the granddaughter's pharmacy stood not far from where Maggie and Yianni had parked, that seemed the appropriate place to start looking for him. The granddaughter told Maggie that he often stopped by the pharmacy unannounced, but at this time of day they'd most likely find him with his friends at a taverna midway along the harbor front.

The taverna took up the first floor of a barely two-story neo-classical building capped by a massive pediment a bit too large for the structure's size. But inside sat a classic old-time taverna, complete with old photos lining the walls, old mismatched tables and chairs resting on a thoroughly scuffed old floor, and old men clustered together in groups with every pair of eyes poised to catch whoever might next come through the front door.

The moment Maggie stepped inside, she heard a loud voice shout out to her from within a group of half a dozen men wedged together at a table for four: "Welcome, lady friend of my newest revolutionary buddy. Please, come join us."

"What's that all about?" whispered Yianni.

"Just keep smiling, and whatever you do, keep your political opinions to yourself. The guy yelling is a ninety-nine-year-old 17 November sympathizer." Maggie smiled all the way to the table. "I'm flattered you remembered me, especially since we never had the opportunity to speak."

"Your friend, Tassos, made quite an impression on us, and of course, we were all great fans of your *yaya*." He and the others at the table lifted their wine tumblers in a salute to Yaya. *"Na zisoume na tin thymomaste."*

Maggie nodded to the men. "Yes, may we all live to remember her. Thank you, I appreciate that very much."

He pointed to two empty chairs at another table, and barked to Yianni, "Grab those chairs for yourself and your mother and come join us."

Yianni smiled broadly, while Maggie struggled to maintain her own.

"He's more like a brother."

"A baby one," said Yianni, still smiling.

"What brings you here?" one of the men asked.

Maggie nodded toward Mihali. "I have some personal things to discuss with Mihali about Yaya."

"What kind of personal things?"

"The kind I keep personal."

The man laughed. "You have your *yaya*'s spirit."

"Thank you once again." She paused. "Actually, there's no mystery to what I have to ask Mihali. It's important for the family to know whether there's anything in Yaya's medical history that we, as her descendants, should be concerned about."

"That makes sound medical sense," said Mihali, rising from his chair. "Let's take a walk, because if we talk in here, they'll all be straining their hearing aids to the breaking point, hoping to pick up on our conversation. Besides, I've heard all their stories a hundred times over."

The men at the table threw an assortment of less-than-gracious hand gestures Mihali's way, smiling as they did.

Once outside, Mihali pointed to a bench across the road, at the edge of the sea. "Let's sit there."

With the aid of his cane, Mihali stepped sprightly across the road, giving no indication of any need or desire for assistance. He sat on one end of the bench, with Maggie next to him and Yianni beside her.

Mihali turned to her. "So, what's your real reason for wanting to speak to me?"

"Sorry. It was the best excuse I could think of at the moment."

"Don't worry, you made them all happy by giving them something new to speculate on for the rest of their afternoon."

He looked at Yianni. "And who are you, young man?"

Maggie answered for him. "He's a detective at GADA. I took my conversation with you seriously and reported your concern about the high number of deaths of elderly people in a two-week period."

Mihali nodded. "Good."

"We have some questions," said Maggie. "Starting with what you think could explain Yaya's change of behavior in her final weeks."

He shook his head. "She wasn't herself. I'd never seen her depressed before, but in my opinion, she was."

"Could it have been a drug-induced depression?" said Yianni.

"Possibly, but I don't think so."

"Then what do you think explains it?" said Maggie.

Mihali's lower lip began trembling, and tears welled up in his eyes. He pulled a handkerchief from his jacket pocket and dabbed at his eyes. "I swore to your *yaya* I would never tell a soul about her deepest secret. One she'd successfully suppressed for more than three-quarters of her life."

Maggie edged slightly closer to him but said not a word.

Mihali sighed. "*Something* happened to her in her final weeks that I pray the Lord agrees frees me from that vow. If I am wrong, may my soul burn in hell."

"Now, Mihali," said Maggie, taking his hand in hers, "don't make yourself ill over this."

He shook his head rapidly. "No, it's time to talk of it."

"Start wherever you feel most comfortable, sir," said Yianni.

Mihali stared out to sea. "I loved your *yaya* from the time I first met her. From afar, mind you, for she was ten years older than I, and married, and when your grandfather died, I was married to a wonderful woman I loved dearly. My wife passed on when your *yaya* was nearing eighty and I seventy. By then we'd been friends for years, and with neither of us knowing how much more time we had left, we simply pressed ahead hoping to enjoy each other's company as best and for as long as we could."

He cleared his throat. "Over those years we reminisced a lot. We agreed that it was good to share our memories while we could still remember them. One day she got off on a dark soliloquy laying out her deepest secret, a haunting burden born of unbearable trauma she'd endured through much of her childhood."

Maggie didn't know if she wanted to hear any more. The genie was still in the bottle. Her hand began to tremble.

Yianni reached over, put his hand on top of Maggie's, and squeezed it gently.

"When Yaya was a child, times were particularly tough, and a childless friend of her mother who lived alone offered to take her, as the youngest child, to live with her until times improved. While Yaya lived away, an older brother and sister died of the Spanish flu. When she returned home, she found her mother consumed by mourning for her lost children. Every day until her mother died—when your *yaya* was twelve--she'd hear her mother questioning the Lord for an answer as to why Yaya had been spared and the two others had not." Mihali paused. "Yaya lived a life infused with guilt and haunted by the thought it was somehow her fault that she'd lived and her siblings had died."

"That makes no sense," said Maggie.

"Trauma often leads to reactions that make no sense to those who've not experienced the event. In your *yaya*'s case, she found salvation in her husband, children, grandchildren, great-grandchildren, and caring friends. They offered her peace and refuge from those painful thoughts of her past. Rarely did any of that surface, except as part of some foggy passing memory of what she'd overcome from her childhood." Mihali jiggled his cane. "That was her deepest secret."

Yianni let go of Maggie's hand. "May I ask, sir, how that tragic past relates to Yaya's death?"

"Sorry," said Mihali. "My mind drifts sometimes."

"No problem," smiled Yianni.

"She hadn't raised that bitter part of her past to me in years. Two weeks ago, out of the blue, she raised it. And not as a passing recollection of a childhood memory, but as a cry from one currently reliving the pain.

"I asked her what had come over her, but she wouldn't tell me. All she said was, she'd made her confession and would serve her penance before joining her brother, sister, and mother."

Maggie's face heated. "What are you saying?"

"Honest, that's all she told me."

"You've already demonstrated you're a savvy man. Just tell me what you made of what she said."

Mihali shrugged. "As I see it, she'd talked about her deepest secret with someone else, someone who rekindled her feelings of guilt."

"You'd have to be a heartless son of a bitch to do that to an old lady," said Yianni.

"Who do you think that might be?" said Maggie.

Mihali stared straight at her. "Someone who accepts confessions and prescribes appropriate penance."

"And who spent weeks alone with her," added Maggie.

"Not always alone. Yaya said that at times he'd show up with a woman he claimed was a nun."

"What do you mean by *claimed*?" said Yianni.

"It came up in a conversation Yaya had with me in her final week, complaining about how much the Church had changed over her lifetime. She said the priest had shown up with a woman wearing ordinary clothes, yet introduced her as a nun. When Yaya asked why she wasn't wearing traditional garb, he dismissed it an example of how changing times had come to the Church."

Yianni said, "Just to make it clear who we're talking about—"

"Papa George."

"I understand he lives in Evdilos," said Maggie.

"Yes, but he no longer spends time working around here as a priest. He prefers the south side of the island, and apparently his superiors are fine with that."

"Why's that?"

"Probably because of sizable donations so many churches on the island receive from grateful families for the attention he shows their oldest relatives."

"But I understood he never asks for donations from the families."

Mihali shrugged. "Perhaps not for himself, but he doesn't discourage donations to a family's church."

"When did you first meet him?" asked Yianni.

"He showed up a couple of years ago as a newly minted priest, full of enthusiasm. He did a terrific job of promoting himself to old folks on the northern side of the island. Then about a month ago, he simply walked away from those he'd worked with in the north for years, and concentrated on tending to those living in the south."

"Any guess as to why he did that?" said Yianni.

Mihali gestured with his cane toward the taverna. "Some of my friends in their wild conspiratorial rants have tied it to a death about a month ago in Evdilos of a centenarian woman named Alki. She'd been the first member of what Papa George calls his flock."

He cleared his throat. "They reason that he was traumatized by Alki's death, for she was someone he'd been close to for as long as he'd been on the island. That now he preferred to deal with relative strangers, so he could tend to them in a detached, clinical manner, particularly when they're not expected to live much longer."

Maggie's face twitched. "With him there to speed along the process."

Yianni leaned in toward Mihali. "There's something about all this that I don't understand, but perhaps you, sir, as a local with knowledge of the medical community, could explain it to me."

Mihali nodded, "I'll try."

Yianni exhaled. "With so many elders dying so close in time to one another, and each exhibiting similar bruising, wouldn't you think a doctor charged with signing death certificates would at some point become suspicious and order an autopsy?"

Mihali rocked forward and back, resting his hands on his cane. "Perhaps, if the same doctor signed all the death certificates. But they died on different parts of the island, and likely had different family doctors. Even if some had the same doctor, I doubt that IV bruises on a very old patient who died peacefully at home in bed would lead the doctor to conclude anything other than death by natural causes."

"In other words," said Maggie, "someone looking to avoid raising suspicions would want to assure that there'd be a different family doctor signing each death certificate."

"But how would Papa George know each decedent's family doctor?" asked Mihali.

Maggie answered through clenched teeth, "By making friends with the island's doctors, who'd let him know when their patients happened to be members of his flock."

Mihali tapped his cane three times on the concrete. "If you're right, I pray God will forgive me for betraying Yaya's confidence."

"I wouldn't worry about that," said Yianni. "The Lord will have a different soul to burn in hell."

Chapter Eleven

Yianni and Maggie had just returned to their parked car when his mobile rang.

"Hello, Detective Kouros?"

"Yes, who's calling?"

"I'm Sergeant Apostolou. I was in charge of collecting the three pieces of garbage that attempted to rob the museum, and in the process killed an undercover officer."

"Oh, yeah, I remember you. What's up?"

"When we searched the three, we found a mobile phone on one of them. We sent it off to the lab to see if they could come up with anything of interest."

"I assume they did."

"Sure did. A photograph of the cop they killed."

"Taken after they'd killed him?"

"No."

Yianni looked over at Maggie, confused. "I don't understand."

"It was a copy of an ID bearing Stavros's photo."

"What?"

"That was my reaction. If these guys were random junkies pulling a smash and grab for jewelry, what was one of them doing with a photo of the cop who supposedly just happened to show up in the wrong place at the wrong time?"

Yianni shut his eyes, his thoughts spinning through possible explanations like a wheel of fortune spinning while bettors waited for it to land on a winning number. "What sort of ID?"

"The kind issued to truckers and their helpers authorizing them to enter the secure parts of the Piraeus docks."

Yianni's eyes opened as his thoughts came to an abrupt halt. "Any idea how the photo ended up on his phone?"

"Not a clue. I hoped you might have one."

"I wish I did. Do me a favor and send me a copy of the photo at this number. And while you're at it, please send one to Chief Inspector Andreas Kaldis at Special Crimes."

"Will do."

"Thanks. Bye."

Yianni put down his phone, shut his eyes again, and leaned back against the passenger seat headrest.

"What is it?"

Yianni opened his eyes. "I came to Ikaria looking for a lead into a drug trafficking investigation at the Piraeus ports, only to find its potential principals are somehow likely connected to the deaths of a half dozen ninety- and hundred-year-olds on Ikaria. Now it appears the coincidental murder of Stavros turns out to be an intentional hit. A hit that, I'd bet my badge, is tied into one or both of those other situations."

"So what do we do now?"

"Call Andreas."

———

Maggie drove while Yianni spoke on the speakerphone with Andreas, relaying the details of their meeting with Mihali and his telephone conversation with the sergeant.

"Jeez," said Andreas. "What the hell have we stumbled into?"

"I was hoping you might have a thought or two on that subject."

"As I see it, our weakest play at the moment is to go directly at Papa George or the Chens. We have nothing on them except deep suspicions. The weakest link looks to be the connection between the three guys involved in Stavros's murder and whatever else is going down."

"So, what do we do next?"

"See if your friend Marco can figure out who's responsible for that copy of Stavros's ID photo ending up on one of the killers' phones. They obviously used it to identify him for the hit. I can't believe that bottom-of-the-food-chain scum played any part in getting access to his ID."

"I'll call Marco, but I'm not sure what he can do."

"Nor am I, but that's why he's a computer detective and we're the head-banging type."

"I assume from the way things are going so far, you're referring to our heads banging against a hard stone wall," Maggie chimed in.

"Have I told you how much I miss you?"

"Feel free to repeat yourself, Chief."

Andreas laughed. "Okay, Yianni, you chase down the origins of the ID with Marco, and I'll pay a visit to the trio jailed in Korydallos."

"Doesn't that risk tipping our hand that we're on to something bigger than a botched robbery?" said Kouros.

"Well, we are. The fact that a photo of the cop they killed appeared on one of their phones makes it a *much* bigger case. In fact, if finding that photo didn't kick things into high gear, that alone would be highly suspicious to their lawyer if not to the killers. My guess is whoever's behind this operation is going to be very unhappy at the ID screwup. I want to shake their cage and see what I can jar loose."

"You get to do all the fun things."

"Yeah, but you get to hang out with Maggie."

"Making me the ultimate winner," she added.

"Bye."

———

Korydallos Prison Complex is Greece's notorious main prison, housing maximum-security and other prisoners in the suburbs of Piraeus. It's repeatedly cited as one of the worst prisons in Europe for overcrowding and alleged inhumane treatment of detainees. Nor is it pretty to look at: a walled, gray amalgam of short, warehouse-like structures crowded into a several-city-blocks area surrounding a tiny central patch of green. Although an uneasy place at best, it's most well known to the public for two separate, great escapes in a rented helicopter—each time by the same notorious kidnapper/bank robber.

When Andreas walked into one of the prison's virtually colorless interrogation rooms, the accused killers sat in a line behind a square metal table anchored to the floor. Two wore slings over one shoulder, their free hands handcuffed to the chair, and their legs shackled to the floor. The third sat in a wheelchair anchored to the floor at one end of the table. At the other end of the table, next to an empty chair, stood a gray-haired, ruddy-faced man in a flashy suit and tie.

"You must be their lawyer," said Andreas, extending his hand to the man. "I'm Chief Inspector Andreas Kaldis of Special Crimes."

The lawyer stepped forward to shake Andreas's hand, introducing himself as he did. "Thank you for having your office alert me that you were on your way to speak to my clients."

"I believe in doing things the right way. Please sit."

The lawyer sat in a chair at the end of the table, and Andreas sat directly opposite the prisoners.

"Let me tell you why I'm here," said Andreas. "It's to do most of you a favor, especially your lawyer."

The lawyer grinned. "We'll see."

"I'm sure you'll agree." Andreas swallowed and, after making direct eye contact with each prisoner, said, "You're in here on several charges, but I'm here to talk about the big one, the murder of a police officer."

The lawyer jumped in. "My clients had no idea the poor deceased man was a police officer."

Andreas nodded. "Yes, I understand your position. In fact. I agree with your concern on that point. For if by chance they did know he was a police officer, they'd face the risk of a much longer prison sentence. And if it should somehow be shown that they not only knew he was a police officer, but came to the museum with the intention of killing him…" Andreas spun his hand in a circle in front of him.

The lawyer smiled. "Yes, but fortunately for my clients, none of that is true. They were high on drugs and one overreacted. That's all."

Andreas nodded again. "And I'm sure you'll agree that if they had shown up with the intention of killing the officer, they're lucky there's no death penalty in Greece. Though, if found guilty on that charge, your relatively young clients would be lucky to get out of prison before they're your grandfather's age."

The lawyer shrugged. "Chief Inspector, I appreciate your assistance in explaining to my clients what their situation would be like if what you said were true, but it's not. So where are you going with this?"

The prisoner to Andreas's left cast a nervous glance at the two others.

"You're right. I'll get straight to the point of my visit." He looked at the nervous one. "Are you the one who showed up at the scene of the murder carrying with you a photograph of the soon-to-be dead officer?"

"Don't answer that," shouted the lawyer, glaring at Andreas as he did. "That's way out of line, Chief Inspector. This interview is over." He stood up.

Andreas calmly signaled for him to sit. "Your clients aren't going anywhere quite yet. They're anchored to the floor. Besides, I was only joshing with you."

The lawyer's face reddened. "I wasn't amused."

"Well then you're just going to love what I have to say next." Andreas cleared his throat. "I know that your client on the left," he pointed at the prisoner, "didn't have that photo with him. In fact, he didn't even have a phone with him."

"What's a phone have to do with anything?"

"The only one who had a phone with him is your client in the middle. The same guy who wielded the hammer."

"Chief Inspector, I don't know what game you're playing, but you're wasting my time."

"I'm here to offer your two clients who did not wield the hammer the opportunity to tell me that they were convinced by their buddy in the middle to join him on an easy score, and that they had no idea whatsoever he'd brought them in to serve as cover for a hit he'd been paid to carry out on the police officer."

"You have no proof of any of that," barked the lawyer.

"Up until now you've been representing all three, claiming there was no need for them to have separate counsel. I'm going to give you the chance of talking with your clients in private to decide if they still want to hang together or would prefer a separate defense."

"This is irresponsible behavior on your part. I'll see to it that you—"

Andreas held up his hand. "Spare me the threats. I'm going to show you something, then leave the room."

Andreas stood and pulled his cellphone out of his pocket. "What I'm about to show you came from a mobile phone found in the middle man's pocket upon his arrest."

Going prisoner by prisoner, Andreas held up the picture of Stavros's ID in front of each of them. The two on the ends studied the photo; the one in the middle looked away.

Next, he showed it to the lawyer. "I'm sure your clients will identify the man in the photo to you if you don't already know who he is."

The lawyer said nothing.

"I now leave you to chat among yourselves."

Once outside, Andreas sat by the door to the interrogation room. About a minute later he heard the screaming begin. First it was the lawyer, then other voices jumped in. Up until that point Andreas wasn't sure if the lawyer was on the up-and-up. For certain, someone else was paying his fees. The only question in Andreas's mind was whether he was honestly defending them, or serving as the eyes and ears of whoever was paying the bills. From the decibel levels of the shouting, Andreas assumed that the attorney had only now learned he'd been lied to. And that two of his three clients had learned the same.

Andreas heard a knock on the door coming from the inside. A prison guard opened the door. The lawyer stepped outside.

"I've resigned my representation of the prisoner you describe as the one in the middle. I shall continue representing the other two. Is there anything else you want to ask my clients?"

"I'll ask you, because I'm sure you already asked them. Do either of them have any idea who hired the third to kill my police officer?"

The lawyer gestured no. "They're as surprised as I was. And angrier."

"Well, then I'll ask the guard to take your remaining two clients back to their cells."

"What about the other one?"

"I'm not done with him yet."

"You won't get anything out of him. He's scared to death. Said he's not safe inside once word gets back to whoever hired him if they think he's going to talk."

"Did he say *they*?"

"Yes."

"Thanks, but I think I'll take a shot at him." He turned to the guard and told him to take the other two back to their cells.

The lawyer shuffled his feet a bit. "One more thing."

"Sure, what is it?"

"You were right, you truly did do me a favor. Thank you."

"There is one favor you could do for me."

"If I can."

"Who's paying your bill?"

The lawyer smiled. "Nice try, but you know that I can't answer that. Besides, I don't know who's paying. Someone just calls my office each day to ask what is owed, and the next day an envelope shows up with cash."

"Not a bad arrangement?"

"It's a living."

"And that doesn't make you curious?" said Andreas.

"Curiosity can kill not only the cat, but the living."

"Profound."

The lawyer patted him on the shoulder and walked away.

Eureka, thought Andreas. Whether intended or not, the lawyer had inspired him on what to do next.

"Guard, keep the prisoner locked up in there until I get back. Do you want anything at the kiosk?"

He gestured no.

Andreas knew the perfect thing to pick up for the guy chained to the floor. Thanks to his ex-lawyer...

———

A half-hour had passed before Andreas returned. He'd given the prisoner more than enough time to build up his anxieties.

Andreas strolled into the interrogation room sipping a coffee. He sat across from the prisoner, and kept sipping his coffee, not saying a word. Nor did the prisoner.

"I understand you're afraid to talk about who hired you to do the hit."

No answer.

"I completely understand why that is. After all, how can you possibly feel safe from guys like that, even in here?" He took another sip. "But there is a way for you to save your sorry ass, because once you're convicted—and you will be convicted—you'll live the rest of your life in here wondering which day is the day that the guys who sent you to kill a cop will send someone to kill you, just to clear up an unnecessary loose end."

No response.

"There is a way out of this for you. Tell us who they are so we can take them out before they take you out."

Dead silence.

"By the way, we already know who they are, but if you don't cooperate, we'll have to build our case against them by interviewing and squeezing people close to them. And once they figure out the pressure's on because of your screwup with the photo... Well, I don't have to tell you what they'll do."

"You don't know shit."

Good, he's talking. "Believe me, we know. And we're going after them. With or without your cooperation. The outcome for you is in your hands alone."

"Like I said, you don't know shit."

Andreas stood up. "Have it your way. By the way, just to show you I'm not a bad guy, I brought something back for you from the kiosk. It's not cigarettes or candy, but reading material. Something I'm sure you'll enjoy."

He reached inside his jacket, pulled out a thin magazine, and dropped it on the table in front of the prisoner.

The man's eyes doubled in size as he bolted upright in his chair.

"I thought you'd like it: Tom and Jerry are my favorites too."

———

It was late afternoon when Marco got back to Yianni.

By then Yianni had settled into the guest room in Spiro's house. Maggie and Spiro had insisted he stay there and not in a hotel. All his protestations ended the moment he tasted the homemade custard pie served by Spiro's wife.

"The way to winning an argument is through my *galakto-boureko*," Sonia confided.

When Marco called, Yianni was strolling through a vineyard heavy with dark red grapes, surrounded by the sounds of warblers, the scents of wild herbs and flowers he could not identify, and thoughts of how drastically different time passed here than in Athens.

"Any luck?" said Yianni.

"Yeah, but not sure if it's the good or bad kind."

Yianni frowned as he turned his gaze from the sea to the ground in front of him. "What's that supposed to mean?"

"I'll tell you what I found, and you tell me whether it's good or bad."

Yianni exhaled. "Okay, I'll play along."

"I accessed the port authority files containing Stavros's ID information."

"Good."

"I also determined that someone recently accessed his file from an SDOE computer."

"Even better. How recently?"

"Four days before he was murdered."

"Was there anything in his file that revealed he was a cop?"

"Not a scrap of a hint."

"Any idea who got into his file?"

"I thought you'd never ask."

"Spare me the drama, please."

"Drumroll," said Marco. "The login credentials belong to Jerry."

Yianni's mouth dropped open. "Of Tom and Jerry?"

"You got it."

"I thought he was the smart one of the two. How could he be so stupid or careless as to sign in with credentials tying him to the murder of a cop?"

"And why would that photo alone justify murder?" said Marco. "It showed him to be a working stiff on the docks."

Yianni bit at his lip. "I can't believe I'm saying this, but it almost makes you think Jerry had no idea that photo would lead to Stavros's murder."

Marco said, "I thought that too. Which is why I did something else. I ran the photo through SDOE's photo-recognition software, and it picked up quite a few hits."

"Damn social media."

"Most were innocent enough, but one stood out."

"Just give me the bad news."

Marco lowered his voice. "I found Stavros's police academy photo."

Yianni froze for an instant. "Very bad news."

"Keep in mind the facial-recognition software I used is very expensive and hard to come by. It's capable of accessing sites the general public cannot reach with off-the-shelf software—such as police academy files."

"What are you telling me?"

"It wasn't ordinary bad guys who got ahold of his academy photo. Whoever it was used sophisticated software. Likely classified, government software."

"Like what was available to Jerry on his SDOE computer?"

"No, he's not authorized to use that software."

"If it wasn't Jerry, then who was it?"

"I don't know, but the search of police academy files came through a computer based in Hong Kong."

Yianni felt goose bumps building on his arms. "And when was that?"

"Three days before his murder."

Goose bumps now were everywhere.

———

As soon as Yianni hung up with Marco, he phoned Andreas.

"Chief, I've got big news."

"So do I, but why don't you go first?"

Yianni told him of his conversation with Marco, and what he'd found that potentially tied Jerry and the Chens to Stavros's murder.

"That fits quite nicely with the news I have from my visit to Korydallos." He told Yianni of his back-and-forth with the lawyer in front of his clients, and how things went better than he'd hoped toward setting up the three perps to turn on each other. When he got to the part where he dropped a Tom and Jerry comic book in front of the killer, Yianni burst out laughing.

"Oh, how I wish I had been there to see his face."

"After that, I couldn't shut him up. He went on and on about how he'd been *set up* by Tom and Jerry to take out Stavros. He said he thought he was just killing a *regular* guy, not a cop."

"What an asshole."

"It gets worse. He said Tom and Jerry had him dead to rights on another homicide and promised to put him away on that charge if he didn't do them this favor."

"I can't believe we share the same planet with those two, let alone a badge."

"They told him the girlfriend of the guy whose picture was on his phone worked at the museum, and he'd find him with her there. He was to arrive at closing time, locate the guy, kill him, and leave. Bringing the two other junkies along was his idea. He figured since it was a jewelry museum, he might as well rob it."

Yianni shook his head.

"Two days later, they showed up at the museum. As things turned out, Stavros wasn't with his girlfriend, so our perp tried scaring her into telling him where he was. First, by grabbing a hammer from a goldsmithing exhibition and using it to smash a display case. When that didn't work, he tried breaking her arm with the hammer, but all she did was scream. That's when he hit her in the head with it."

"How did you restrain yourself? I'd have wanted to kill the sucker right then and there."

Andreas spoke calmly. "Easy. I just kept saying to myself, everything we're saying is being recorded. He'll get what's coming to him later."

Yianni sighed. "Yep. There's a bigger picture to consider."

"Just after he'd knocked her out, Stavros came off the elevator. He described that moment as a gift, one that made everything he'd planned fall into place. But instead of shooting Stavros, he killed him with the hammer, which made it look like random violence committed by druggies robbing the place, not a planned hit."

Andreas paused. "But then you jumped into the middle of it all, wrecking his plans."

"Not soon enough," said Yianni between clenched jaws. "When do we arrest the two piece-of-shit cops?"

"As soon as we have hard evidence and witnesses sufficiently believable to convict them and whoever else was involved in the murder."

"And when do you suspect that will be?"

"You tell me. I'd say we've come pretty far in a short time, but we still have nothing tying the Chens into any of this."

"The Hong Kong computer?"

"Come on, you know better than that. There are seven and a half million people in Hong Kong. Yes, if I had to bet, I'd agree they're involved, from the tips of their Gucci loafers to the tops of their perfectly coiffed heads. It seems to me that Jerry obtained a copy of Stavros's ID photo for the Chens, thinking it was for some other, more innocent purpose. That's the only sensible explanation I can come up with for why Jerry used a computer so readily tied back to him."

Andreas drew in a deep breath. "But then someone in Hong Kong discovered Stavros's police academy photo and sent Tom and Jerry on a quick mission to find an assassin to murder him."

"We gotta nail those bastards."

"To do that, we'll need to find a motive for the Chens ordering his murder. And why they made it so urgent."

"How do you suggest we do that?"

"By turning you loose on Ikaria."

"What are you talking about?"

"You and Maggie are on to something with this Papa George character, even though he's checked out to be a real priest. I've no idea how he's involved with the Chens, or if he has anything to do with what got Stavros killed, but there's sure as hell a lot more to his boat ride with the Chens than coincidence. I think we concentrate on Papa George. And through him, them."

Images popped into Yianni's imagination. "Meaning?"

"Shake him up. Tell him whatever it takes to set him off, because we've no doubt he's involved in something rotten. And whatever it is, I don't see the Church backing him up, certainly not if he has anything to do with so many loyal elderly followers dying like flies around him."

"What if he's innocent?"

"We're not going public with any accusations, and I doubt he'll want to make them public. So, if we're wrong about him, the most he'll likely do is lay some heavy-duty curses on you."

"Great."

"Think nothing of it. Besides, you have a far greater power on your side than he could ever muster."

"And what would that be?"

Andreas chuckled. "Maggie. Go get him."

———

Yianni sat on the stump of an ancient tree, staring off between neat rows of sturdy old trees laden with olives. Soon it would be harvesttime, and the peace and quiet of this place would yield to the clatter and rush to gather and process the crop.

A falcon burst out across a cobalt-blue sky, soaring high above the treetops and triggering sharp warning calls among its potential prey, breaking the silence of the moment.

Yianni had concluded that no matter what story Papa George might spin to justify his behavior, his flock and all other likely targets had to be warned of the potential danger they faced.

We can't remain silent.

But how to locate the members of Papa George's flock without his cooperation? And even with his cooperation, could he be trusted to turn over the names of any who might possibly implicate him in six deaths—if not more? Worse still, without proof supporting his and Maggie's suspicions, going public with an island-wide alert was not a viable option.

Yianni cursed aloud and kicked at the dirt. There must be some nonpublic way to reach out to his flock without going through Papa George.

Yianni ran the fingers of his right hand across his day-old beard. Maggie was pressing everyone she knew on the island for the whereabouts of Papa George. But he'd not been seen since jumping on the Chens's yacht in Evdilos.

He and the yacht had vanished.

That made it even more urgent that they find a way to locate his flock, if only to assure themselves that all in his flock are safe.

But how?

Yianni shut his eyes, allowing his other senses to shift through the scents and sounds of the hillside, waiting for one to outdo the others and win this impromptu lottery of the senses.

Lottery.

Yianni's eyes popped open. He'd found his answer.

Chapter Twelve

Yianni hurried back from the olive grove to the main house, hoping to find Maggie there. Spiro told him she'd gone to Yaya's cottage but said she'd be right back.

"Thanks, I'll catch up with her there." He turned to leave, then paused, and looked at Spiro. "Perhaps *you* can help me."

"If I can, sure."

"I understand there's an old man on the island who runs a lottery where the winner is based upon when the next Ikariot over ninety will pass away."

Spiro smiled as he shook his head. "Poor old Ilias. His heart's always in the right place, but his head... Well, what can I say? Yes, I know him. He was kind enough to deliver one of his wreaths to Yaya's funeral."

"Do you know where I can find him?"

"He lives out by the southwestern end of the island, in the fishing village of Karkinagri."

"Karkinagri?"

"It's an ancient Greek word for crab, which fits its fishing history. These days it draws a lot of tourists seeking peace and quiet. If you're into rocky places, you'll love it there, because it's surrounded by giant rocks, sheer cliffs, and off in the background, the Atheras Mountains range."

"Sounds isolated."

"Ilias loves it there, mainly for its *kafenion* life. If he's not sailing his caïque to Agios Kirykos or Evdilos on visits to the elderly, or off selling lottery chances somewhere, he's either attending a funeral or hanging out around Karkinagri's town square."

"How do I find out where he's going to be tomorrow morning?"

Spiro smiled. "It's simple. You ask me to make a call."

Yianni laughed. "Thanks."

"What's so funny?" said Maggie coming through the front doorway. "I could use a laugh myself."

"We can't seem to find Papa George, but I came up with a thought on another possible way of locating the members of his flock and others at risk." Yianni nodded at Spiro, "With your cousin's much-appreciated offer of help."

"Let me try to get you your answer." Spiro pulled his mobile out of his pocket and stepped outside to make the call.

"What's your plan?" said Maggie, closing the door.

Yianni told her of his conversations with Marco and Andreas, and of how he remembered hearing about an old Ikariot man who dedicated his life to keeping track of his island's nonagenarians and centenarians. "Ilias could be our best chance at finding who might be next on Papa George's hit list."

"Who told you about Ilias?"

Yianni coughed. This was not the moment to reveal Tassos as his source. "I overheard it somewhere, and it just stuck with me. When I mentioned what I remembered about him to Spiro, he identified the guy immediately."

Maggie fixed her stare on him. "I see."

Yianni looked away, just as Spiro opened the front door.

"I have your answer. Ilias will be with his friends for coffee at their regular meeting place in Karkinagri at around nine thirty tomorrow morning. He's usually there until eleven."

Yianni looked at Maggie. "Do you know how to get us there?"

"I can figure it out."

Spiro gestured no. "Don't even think about driving there. I'll borrow my friend's boat and get you there far faster and easier than driving. Besides, Ilias will be more likely to talk to you if I'm with you."

"How's that sound, Maggie?" said Yianni, still not making eye contact with her.

"Fine with me."

"Good," said Spiro. "I'll make the arrangements. The only thing is, my friend will want to be paid for his petrol. But it's an inflatable."

"No problem," said Maggie. "Right, Yianni?"

Yianni saluted her. "Whatever you say, Boss. Especially since you administer our unit's expense account."

"What time should we be ready to leave?"

"Let's be out of here by eight thirty."

"Is that real time or Ikarian time?" said Maggie.

"If we want to catch Ilias tomorrow morning, we'd better operate on real time." Spiro smiled. "Then again, if we go according to Ikarian time, I'm sure we'd make it there in time to catch him the day after."

"Why's everyone in my family a wiseass?"

"I hope you're not asking me that question," said Yianni.

She feigned a glare. "And I hope you're not considering answering it."

Yianni winked. "Not in this life."

———

The next morning, Maggie, Yianni, and Spiro made it down to the boat and were off to Karkinagri by nine. The "inflatable" turned out to be a ten-meter Brig Eagle equipped with twin Suzuki three-hundred-fifty horsepower engines.

"My God," said Yianni. "How did you get your friend to loan you this baby? Not that I object, mind you, but paying for the petrol she burns could bust our unit's annual budget."

Spiro smiled. "It belongs to a doctor who only uses it when he's here on holiday. Our deal is, I take care of it while he's away and get to use it if I pay for the petrol. But don't worry, as long as the sea remains calm, I'll keep the speed down to where it doesn't burn a lot of fuel, and still have us there by ten."

Once underway, Maggie lay on the stern bench, while Yianni sat beside Spiro on the cockpit seat, listening to his running commentary on the areas of the island they passed and what roles they'd played in Ikarian history.

From the sea, much of the island seemed untouched, almost virginal, but islands often appeared that way along their shorelines, no matter how developed they might be elsewhere. Shades of brown, gray, rust, and random patches of green cascaded down from Ikaria's pronounced mountain spine, along stone gullies and ridges, toward a rough and rocky coastline of massive granite boulders and isolated bits of beach and coves. Glimpses of a church or even a village did not intrude upon Yianni's sense that what he saw today might be much the same as what had greeted the island's first settlers—less its once-ubiquitous forests.

He'd long held the belief that Greek islanders, despite where they hailed from, shared a lifestyle and ethos much in common with one another, no matter how different one island's architecture might be from another's. In part, those differences correlated to an island's naturally available building materials, be they forests, stone, or marble, but in larger measure, they undoubtedly related to which foreign culture had occupied an island long enough to imprint its tastes upon the islanders.

Yianni wondered how successful today's islanders would be at resisting the temptation to abandon their historical commonality in exchange for the promise of great wealth dangled before them by a new breed of foreign conquerors. The new came equipped with capital, not armaments, but were driven by the same merciless goal shared by all conquerors: to exploit the conquered, their island, and their nation.

"We're almost there," said Spiro. "Karkinagri is off to the right, about two kilometers around that bend. It's one of the few decent anchorages west of Agios Kirykos, so we might have to search a bit for a place to tie up along shore."

Yianni looked at his watch. "You made good time."

Spiro nodded back at Maggie. "I'd have made better, but I didn't want to wake her."

"I think I better do that now."

Yianni went back and gently jostled Maggie's arm. "Wakey, wakey, we're almost there."

Maggie shook her head, batted her eyes a few times and sat up. "Where are we?"

"Close to Karkinagri."

Spiro yelled. "Looks like we'll have no trouble finding a place to dock. Not many small boats here this morning, and just a couple of yachts anchored in the deeper water."

Spiro and Maggie sat in the cockpit seat, with Yianni standing behind them, as their boat closed in on the town. Karkinagri stood as a village of three hundred in the most remote and inaccessible part of Ikaria. It occupied what seemed to be every bit of a coastal plain, bounded by the water to the south and rocky hillsides, cliffs, and mountains in all other directions. Compared to other island seafront towns, Karkinagri was far from crowded or overbuilt. Perhaps because lush gardens adorned so many of the neatly maintained whitewashed homes, providing welcome sanctuaries for lives happily lived within the village's isolated rocky nest.

As they passed an anchored fifty-meter yacht, Spiro pointed to a smaller yacht that had been moored unseen behind the larger one. "I love that boat. A seaworthy beauty of manageable size that you can take practically anywhere."

Yianni turned to look at what had caught Spiro's attention, then tapped Maggie on the shoulder. "Look at what your cousin just found." He paused until she turned. "Our missing Uniesse 56SS."

"What do you mean missing?" said Spiro.

Maggie practically shouted, "I don't believe it's here."

"It vanished from my yacht-finder app right after it departed Evdilos harbor."

Spiro smiled. "That's an old smuggler's trick for avoiding detection in Greek waters. Simply turn off your GPS and, poof, you vanish."

"Son of a bitch," said Yianni.

"Should I take a spin around it?" asked Spiro.

"Yes," said Yianni, "but don't make it too obvious."

"Don't worry, we poor islanders are expected to ogle expensive boats."

"Not sure you qualify as *poor*, piloting this boat," said Yianni, his eyes glued to the Uniesse.

Spiro slowly circled the boat once before heading toward shore. "It doesn't look like anyone's on it."

"Let's find Ilias ASAP," said Yianni. "I've got a bad feeling about this, and I don't know why."

Maggie looked back at the boat. "Me too."

———

They tied up alongside a concrete pier on the eastern side of the harbor and quickly made their way west to a taverna overlooking the water. Beneath salt pines, olive trees, and a tented canopy, in a space wide open to the sea, five elderly men sat around a table covered by a green-and-beige checked tablecloth. Two played *tavli*, while the other three talked among themselves, tossing out random observations on one or the other player's choice of moves on their backgammon board.

"Ilias!" shouted Spiro from the entrance to the taverna. "How are you, my good friend?"

Ilias seemed confused for a moment, then his face lit up. "Spiro, what are you doing here?"

"My cousin and her friend wanted to see Karkinagri, so I offered to bring them."

"Come, join us."

Spiro, Maggie, and Yianni pulled up chairs, and Spiro made the introductions, as Ilias gestured to the waiter to bring his guests coffees.

"I used to come here with my *yaya* to visit her friend," said Maggie. "We'd always meet her in the village, and it looks much as I remember it."

"Your memory is far too kind," said a snow-white-bearded *tavli* player. "These days we survive more on tourism than fishing."

"Life moves on," said the other player.

The coffees came, together with glasses of water and a plate of *koulourakia* cookies, followed by a back-and-forth discussion on the advantages and disadvantages of expanded tourism, the classic off-season islander debate.

Yianni pointed to the two boats anchored offshore. "They must bring money to the village."

Ilias shrugged. "I always try selling my lottery tickets to people off those sorts of boats. I tell them it's for charity. Some buy, some don't."

"Any luck with those two out there?"

"Two people off the big boat each bought a ticket. The three off the smaller boat ignored me like I didn't exist."

"Got Ilias right angry too," said the bearded *tavli* player. "He actually cursed a priest."

"A priest?" said Maggie.

Ilias sighed. "Yes, and worse yet, I know him. But to be fair, he seemed distracted. Not his normal charming self."

"What are they doing here?" asked Yianni.

"I've no idea." Ilias pointed to the other *tavli* player. "He told me their boat arrived in port just after sunrise, but no one got off until around nine. That's when I saw the three of them in a dinghy, and so I hurried over to meet them when they came ashore. Like I said, they just ignored me and walked away."

"Did you see where they went?"

"To the car-rental place."

"Where they were just as rude to me," said the bearded *tavli* player.

"He owns the rental place," explained Ilias.

"Those three were a strange mix of terribly anxious and utterly self-important folk," the player explained.

"What do you mean?" asked Yianni.

"The Chinese couple wanted a BMW, and when I told him the best I had was a Fiat, you'd think I'd insulted their family heritage. The priest was just plain abrupt. All he wanted from me were directions, and when I explained it's a little hard to give directions to where he was trying to get, he insisted I draw him a precise map."

"Directions to where?" asked Ilias.

"Anna's house."

"Anna Moraitis?" exclaimed Maggie, bringing her hand to her mouth.

"Yeah, she's a legend around here. One hundred four and still going strong. As if she weren't a day over ninety."

"She's the friend Yaya and I used to visit," said Maggie. "They met when Anna came to live with Yaya's family while Anna was attending high school in Agios Kirykos. That was the only way children who lived so far from Agios Kirykos could attend school in those days. I remember Yaya telling me how Anna had lied about her age because she was too old to go to high school when it was built, but she wanted an education."

"That old high school is now the Archaeological Museum," said Ilias.

Maggie jerked herself back from the memory, then said to the bearded man, "Sir, it's urgent we get to Anna's home immediately. Can you rent me a car and give me those same directions as you gave the priest?"

"What's going on?" asked Ilias.

"Her life could be in danger," said Spiro.

Yianni shot Spiro a critical look. "We can't say that. It's just important that we get to her immediately."

Spiro shook his head. "Trust me, Anna's life is at risk."

"You'll never find her on your own." Ilias stood up. "Come, we'll take my car."

"What about us?" asked the bearded player.

"Just hang around until I get back. Then I'll tell you whether or not there's a story here for you to spread around."

Yianni whispered to Maggie, "This is getting out of control."

"What makes you think it ever was under control?"

Yianni rolled his eyes.

"Don't worry, on Ikaria we always find a way," Maggie whispered back.

"I have a different attitude, but it lands both of us in the same place."

"What's that?"

"When it's the only game in town, play it."

———

The sun-bleached olive tone of Ilias's forty-year-old Land Rover Defender 110 nicely complemented much of the foliage they passed on their way to the mountain village of Lagkada.

"How far is it?" asked Yianni, sitting up front beside Ilias.

"About a half hour from when we left town. That's assuming we don't run into a herd of goats on the way."

"Great, that's all we need."

"We're pretty isolated out here from the rest of the island," said Ilias. "It's over two hours to the airport and, with the southern road east of Karkinagri washed away, it's as if we have to drive in circles to get anywhere. Just to reach where we're headed now, we go west practically to the end of the island, before winding back northeast to a place due north of where we started from."

"Sounds frustrating."

"It's why I have a caïque to get me to villages along the coast-line." He looked at Yianni. "May I ask you a question?"

"I'm sure you must have more than one."

"What makes you think Anna is in danger?"

"Just a hunch."

"I see. So, it has nothing to do with so many of Papa George's flock passing away in bunches?" Ilias stared at Yianni.

"What makes you say that?" said Yianni, trying to show no emotion.

With his eyes still fixed on Yianni, he said, "It's my business."

The blare of a horn shook Ilias's eyes off Yianni and onto a truck headed straight at them. Ilias yanked the steering wheel hard to the right, bringing the Defender wobbling back onto its side of the road. "This old truck isn't the best in tricky-handling situations."

"Then may I suggest you keep your eyes on the road," lectured Maggie.

Ilias kept talking. "Like I said, it's my business. I had to change my lottery rules when so many over ninety began dying so close to one another. Along the way, I noticed Papa George showing up at their funerals, and I wondered why a priest from Evdilos was attending funerals all over the island. That's when I learned he'd been counseling those who'd died."

"But you never asked anyone about that?" said Maggie.

"What should I have said, and to whom? The Church? The police?"

"Have you ever seen him in Karkinagri?" asked Yianni.

"Not until this morning. Like I said, it's hard to get here by car. Most come by boat. Which is how he arrived today."

Ilias turned right onto a dirt road bounded by views down to the sea and orchards growing thicker and greener the higher up the mountain they traveled.

"It's beautiful up here," said Maggie.

"We've got a way to climb yet. There's only one village on Ikaria at a higher elevation than Lagkada, and just slightly so."

"You haven't been here before?" said Spiro.

"I vaguely remember coming up here for a *panegyri*."

"That would have been on an August fifteenth," said Ilias. "Lagkada is famous for its *panegyri* in honor of the Virgin Mary, after which its church was consecrated. It's also revered as the oldest of our anti-pirate villages. Thousands of Ikariots flocked to Lagkada for safety as far back as the Middle Ages. But today, only about a dozen live there."

Maggie stared out her side window. "I'd forgotten how utterly idyllic, wild, green, and fertile this part of the island is."

"That's precisely why Anna has refused to move," said Ilias, his eyes now firmly fixed on the road. "Enough of her children and grandchildren live in the area for someone to stop by every day to check on her, bring her whatever she needs, and take her wherever she has to go." He smiled. "But she's a tough one, that Anna, and even if they didn't live around here, my money would be on her finding a way to survive. Up until a couple of years ago, several times a week she'd walk three kilometers each way along a mountain path over to the village of Vrakades, but her grandchildren put a stop to that."

"God bless her," said Maggie.

"Well, here's where we get out." He drove up onto a basketball-court-sized concrete plateau and parked. Directly ahead of them stood a simple white church, and farther on to the left, what looked to be a kitchen facility. Beyond that opened a view across orchards out to the sea, and a gathering mist drifting in to mask the region's rugged landscape and bring moisture to the orchards.

"This is where they hold the dancing, praying, and cooking."

"But where's Anna's house?"

Ilias pointed north. "We have to walk a bit. She lives in one of the few anti-pirate stone houses that remain."

"Ilias, what are you doing here?" called a voice. "I'm not buying any more lottery tickets."

Ilias laughed and waved at the man.

"Who's that?" said Yianni.

"He's the caretaker who watches over the place," said Ilias, before yelling to the man, "We're here to visit Anna."

"She's pretty popular today. Three others came to see her about two hours ago."

"Are they still here?" said Yianni.

"No, they left about thirty minutes ago."

"What did they look like?" said Ilias.

"Two Chinese and a priest. Come sit with me, my friend, have some wine, and tell me the news."

Yianni took Ilias by the arm. "You've got to get us to Anna *now*."

Ilias yelled back to the caretaker, "I'll stop on our way back."

Yianni steered Ilias in the direction he'd pointed. *"Hurry."*

Maggie faced the church, bowed her head, and crossed herself three times. *"And pray."*

———

But for the pots of geraniums by the front of Anna's house, one could easily walk right past it without noticing anything more than a larger boulder leaning up against a rocky hillside.

Ilias had not said a word since leaving the parking area for a well-worn dirt path. Instead, he concentrated his efforts on leading the four of them along the path at as brisk a pace as his body allowed.

Panting, he stopped and pointed at the geraniums. "Her front door is in there." He pointed to the space between the boulder and the hillside.

Yianni hurried to where he'd pointed, found a wooden door, and knocked. *"Kiria* Moraitis?" he shouted.

No answer. He went to a window, but it was shuttered closed. He returned to the front door, pounded harder and yelled louder.

Still no answer.

"Force open the door," said Spiro.

"Wait," said Maggie. She walked up to the door, pressed down on the latch, and pushed, sending the door swinging into the room.

She peeked inside. "Oh no," and ran toward a bed on the far side of the room.

The others piled into the room behind her.

Anna lay flat on her back with her eyes closed, a light blanket tucked neatly under nightgown-covered arms resting across her chest.

"Is she breathing?" asked Spiro.

"I can't tell."

Yianni pushed past Maggie, reached for Anna's wrist, lifted it up, and felt for a pulse. "She has a pulse but a very weak one."

He put down her wrist and gently pulled up the sleeves of her nightshirt. He shut his eyes and cursed. "She has the same bruising."

Maggie leaned in to take a closer look. "The puncture is fresh."

"Damn it," said Yianni. "We've got to get her to a hospital right away." He looked at Spiro, then Ilias. "We need an ambulance."

Ilias shook his head. "Forget about getting an ambulance, and even if we did, it's at least two hours to the general hospital in Agios Kirykos."

"Isn't there a clinic in Karkinagri?"

"Not for something this serious," said Ilias. "And if they have to fly her to Athens, it would be from Agios Kirykos."

"She'll never hold on that long," said Yianni.

"There must be something we can do," cried Maggie.

"There is," said Spiro. "Let's get her back to the boat and I'll get her from there to the hospital in a half hour." He looked at Maggie. "Call your friend the police chief and tell him to have an ambulance at the port in Agios Kirykos ready to transfer a hundred-plus-year-old woman in shock to the hospital."

"How do you know she's in shock?" Maggie asked.

"Because I've seen people die from it in accidents. We'd better keep her warm. Grab another blanket, Maggie. And Ilias, get your buddies in town to meet us at my boat with an oxygen tank so we can hook her up to it until she's at the hospital."

"Is it safe to move her?" Ilias asked.

"No, but considering the alternative, what choice do we have?"

"I'll carry her," said Yianni.

"Her bed's basically a cot," said Spiro. "You and I can carry it like a stretcher, and that way we can keep her legs elevated."

"Let's go," said Maggie, gathering up a blanket and a well-worn fabric shopping bag. She moved aside to let Spiro and Yianni get by with Anna on the cot. As she waited for them to pass, she glanced up at the wall at the foot of Anna's bed. Only one item occupied that wall: a simple Byzantine cross. It would be the last thing Anna saw when she laid down at night, and the first thing she saw when she rose in the morning.

Maggie reached up, took it down, and carefully wrapped it in the blanket before putting both into the bag.

"We'll need this for your journey," she told Anna.

———

Spiro drove, with Maggie and Yianni crowded next to him in the front seat, while Ilias sat in back steadying Anna in her cot on the ride back to Karkinagri.

"Have you reached the police chief yet?" said Spiro to Maggie.

"My call went to voicemail, but I left a detailed message for him." She struggled to pull her phone out of her jeans. "This is one of those times when I wish I carried a purse." She looked at her phone. "No reply yet." She put her phone into the bag with the extra blanket and the cross.

When they reached the port, Ilias's friends were waiting with a portable oxygen unit. They said not a word, just watched as Yianni and Spiro carefully carried Anna on her cot from the truck to the edge of the pier.

"I don't think it will fit," said Yianni, looking at the stern seat. "It's too long."

"I'll make it fit," said Spiro, jumping into the boat.

He tinkered with a table mounted in front of the stern seat, and in seconds had it removed and stowed away.

"You're a magician," said Yianni.

"Nope, just an out-of-work fisherman." He reached up to take one end of the cot, and together with Yianni, maneuvered it into the space formerly occupied by the table.

"Let's get underway," said Spiro.

"Just a second," said Yianni. He waved for Ilias to come to him, then leaned forward so as not to be overheard by the others on shore. "Thanks for all you did. I only have one more favor to ask of you. If you share with your friends any of our obvious suspicions over what happened to Anna, we may never be able to catch those responsible. I trust you to do the right thing."

"Come on," said Spiro, "we've got to get underway."

Ilias nodded as the engines roared to life. Two of Ilias's friends undid the mooring lines and tossed them into the boat. Yianni gathered up the lines and pulled in the bumpers, while Maggie made her way to the stern seat beside Anna. With the oxygen tank cradled between her legs, Maggie adjusted the mask over Anna's face, pulled up her blankets, and whispered to her as she held Anna's hand.

Spiro slowly pull away from the dock, taking care not to disturb the nearby boats with his wake. "I see the Uniesse is gone."

"Yes. But I can assure you not forgotten," muttered Yianni.

"How are you doing back there?" Yianni called to Maggie.

"Fine, but keep moving." She mouthed the word *PULSE* and pointed downward.

He looked back at Maggie. She was holding the cross between her hand and Anna's.

"Okay, here we go," called Spiro, and the engines roared.

Yianni kept looking back at Maggie, and she kept giving him a thumbs-up. Anna remained motionless.

For twenty minutes they cut through the water as if on wings, the sun at their backs, the engines humming, the promise of salvation dead ahead.

As they approached Agios Kirykos, Spiro pointed ahead to the right. "Look what we're coming up on off starboard."

"You've caught up with the bastards' boat."

"I wish I could ram them," said Spiro.

"Some other time."

As they passed the Uniesse, Yianni yelled to Maggie, "We're passing our friends."

Maggie looked over as Papa George waved to them.

She waved back.

Yianni yelled to Maggie, "I don't think it's proper maritime courtesy to wave back with the middle finger."

Maggie feigned a smile and went back to stroking Anna's hand.

They roared into the harbor, headed straight for an ambulance waiting on the quay. Spiro brought the boat close enough for Yianni to toss the mooring lines to the ambulance driver and a policeman. They secured the lines as Yianni dropped the bumpers between the boat and pier and Spiro cut the engines. Together Spiro and Yianni lifted the cot and transferred Anna and her oxygen to the cop and ambulance driver.

The two hustled Anna into the ambulance, and in seconds it was on its way to the hospital. The police officer strolled back to the edge of the pier and looked down into the boat.

"You sure do live an interesting life," he said to Maggie.

"Oh, hi, Dimitri. I do, don't I?" She introduced him to Yianni and Spiro. "I see the chief got my message."

Dimitri smiled. "And once again he volunteered me to be your driver. Where can I take you?"

Maggie looked at Spiro. "Yianni and I are heading to the hospital. What about you?"

"I'll join you. Just give me a couple of minutes to lock up the boat. One can't be too careful with the sort of people the island's attracting these days." He nodded toward where Papa George and the Chens stood on the bow of their boat, looking down at them.

"No more fingers, please," Yianni told Maggie.

"Oh, don't worry. I wouldn't be so unladylike as to do anything like that twice."

She reached into the bag holding the blanket she'd clutched around Anna, and pulled out the cross. She looped the straps of the bag over one shoulder and, staring straight at Papa George, lifted Anna's cross high above her head and shook it at him, shouting over and over, *"May you rot in hell."*

Papa George turned and walked away, but the Chens never moved or took their eyes off Maggie.

Chapter Thirteen

Five minutes after they left the harbor, Dimitri had them at General Hospital and back in the reception area where Maggie first met Papa George. Dimitri went straight to the receptionist.

He returned grim-faced. "Anna's in deep shock, but alive. If she'd arrived twenty minutes later…" He shook his head.

Maggie crossed herself. "When will they know if she's out of danger?"

"I didn't ask, but my guess is once they figure out what put her into shock."

"If the doctor can safely spare a few minutes to speak with Maggie and me, we might be able to help him answer that question."

"I'll be right back." Dimitri went back to the receptionist, and a moment later waved for them to join him.

"I'll wait here," said Spiro.

The receptionist led them into the emergency room and pointed to a group in white gathered around Anna. Yianni and Maggie started toward the bed, but a doctor held up his hand for them to stop, stepped away from the group, and stepped briskly to them.

"Ah, *Kiria* Maggie, I'm happy to see you've recovered from your accident."

She shot a nervous glance in Yianni's direction. "Oh, yes, it was nothing, and I'm all better, thanks to you."

"I wouldn't exactly say flying off a mountaintop on a motorbike in the middle of a rainstorm is *nothing*, but I'm glad you think that."

Maggie didn't dare look at Yianni.

"So, I understand you may have some information that could help us in treating *Kiria* Anna?"

"Yes," said Yianni. "We believe she may be the victim of a crime."

The doctor's face turned grim. "Who are you, sir?"

"Detective Yianni Kouros of GADA's Special Crimes Unit." He pulled out the ID he wore on a cord around his neck, under his shirt.

"Let's talk over there," said the doctor, steering them to a corner of the room away from potential eavesdroppers. "What kind of crime?"

"All I can say at this point is that we believe she may have been poisoned."

"Why?"

"We don't know."

"I meant, what makes you *believe* she was poisoned?"

Yianni gestured at Anna with his head. "From the IV marks on her arm. They're consistent with marks found on a half dozen other Ikariots above the age of ninety who recently passed away."

The doctor paused. "I'm sure you appreciate the significance of such a serious accusation, Detective, but frankly, if someone were looking to kill by a lethal injection, there are far simpler and less conspicuous ways of doing that than with an IV."

"We understand that, Doctor," said Maggie. "Maybe they were simple injections. But what else could explain identical bruising on six otherwise-healthy souls who seemed to have passed away peacefully at home in their beds?"

The doctor stroked his chin with his right hand. "I have a thought, give me a minute."

They watched him hurry back to Anna's bedside, lean over, and intently examine her arms. He spoke to a nurse who immediately picked up a phone, talked for a moment, and said something to the doctor. He replied and the nurse raced out of the ER.

"What you said looks to have been inspirational," Yianni said to Maggie, sotto voce.

"Stop trying to make me feel better."

"Speaking of feeling better, what's this about you flying off a motorbike in a rainstorm?"

"He's talking about when I was a child."

Yianni laughed. "That's interesting, since he's at least ten years younger than you."

Maggie's face reddened.

"You were right!" the doctor called to them.

"We were?" said Maggie, as the doctor walked toward her.

"She was poisoned?" Yianni asked.

"No, not poisoned."

"Then I don't understand," Yianni said.

"The needle marks are the key. Yes, they're from an IV, but for a needle far larger than we'd normally use on a person of her age. If fact, it's larger than what we'd normally use on any patient."

"When would you use it?" Yianni asked.

"Only for the most rapid of transfusions."

"Someone gave her blood?" said Maggie.

The doctor gestured no. "I had my nurse call the lab to check on her hemoglobin results. Those results explained a lot of things."

"What things?"

"She's critically anemic. As if she'd lost liters of blood."

"*What*?" said Yianni.

"Those marks on her arm? Blood was drawn from her there."

"This is insane," Maggie breathed, stunned.

"Insane or not, I've sent my nurse to get us as many units of her blood type as we can, STAT."

"Why would anyone want to drain a hundred-year-old woman of her blood?" asked Maggie.

"Not to mention the others." Yianni looked at the doctor. "I assume I can trust you not to mention this to anyone until we find who's responsible."

"I understand," he said. "The last thing we need is the media picking up on rumors of vampires roaming our island."

"Come on, I wouldn't call them vampires," said Yianni.

"Nor would I," said the doctor, "but unless you can come up with an explanation for why so many of our oldest citizens are unexpectedly and suddenly dying because of blood mysteriously drained from their bodies, my money's on the gossip mill backing vampires."

Maggie looked at Yianni, and shrugged.

"One question, doctor," said Yianni. "What sort of equipment and expertise do you need in order to collect blood the way it was done on Anna?"

"It's relatively simple if you know how to insert a needle into a vein and connect a tube to the collection container. Gravity and blood pressure do the rest."

"Any idea why someone would do this?" asked Maggie.

"Not a clue, though I once had a professor who used to tell us that in virtually every part of the developed world, if you drew a kilometer radius circle around wherever you happen to be, somewhere within that circle, the worst and most unimaginable things were being perpetrated by one human being upon another."

"That's not very comforting," said Yianni.

The doctor frowned. "It's not meant to be. It's reality. Now, if you'll excuse me, I've got to get back to dealing with reality's consequences."

As the doctor walked away, Yianni turned to Maggie. "So do we."

"Right," said Maggie, still staring at Anna's bed. "Starting with Papa George."

———

"What's the news?" said Spiro as Yianni and Maggie walked into the reception area.

They dropped into chairs on either side of him.

"It's still touch and go," said Yianni.

"But at least they now know what happened to her," added Maggie.

Spiro stared at his cousin. "Blood loss."

Maggie blinked. "How did you know that?"

"When I saw her in the cottage, she reminded me of loggers I'd seen who'd bled out from chainsaw or log-skidder accidents... swimmers hit by an engine prop. But I wasn't sure, because in those situations the bloody mess made the reason obvious." Spiro sighed. "As I was sitting here, I got to thinking about all those questions you'd asked me about Yaya's bruises and IVs. That's when I started to think about how the needles could account for the blood loss." He paused and swallowed. "Who do you think did it?"

"We've got a pretty good idea of that, but the question is why."

"How do you plan on getting that answer?"

"From Papa George," said Maggie.

"Well, that should be easy."

"How's that?" said Yianni.

"Five minutes after you left reception, he walked in through the front door, all smiles and hellos."

Yianni jumped up. "Where did he go?"

"No idea, he spoke to the receptionist, then went inside as if he owned the place."

Yianni ran to the receptionist, and interrupted her conversation with Dimitri. He spoke to her for a few seconds before waving to Maggie.

"We've got to run. He's alone with another member of his flock." Yianni turned to Dimitri. "Get in the ER and keep an eye on Anna until I get back. Under no circumstances let Papa George anywhere near her."

Maggie caught up to Yianni as Dimitri asked, "What if he doesn't listen to me? After all, he's a priest."

"That's easy" said Maggie as Yianni raced down the hallway. "Shoot the bastard."

———

Yianni stopped beside a door adjacent to a small sign marked QUIET PLEASE. He had his ear against the door when Maggie caught up to him. He nodded at the door. "He's in here."

"Then what are we waiting for? Open the door."

Yianni carefully pressed down on the door handle with his left hand, his right ready to grab his gun. Slowly, he pushed the door open. An elderly woman lay on the only bed in the room. They saw no one else inside.

"Try the bathroom," said Maggie.

As Yianni stepped into the room, the woman began to stir.

"Thank God you're here," came a voice from behind them.

Maggie and Yianni swung around to see a smiling Papa George.

"Please, close poor Maria's door. Let her rest. We can talk in the next room. It's empty."

Neither moved.

"I know you'll want to hear what I have to say, and we can't talk in front of her, so…"

Yianni gestured for Papa George to lead the way. Once in the adjacent room, Papa George closed the door behind them and walked to the far side of the empty bed.

"I don't believe we've met before, sir," he told Yianni.

"I'm Detective Yianni Kouros of GADA Special Crimes."

"Terrific," said Papa George, clapping his hands together. "Precisely the sort of person I prayed for the Lord to send me."

"Funny, you're the answer to my prayers too," said a stone-faced Yianni.

Papa George cleared his throat. "Before we begin, there is a preliminary matter to resolve."

"Preliminary to what?" asked Maggie.

"Your hearing my confession."

Maggie looked at Yianni, but he kept his eyes glued to the priest.

"Please turn off your mobile phones and place them here." He patted the bed. "This is a private confession. There's no need for what I tell you in confidence to be recorded."

"What about your phone?" said Yianni.

Papa George reached into his pocket, pulled out a phone, and tossed it on the bed. As Yianni fumbled through the pockets of his jacket looking for his phone, Maggie slid Anna's bag off her shoulder onto the bed and rooted around inside it. Yianni tossed his phone on the bed beside her bag.

"Ah, here's what I'm looking for," said Maggie. "I left my phone in the boat, but here's what I need you to do." She pulled Anna's cross out of the bag and placed it on the bed directly in front of Papa George.

"Swear upon Anna's cross and before God Almighty that what you're about to tell us is true."

He bowed his head. "I so swear."

Maggie crossed her arms. "Then start talking."

He looked at her with compassion, his eyes almost tearful. "If I'd heard what you've heard, seen what you'd seen, and yes, suffered the loss you suffered, I'd be just as angry and convinced of my complicity in whatever you imagine led to the deaths of so many."

Maggie glared.

"Please, just hear me out, for once you do, I believe you'll understand I am not at fault, so help me God." He crossed himself.

Yianni exhaled loudly, "As the lady said, start talking."

Papa George leaned forward, touched the cross, and looked up at Maggie. "Before I answered my calling to the priesthood, I worked as a jewelry salesman on Santorini. That's where I first met the Chens. You saw me with them on their boat earlier today. They were very good customers, and as is the way of jewelers with such customers, I spent a lot of time with them whenever they were on the island. I took them to the best restaurants and places to party. Whatever they wanted, I provided for them.

"We were close in age and became good friends. I'd even visited them in Hong Kong, and knew them to be part of a very powerful and wealthy family, with a hugely successful pharmaceutical business."

He sighed. "I had no idea of the dark side of their business."

"What dark side?" said Yianni.

"I'm about to tell you."

He swallowed. "Early in my life I'd studied for the priesthood, but became distracted by secular temptations and found myself lost amidst all the craziness of youth. A few years after meeting the Chens I realized I'd lost direction and returned to my studies.

Within two years I was ordained. Over those years, the Chens and I lost track of each other."

He turned to look out a window. "Though I thought I'd left the secular world behind, I soon realized that in seeking to do God's work, one needed charitable souls willing to finance those labors."

He turned back to face them. "I thought the Chens were those kind of people, and so I wrote to them explaining what I had become, where I was, and what I needed from them to aid my flock."

He shook his head. "About a week after I sent my letter, the brother called me to congratulate me on my choice of career and asked if I was on the island where so many people lived to be over one hundred. I was impressed they knew so much about Ikaria, but then again, they're both brilliant. I replied yes."

Maggie began tapping her foot.

"Sorry," said Papa George. "It's just that when I think of how stupid I've been, I have a hard time getting to the point."

"Then why not try getting there directly?" she said.

He nodded. "A week or so later the sister called with congratulations and asked if I'd be available to meet with them the following week at their hotel in Athens. He said they had a business proposal to make to me. So, I went to Athens and we met."

Again, he looked to be holding back tears. "Here comes the hard part. They asked me if I knew any of the very old Ikariots. I told them they were the focus of my ministry. The two of them literally jumped up and down like children, saying God must have chosen the three of us to bring forth a miracle on earth."

"What are you talking about?" said Yianni.

"That's exactly what I asked them. They told me that our becoming friends, my going into the priesthood, my ending up with a ministry on Ikaria tending to its oldest souls, and their pharmaceutical expertise, must be part of some heavenly plan calling upon those who are about to depart for their reward to save our world from great pain and suffering."

"You're sounding a bit deranged," said Maggie.

"More than a bit, if you ask me," said Yianni.

"I'm sure I do, but I'm not at the truly crazy part yet."

"Can't wait to hear this," said Yianni.

"They told me what we all know is true. Our planet just experienced a horrific pandemic. All of us pray it has passed, but even assuming it has, fear still haunts the world that another more virulent virus could appear and take hold at any time. People are desperate for a preventive solution, and the Chens' scientists believed the answer could be found among the very oldest of Ikariots."

"If you're not insane, they're insane," said Maggie.

"Maybe both," said Yianni.

"Believe me, I thought the same way at first. They bombarded me with facts, and interviews with their most respected scientists. All in support of their supposition that those who'd lived through the Spanish flu of 1918–1920, the pandemic of 2020–2022, and the myriad of epidemics in between, yet still remained in good health into their centenarian years, could hold the secret to what might spare the world another pandemic catastrophe."

He paused. "Considering the millions who died, and hundreds of millions infected, how could I dismiss their claims out of hand? They were responsible, respected professionals. Or at least I thought they were."

"So you helped them murder innocents. Just following orders, perhaps?" barked Maggie.

"It wasn't like that at all. The Chens insisted it all be aboveboard. That we obtain the formal written consent of any anyone who agreed to participate in their study. In exchange for their cooperation, the Chens promised to contribute a hundred thousand euros to my ministry, and if they developed a success-ful vaccine, one percent of worldwide sales."

Yianni stared at him. "Are you saying you have written consent from every one of your flock who died?"

"Yes, they're back in my office, all fully explaining the risks each one faced." Papa George dropped his head. "But they shouldn't have died."

Maggie spoke through a clenched jaw. "Then why did they?"

He shut his eyes and shook his head. "The first person I approached I'd known since practically my first day on Ikaria. Her name was Alki, and she suffered with depression over a life that had not treated her well. I told her of how she might possess within her being the salvation of generations to come." He opened his eyes. "She came alive at the thought. I'd never seen her happier or more upbeat. All because this sweet soul now saw within herself the means for potentially helping to save the world."

"What went wrong?" asked Yianni.

"At first nothing. The Chens supplied a nurse to accompany me and draw Alki's blood. She donated a unit, and the Chens said their scientists found it very promising. They wanted more. I said Alki was very old and that didn't seem prudent. They said the nurse would know what's best, and if I preferred not to be with her when she drew the blood, that was okay with them."

He straightened up. "But that wasn't okay with me. I'd known her longer than anyone else in my flock. I saw it as my duty to be with her each day the nurse drew blood."

"How often was that?" said Yianni.

"Twice a week. For two weeks."

"Or until she died," said Maggie.

"The nurse assured me she would be fine, because the schedule gave her body sufficient time to regenerate her blood."

"And what did you do after you saw that she wasn't fine, and in fact had died?" said Yianni.

"I told the Chens I was done recruiting for them. Finished. They told me that Alki's donation stood to save countless lives, and there were undoubtedly many more on the island who could provide the same sort of protection. I said the old had as much right to live as the young. They agreed and said we could seek younger donors, for even if the heart of the 1918–1920 pandemic had passed before they were born, there was still the chance they'd have been infected by some remnant or variant of that virus."

"Is that when you started in on the ninety-year-olds?" asked Yianni.

"Yes, and at first they held up well, but the Chens said nonagenarian blood did not appear as promising as Alki's, and I should seek out volunteers from among those who had lived through the earlier pandemic."

"Which is when you approached my *yaya*."

"Alki's death had been a terrible tragedy, but as the Chens kept insisting, she knowingly chose to use her final days to contribute toward the potential welfare of millions. The Chens asked why others similarly disposed should be denied that opportunity if they voluntarily decide to take a fully disclosed risk."

"How did you convince my *yaya* to participate?"

"Actually, I didn't have to convince her. I simply explained the purpose of the study, and she immediately volunteered. She said it gave her the chance to redeem herself for living through the earlier pandemic when other members of her family had succumbed to it."

Maggie gritted her teeth. "I see."

"I get it, saving the world is your excuse for allowing six in your care to die." Yianni didn't try to disguise his disgust.

Papa George looked down at his hands. "I offer no excuse for failing my flock. I became too busy to accompany the nurse each time she drew blood. I did not realize she'd been instructed by the Chens to maximize the blood donations, no matter the risk to the donors."

"How do you know the Chens told the nurse to do that?" asked Maggie.

"After your *yaya*'s death, I demanded a meeting with them on Ikaria. I wanted to show them firsthand the grief they'd brought to so many families. Yesterday, they picked me up on their boat. I told them of my anger at their incompetent nurse who'd killed so many innocents by drawing too much blood. Their response rocked me to my core. People I thought I knew well showed not even a modicum of remorse. They simply shrugged and said I obviously didn't understand how many trillions could be made off this project, should it yield anything close to what they anticipated. I couldn't believe what I was hearing."

"Nor can I," said Yianni. "You expect us to believe that six people in your care had died, and you weren't even slightly suspicious until your boat ride yesterday?"

"That is a curse upon my soul that I shall bear beyond my dying day. Yes, I held suspicions. How could any rational person not? But as I said, I thought I knew these people, and it never entered my mind until yesterday that the Chens were following a premeditated plan to bleed those poor souls to death."

Maggie dropped her hands to her sides. "That's some story, but what about today?"

"You mean with Anna?"

Maggie nodded.

"I insisted we immediately go to Anna and warn her to donate no more blood. The Chens' nurse had visited her once with me, and I feared she might go on her own to draw more. They refused my demand, saying they considered Anna a true prize. I said if they wouldn't warn her, I'd tell the police everything." He gave them a helpless shrug.

"They said they didn't care. Everything was legal and above-board. Their lawyers would handle any issues with the law. A small price to pay for a trillion in profits. I told them if that's how they wanted to be, I'd take the story to the media. The horren-dous press that would rain down on their heads would indelibly stain their family name for eternity, and incur the unforgiving wrath of their family, most notably their powerful father's. That frightened them, or so I thought. They suggested I spend the night with them on their boat so that we could be in Karkinagri first thing in the morning."

He bit his lip. "Once we got to Anna's house, I realized I'd made a grave mistake. The Chens told her that today was the last day of their project on Ikaria, and they had come to her home to personally thank her for all she'd done toward bettering the world. Then they asked her if she'd like to make a final donation."

He punched a fist into his other hand. "I went berserk, telling her not to do it, that she could die from it. But she refused to lis-ten to me and allowed the sister to draw blood. When I saw you in the harbor with Anna and the ambulance, I realized God had sent me a message that you were the people who could bring the Chens to justice for what they'd done to so many."

He bowed his head. "I acknowledge my moral complicity in lacking the courage to speak up when my heart told me I should, and instead listened to my head telling me to believe the words of people I thought I could trust."

"Let me get this straight," said Maggie. "You're saying that this morning you witnessed the Chens drawing blood out of Anna Moraitis at her home in Lagkada. And Anna is the same woman who was just admitted to this hospital on the edge of death due to blood loss?"

"Yes, but only the Chen sister actually drew the blood. Her brother stood by, encouraging her to draw more."

Maggie stared straight at him. "And the Chens did this after you'd warned them that drawing Anna's blood might kill her?"

"Yes."

"Do you have anything else to say?" asked Yianni.

He gestured no.

"That nurse they used. Where's she now?" said Maggie.

"I don't know. The Chens told me they fired her."

"Do you have a name, an address, a telephone number?"

"The name's Sudha, and I have a mobile number, but no address." He gave Yianni the phone number.

"It's an Athens mobile."

Papa George shrugged. "It's how I reached her."

"What more do you know about her?"

"She's an immigrant. That's all I know. We didn't talk much. Her Greek was very poor."

Yianni pointed his finger dead center at Papa George's forehead. "Don't even think of coming anywhere close to Anna, unless you want to be arrested on the spot."

He nodded. "Understood, Detective."

"And we need the names, locations, and telephone numbers of everyone in your flock."

"Yes, *Kiria*."

Papa George bent over and kissed Anna's cross. "May the Lord forgive me."

"Perhaps the Lord will, but I won't." Maggie grabbed the bag, put Anna's cross inside it, slung the bag over her shoulder, and walked out.

"Some people just aren't so forgiving of those involved in the murder of their loved ones," said Yianni. He paused at the door and fixed his eyes on Papa George's. "I know that I sure as hell wouldn't be."

———

"How did your boat ride from Karkinagri turn out?" said Andreas.

"We got her to the hospital in record time."

"Thank God, I was wondering when I'd hear back from you. How's she doing?"

"It's still touch and go," said Maggie, jumping in via Yianni's speakerphone.

"Sorry to hear that."

"There's a lot more to tell. The question is where to start."

"Sounds ominous."

"It is," said Yianni. He told Andreas of their encounter in the port with the Chens and Papa George, their conversation with the doctor who linked the likely cause of death to blood-loss-induced shock, and finished with their confrontation with Papa George.

"Ominous sounds like an understatement to me," said Andreas. "What's your take on Papa George's confession?"

"I'd hardly call it a confession," said Yianni. "More like an effort to portray himself as a poor shepherd seeking to do good for his flock by helping them save the world, but who was cunningly led astray by a conniving pair of criminals."

"It was all BS," said Maggie. "I don't trust him as far as I can throw the boat he rode in on."

"Me either, Chief."

"I get you. But you have to admit he's pretty smooth. When he saw you in the harbor at Agios Kirykos he must have realized you were on to him. If he's lying, he came up with a good story quickly. The bad guys are foreigners, and not just any foreigners, but Chinese, who already are vilified in the minds of many Greeks."

"Like I said, it's all BS," said Maggie.

"That's certainly a possibility, but some might say the more likely explanation is that everything he said was true."

"That's ridiculous," she shouted.

"Keep your voice down," said Yianni, "We're still in a hospital."

"Well, let's start with the obvious," said Andreas. "Instead of fleeing, he went directly to the hospital, knowing full well you'd find him there. And if he does have those signed consent forms, that goes a long way toward supporting his story."

"I know he's dirty."

"I do too," said Yianni. "We just have to prove it."

"What I can't figure out is why he didn't want you recording his confession," said Andreas. "Everything he said was intended to exonerate him and bury the Chens."

"Maybe we missed something he said. It was a rather tense confrontation," added Yianni.

"I don't think we missed a thing," said Maggie.

"A good place to start is with the Chens," said Andreas. "I'll see if we can get the Coast Guard to find their boat and detain them. Do you have its name and location?"

Yianni gave its name, make, and model. "Someone turned off the boat's GPS, so I've no idea where it is or where it's headed, but maybe the hotel in Athens that chartered the boat for them can find out. I'll give the hotel a call."

"Good. What about finding the nurse?"

"I think that will be a waste of time," said Maggie.

"Why's that?" asked Andreas.

"Because I just tried the number Papa George gave us for her, and the line's been disconnected."

"How convenient," said Yianni. "Hey, wait a minute. I thought you told Papa George you'd left your phone on the boat."

"Okay, so I lied. It was in Anna's bag. While I rummaged through the bag for her cross, I turned on the phone's recording app."

"You're so sneaky," said Andreas. "Which is why I love you."

"We both do," said Yianni.

"I still wonder why he didn't want it recorded," said Andreas.

"I'll send you a copy, and you can listen for yourself."

"Perhaps the Chens can answer that question," said Yianni.

"Which is why we better get cracking on finding them before they leave Greece. If they get to Hong Kong, we're not likely to see them back here anytime soon."

"Speaking of bad guys, what's happening with Tom and Jerry?" asked Yianni.

"The prosecutor is mulling over the evidence linking them to Stavros's killer. He's not particularly thrilled that the key witness against Tom and Jerry is a junkie tied to multiple murders. Much less that he accuses them of blackmailing him into killing Stavros because they had him dead to rights on another murder charge for which they'd not yet arrested him."

"Shit," said Yianni.

"Exactly. It doesn't take much imagination to see Tom and Jerry's defense counsel painting Stavros's killer as desperate, and willing to say whatever the prosecution wants him to say in hopes of somehow saving his ass."

"Do Tom and Jerry know we're on to them?" said Yianni.

"Not yet, and hopefully not until the prosecutor decides whether to go forward with a case against them. He's worried if word gets out too soon, they might start eliminating potential witnesses. As they did with Stavros."

"Don't tell me those dirtbags are going to get away with murder too," moaned Maggie.

"No one's getting away with anything. Smart guys make mistakes the same as dumb guys. It just takes longer to figure out where they screwed up. You and Yianni have brought us to the verge of unmasking who's responsible for at least six deaths on Ikaria and the murder of a good cop in Athens. We'll just have to keep plodding along until we nail the bastards."

"Nice pep talk, Chief," said Maggie.

"Well, let me add something to that. There's a lot of moving parts to whatever's going on here, and a lot of dead bodies, so until we sort this out, be careful."

"What are we going to do about Papa George? We can't just let him continue on as he has," said Maggie.

"Agreed," said Andreas. "But if he has those signed consents from the elders, I doubt we'll get anywhere with an arrest. For now, at least, he seems willing to cooperate, but before either of you say it, I'm not about to take his word on anything. I'll brief the Ikaria police chief, and ask him to keep a subtle but strong eye on Papa George."

"What should I do now, return to Athens?" said Yianni.

"No, stay with Maggie, at least until we know where the Chens are, and how they fit in with Papa George and Tom and Jerry."

"I don't need Yianni to protect me."

"No, but he needs you."

"You're patronizing me."

"Would you rather I tell Tassos what you've been up to?"

"And now you're threatening me."

"You've got that right."

"Just wait until I get back to the office."

"Now you're threatening *me*."

"You've got that right."

Chapter Fourteen

The Hellenic Coast Guard bore responsibility for law enforcement on Greece's seas and in the nation's ports. Also known as the port police, they kept a close eye on what sailed into and out of all major harbors. Andreas's call for assistance in locating the Chens' boat and detaining its occupants for questioning by Andreas's unit yielded quick results.

The boat had docked in Mykonos's new port. When port police questioned its captain, he said his two passengers had disembarked immediately. They'd said nothing to him about their plans, but simply jumped in a taxi and driven off. He assumed they'd be returning because they'd left all their luggage. Then he found a note telling him that urgent business required them to cut short their holiday and asking him to deliver their bags to their hotel in Athens. The port police impounded the luggage.

Andreas's next call was to the Mykonos airport police. They confirmed what Andreas suspected. Thirty-five minutes earlier, a Gulfstream G700 private jet had arrived at the airport. Fifteen minutes later, the Chens boarded the plane, and ten minutes later, the plane took off. When Andreas asked for the plane's destination, he received the anticipated answer: Hong Kong.

With its range of 7,500 nautical miles, the Gulfstream could easily fly straight to Hong Kong, delivering the Chens safely home and beyond the reach of Greek police.

Andreas picked up a pencil from his desktop and began twirling it between his fingers as he tried to think of what to do next. Nothing came readily to mind.

So, he snapped the pencil in half and cursed.

————

While Yianni and Andreas commiserated over the Chens escaping justice so easily, Maggie railed at any suggestion that by fleeing the country, the Chens gave credence to Papa George's story.

"Well, let's look at the facts," said Andreas in another speakerphone conversation. "The Chens saw a woman they'd left to die in her bed in an isolated part of the island lifted out of a boat and put into an ambulance in Agios Kirykos under the supervision of the Greek police. Then they watched Maggie curse Papa George to rot in hell, ferociously enough to send him scurrying out of sight.

"Next, we have Papa George racing to the hospital to tell you his side of the story. Who knows what he told the Chens he was planning to do once he left them in the port?"

Yianni spoke up. "Papa George told us that the night before they went to Anna's house, he threatened to tell the police everything if the Chens didn't join him in personally warning Anna to stop her blood donations."

"Right," said Andreas. "I've listened to the recording. So, I'm thinking that the moment Papa George left the boat, the Chens raced off to the nearest island with a runway capable of accommodating the jet they'd summoned to whisk them back to Hong Kong. I hate to say it, Maggie, but that sure sounds suspiciously guilty to me."

"I get that, Chief, but it doesn't mean Papa George isn't at least as guilty as the Chens."

"Maggie, I know how invested you are in this, but you've also told me how virtually everyone you've spoken to about Papa George has nothing but the highest praise for him."

"All that means is that I have to talk to more people."

"You're like the proverbial dog with a bone."

"You better believe it."

"What do you think, Yianni?"

"I share Maggie's instincts but agree his story is convincing enough to likely avoid conviction, if not prosecution. After all, he is a priest with a long line of character witnesses singing his praises, and on top of all that, you have the Chens fleeing the country."

"Do either of you have even a bit of concrete evidence that Papa George is as much a bad guy in all this as the Chens appear to be?"

"I don't," said Yianni.

"I might," said Maggie.

"Okay. What is it?"

"Did the Mykonos port police find anything suspicious in the luggage the Chens left on the boat?"

"No," said Andreas.

"Papa George said the sister mercilessly drained the life out of Anna as her brother encouraged her. If that's true, where's the blood?"

"They could have dumped it into the sea," said Yianni.

"If what they took from Anna was the *true prize*, worth the *trillions* Papa George claimed the Chens said it was, I doubt they'd do that."

"So where is it?" said Andreas.

"My guess is with Papa George on Ikaria," said Maggie, "but you're the detectives. Start detecting."

Andreas obtained the mobile number of the yacht captain from the Mykonos Port Police and reached him at his home in Piraeus He sounded appropriately nervous for an innocent suddenly the focus of the Greek Coast Guard and the Greek police.

"Sir, I appreciate your anxiety, but this has nothing to do with you. I understand all the arrangements for the use of your ship were made through your clients' hotel, not directly with you."

"Yes, that's correct."

"You told the port police that, when the Chens disembarked in Mykonos, they left all their belongings on board with instructions that you deliver their things to their hotel in Athens."

"Yes."

"They carried nothing with them when they left you on Mykonos?"

"Yes, nothing."

"What about the woman? Was she carrying one of those big bags with her?"

"No, she had a tiny purse, about the size of a paperback book."

Andreas sighed. "Are you sure they left nothing else on the boat?"

"Nothing more than what your guys picked up."

"You mean the luggage?"

"Yes, and later, the cooler."

Andreas froze. "What cooler?"

"The one that the cops picked up the moment I docked in Piraeus."

"Let's back up a bit here. Why didn't you mention the cooler to the port police in Mykonos?"

"It was one of those throwaway Styrofoam coolers that fancy

food deliveries come in. I didn't think of it as luggage, more like garbage they'd left behind."

"Who brought it on board?"

"A delivery guy. The Chens made a big fuss over ordering a gourmet dinner from some five-star restaurant in Raches that Papa George had recommended. But it was six kilometers away from where we anchored in Armenistis, and they didn't want to go through the hassle of getting a taxi back and forth. Instead, they paid the restaurant a hefty premium to deliver to the boat. Everything arrived in that cooler."

"So, you're saying port police picked up the cooler from you in Piraeus?"

"No, not port police. But they were cops. They were waiting for me when I arrived. They showed me their IDs and told me they were there to pick up a cooler left behind by the Chens. I figured that since they knew my clients' names and already knew about the cooler, it was okay to give it to them."

Andreas smacked at his forehead with his free hand. "Did you happen to get the cops' names?"

"I saw their names but don't remember them. I was in a hurry to close up the boat and wanted to get rid of them as fast as I could."

"What about a description?"

"Uh, sure. Let's see… One was a big guy with short gray hair. The other was shorter and skinnier, with brown hair. He looked a little…" The captain searched for the right word.

"Mousy?" offered Andreas.

"Yes, that's the word. Do you know them?"

"I think so."

"Whew, I was worried I might have turned the cooler over to the wrong people."

"It's okay. No need to worry about that. Was there anything in the cooler when they took it?"

"I wouldn't know. They knew where to look for it, and found it sealed with packing tape. I never touched it, but from the way the mousy one carried it in both hands, I'd say it had weight to it."

Crafty and careful, thought Andreas. "When your passengers returned to the boat back in Karkinagri, were any of them carrying a bag, a box, or some kind of container?"

"I wasn't onboard when they returned. I'd left to have a coffee in town. The brother called me to tell me they were back and wanted to depart immediately."

Andreas paused to process his latest bit of bad luck. "One last question, sir. Any idea what was in the cooler?"

"Not a clue, and from all the attention it's getting, I don't think I want to know."

That got a sad chuckle out of Andreas. "Thanks for your time and cooperation, sir. Goodbye."

Andreas hung up, convinced Maggie was right about the blood not being dumped. But it wasn't on Ikaria with Papa George. It was with Tom and Jerry, acting once again as errand boys.

When they weren't arranging to murder a cop.

———

Maggie refused to leave the hospital until she knew if Anna's condition had improved. She sat with Yianni and Spiro in the reception area, waiting to hear from Anna's doctor.

Papa George left about an hour after his confessional presentation, offering nothing but smiles and cheerful goodbyes as he did. Yianni acknowledged him with a nod; Maggie turned away.

A little later, they sent Dimitri off, after thanking him for all his help. Spiro said he could stay until an hour before dark, by when he must leave to return the boat to its mooring. But he promised to pick them up with his car should they need a ride home.

When Andreas called to tell Yianni and Maggie about his conversation with the ship captain, Yianni's first reaction at the mention of Tom and Jerry was concern for Anna's life.

"If someone out there is nervous about what she could say, and those lowlifes are working for whoever that is, I'm worried about what they might try to do to her."

"I doubt we could get the Ikarian police force to provide round-the-clock police protection, but if they did, there's no way we could pull that off without triggering a massive spike on the island's gossip mill."

"But there is something we can do," said Maggie. "I'll ask the Church to provide 24/7 companionship for Anna while she's in the hospital. After all, she is a well-known, much-loved representative of the centenarian class that Ikaria is famous for. And I doubt those two dirtbags are going to risk turning some third party's imagined problem with what a very old woman might say into a very real and personal problem for themselves by tangling with a church lady watching over Anna."

"If you think you can make that happen without Papa George getting involved, it's fine with me."

"Don't worry about him. I'll get right on it."

"What about me?" said Yianni.

"I think it's time to go straight at Tom and Jerry. They're crawling out from under every rock we kick over, but they don't know we're on to them yet. Letting them know we are might rattle them into making a mistake."

"Like running to whoever they're working for?"

"That's one scenario."

"Dare I ask about the others?"

"They're all blinking BE CAREFUL. The pair's already responsible for the murder of a cop they *thought* might be on to them. Imagine how they'll react to cops they *know* are on to them."

"That's comforting," said Yianni.

"So enjoy your final night of peace and tranquility on Ikaria. I want you back here tomorrow so we can go after those two scumbags."

"What, and leave me all alone?" quipped Maggie.

"Not quite. I think it's time you invited Tassos to join you. After all, why should Yianni have all the fun?"

Maggie sighed. "Okay, I agree. Just let *me* tell him what's happened. That way I won't get the 'Why did I have to hear this from somebody else?' lecture along with everything else he'll be unloading on me."

Andreas laughed. "You're a woman who certainly knows her man. Just promise me you'll call him and tell him tonight."

"Will do."

"Yianni, were her fingers crossed?"

"Not that I could see."

"Good. Until tomorrow then."

"Until tomorrow."

———

Maggie had no trouble finding volunteers from Yaya's local church to stay with Anna. In fact, so many wanted to participate that a team of two showed up to spend the first night with her. Even better, her vital signs had improved markedly. On that good news, Maggie and Yianni arranged for a taxi to take them home.

Though it was close to ten when the taxi dropped them off, their path through the orchard was lit by the reflected silver of a full moon. Random shadows of passing clouds turned gnarled olive trees into demons and tall cypresses into sentinels.

"I find all this terribly romantic," said Yianni.

"Hey!" She punched him in the shoulder. "I'm old enough to be your mother."

"Thank God you reminded me." Yianni laughed. "I miss Toni. I'll have to call her as soon as I get back to Spiro's."

"Don't bet on that. Knowing my cousin, they've been holding dinner for us."

"By the way, have you called Tassos yet?"

"I left a message."

"That's not good enough. The chief said you had to speak to him."

"My message was that I'd like him to join me whenever it's convenient for him, and to call me whenever he has the time."

"That sounds clinically ominous."

"Don't worry, everything's under control."

A black cat shot out and crossed directly in front of them, chasing after prey only it could see.

"Now, *that's* what I call ominous," said Maggie, crossing herself and spitting three times.

"You and your superstitions."

"Don't knock them. So far they've kept me and millions of Greeks safely out of trouble for thousands of years."

"Do you think any of that mumbo jumbo would work for the mouse, or whatever the cat was chasing?"

"That's something between the mouse and its Maker."

"Welcome," called out Spiro, standing in front of his house. "We've been saving dinner. And bring your appetite, because my wife has a whole carton of new plates she's been dying to use."

Maggie looked at Yianni. "Do I know the men in my life or what? Like I said, stop worrying. Everything's under control."

———

Maggie didn't manage to get back to Yaya's cottage until after midnight. Dinner with Sonia was never an abbreviated affair. But tonight, she'd taken special care to impress their guest, Yianni, with a parade of dishes ranging from stuffed tomatoes and zucchini balls to just-picked greens, tzatziki freshly made from homemade yoghurt and garden dill, to her secret *katsikaki* recipe for goat with French fried potatoes. On top of that came Spiro's endless pours of his homemade wine.

After all the food and wine, Maggie was surprised she'd made it home to the cottage at all.

She'd still not heard back from Tassos, but now was not the time to have the detailed sort of clearheaded conversation that call would require. She washed her face, put on her nightgown, turned off her phone, and collapsed onto the bed. Tomorrow would be another day. She fell asleep to memories of her mother and Yaya playing hide-and-seek with her in the cottage.

Those were happy times, a childhood tied to nature with not a care in the world. Not like her adult life today in Athens. Instead of the songs of birds and the fragrance of flowers and herbs coming to her on winds whistling around the cottage, in Athens she endured the incessant din of cars and motorbikes spewing their noxious fumes outside her apartment. She far preferred those gentler dreams and memories of times spent with her loved ones, so she tried to banish the sounds and smells of Athens from her subconscious. But she couldn't. They were part of her makeup now and followed her everywhere. Even to Ikaria, while she slept.

"Maaah, maaah, maaah," sounded in her head, as if a chorus of Yaya's goats were bleating out to her. If only she could understand their meaning as Yaya did. Yaya used to say she could tell from the cadence of their cries whether they were happy, hungry, or frightened. Maggie had not cultivated that skill; at least not with four-legged creatures.

With a motorbike so close to them, they must be frightened.

Maggie's eyes popped open. She wasn't dreaming. The goats *were* braying and a motorbike *was* idling nearby. Indeed, right outside her front door. She sat up, gagging as she did. It was hard to breathe. She staggered to the front door to pull it open, but it wouldn't budge.

The acrid odor panicked her. Exhaust fumes meant carbon monoxide. And that meant someone was trying to kill her. She thought to scream for help, but from within this stone fortress, no one would hear her but her killer. She had to stop the fumes from getting into the cottage. But how? There must be a hose. She searched around the door. Nothing there.

She made it as best she could to the open window to push open the shutters. They wouldn't budge. She placed her ear next to the shutters. She could hear the hiss. Fumes were coming through the shutter slats. Carefully, quietly, she slid the interior window shut. Now, no more fumes could get through.

She found her way back to her phone and called Yianni. No answer. She left a frantic message that someone was trying to kill her. She tried Spiro. No answer. She left the same message. She looked at the time. It was four in the morning. Their phones must be off.

Suddenly, she heard the shutters pry open as moonlight flooded the room. She fell to the floor on the far side of the bed to hide. They were coming for her. She heard the glass of the window shatter. She had no way of defending herself. This was the end. She was going to die in the home where her mother and Yaya were born.

She shut her eyes and prayed. The room grew dark again. She heard the shutters close, followed by the hiss of the fumes from the hose.

This was how they intended for her to die. Slowly, in her sleep. Like Yaya.

She was no longer frightened or panicked. She was angry.

———

Minutes later the door to the cottage swung open. A man dressed in black crept in, a flashlight in his hand, a respirator mask over his face. He went straight for the bed, shining his light on it as he did. Then he knelt down and looked under the bed. He jumped up, wildly flashing his light over every nook and cranny of the room, and inside every door and cupboard.

He ran to the front door and said in loud whisper, "She's gone."

"As in dead?"

"No, as in no-fucking-where to be fucking found."

"That's impossible. We heard her close the window. She must be in there."

"I'm telling you she's fucking gone. Here, take the flashlight and look for yourself."

"I'll need the respirator too," he said, reaching up and ripping the respirator off the head of his gray-haired colleague.

Gray Hair stood outside. "You're such an asshole," he yelled to the shorter man entering the house. "She's not in there, I tell you. We've got to get out of here before someone finds us."

"No way," said the shorter man. "You heard the same thing I did when we delivered the cooler. She's gonna kill our deal, and she won't stop as long as she's alive."

"She can push whatever damn investigation she wants," said Gray Hair. "They don't have a thing linking us to anything… unless we do something stupid." He paused. "Like getting fucking caught trying to kill some old broad out in the middle of nowhere."

A shout came from the top of the steps. "Hey, what are you doing down there?"

Gray Hair drew a gun, swung around in the direction of the voice, and fired three rounds. He likely would have emptied the magazine but for the double-barrel shotgun blast the unseen figure fired in response.

A wet moan, then silence.

Another voice from up above yelled, "Spiro, are you okay?"

"Yes."

"Stay away from the steps," said Yianni, coming up behind Spiro. "There might be others."

"He was talking to somebody inside the cottage about a cooler and going after Maggie for threatening some deal they're involved in."

"Just let us handle it," said Yianni.

"Where's Tassos?"

"He was here a minute ago." Yianni looked around. "He's disappeared."

"It's almost dawn, and this is the only way out," said Spiro.

"We've got a serious hostage situation here. The guy you just emptied your shotgun into has a partner at least as dangerous as he is. And, by now he's desperate. No telling what he'll do to Maggie if he thinks he's cornered."

"But that's exactly what he is."

"Hold on a second," said Yianni.

"What is it?"

"A text message from Tassos. He says in five minutes do something that brings the other guy to the front door."

"What's that mean?"

"It means I'm about to experience the longest five minutes of my life." He paused. "But I have an idea. One that I hope your wife will forgive us for."

Precisely five minutes later, a plate broke in front of Yaya's cottage's door, followed ten seconds later by another, then another, and another. After two minutes of this constant barrage of crockery, the door opened enough for a respirator-cloaked head to peeked out and up the stairs in the direction of the incoming plates.

He likely never heard the shot that killed him.

Yianni raced down the stairs as Tassos came from the other side of the cottage.

"Why did you have to kill him?" asked Yianni.

Tassos pushed past him into the cottage, his gun still drawn. "We both know what he's capable of. Imagine if Toni were inside. Would you risk living with yourself if you just wounded him, and he started in on Toni to make us let him go?"

The two men looked around the room.

"She's not here," said Yianni.

Tassos began shouting, "Maggie, Maggie, where are you? It's Tassos. If you're here, do something, make a sound."

The two fell silent.

Tassos frantically shouted her name again.

"She must be in here somewhere."

Spiro came through the doorway carrying an oxygen tank. "As soon as I smelled the exhaust fumes, I thought Maggie might need this. It's what she used to help Anna breathe on the boat ride."

"We can't find her," said Tassos, almost in tears. "She's not here."

"God bless her, she remembered. Let's just pray she got out in time."

"I don't know what you're talking about," said Yianni. "But if you think you know where she is, let's go."

Spiro stepped toward the rear wall of the cottage and stopped in front of a solid oak cupboard. It stood a half-meter away from a tall stone fireplace, its other side flush against the end of a stone wall running parallel to the rear of the cottage. Spiro opened the cupboard, reached down, pulled a spring-loaded latch fitted into the stone floor, and slid the entire cupboard toward the fireplace. A half-meter of open space now sat between the cupboard and the wall—opening into a narrow passageway running between the stone wall and the true rear of the cottage.

"The cupboard was where it should be, so if she's in there, she still had enough strength to pull it back into place." Spiro pointed to a handle mounted on the side of the cupboard.

"Here, use this," said Yianni picking up one of the dead guys' flashlight and handing it to Spiro.

Spiro shined the light down the passage. "She's not in here, but it turns to the right at the far end and runs halfway up the side of the house to a hatch at the bottom of the exterior wall. It's camouflaged to look like a part of the wall."

"I took my shot from there," said Tassos. "I didn't see her."

"How did you get there?" asked Spiro, edging his way into the narrow passage.

"Maggie told me that Yaya kept her goats in a shed on a plateau below that side of the house. I figured that, being goats, they must have a way of getting up and down the gorge wall behind their shed. To me, it was worth the risk of a fall if it meant finding a way of coming up on the bad guys from behind."

Spiro took a quick deep breath and slid sideways along the passage. At the end, he crossed himself and stared around the corner.

"She's here!" he shouted. "On the floor with her face up against the hatch. It's pushed open a bit."

"How do we get her out?" shouted Tassos.

"Get outside and pull open the hatch."

Fifteen seconds later, Yianni and Tassos had yanked open the hatch, and in as many seconds had Maggie out in the fresh air.

"She's still breathing," said Yianni.

"And I can feel her pulse. Thank God," cried Tassos.

Spiro came around the corner of the cottage carrying the oxygen tank. "Here, put this on her."

Tassos gently pulled the mask over Maggie's face and adjusted the flow of oxygen.

"I'll call the police and tell them to rush a doctor and ambulance here," said Yianni. "And while they're at it, to send someone to start in on the paperwork covering two dead guys who just happen to be cops." He looked at Tassos, thinking. "And then I'll call Andreas, to break the news to him that our best hope of finding answers for half a dozen deaths on Ikaria, and an assassinated cop in Athens, just died in a gunfight over Maggie."

Tassos held Maggie's hand and stared at Yianni.

"Two of the most righteous and justifiable killings ever, I might add," said Yianni.

Tassos rubbed Maggie's hand and kissed it as a tear rolled down his cheek.

Chapter Fifteen

Maggie woke to the sound of Tassos snoring in a chair beside her hospital bed. That was not how she imagined Prince Charming stirring Snow White from near-eternal rest, but this was Maggie's fairy tale come true.

"Tassos," she said through the mask covering her mouth and nose.

He didn't budge.

She smiled. He was here, and she was alive. That's all that mattered. Daylight streamed in through a window, but she had no way of knowing if the craziness she recalled had happened today, yesterday, or on some other day.

The last thing she remembered was crawling in the dark along the stone floor of the cottage's centuries-old pirate escape passage, pressing on the exterior wall hoping to find the secret exit that Yaya told her was there, and once finding it, frantically pushing hard enough against it to feel a breeze on her face before she passed out.

A nurse stuck her face through the doorway. Maggie lifted her hand in a faint wave.

"You're awake and back with us. Wonderful," said the nurse, coming up to the bed. "How do you feel?"

"Exhausted. How long have I been here?"

"Since just before dawn. We almost transferred you to Athens and a hyperbaric chamber, but your cousin's quick thinking had you on oxygen early on, and it saved you that trip."

"How long has he been here?" nodding at Tassos.

"He arrived with you and has been by your side since you got here." She smiled. "I'm happy he's finally getting a little sleep himself."

"How could he have come with me?" Feeling stronger, she raised her voice. "Tassos, wake up."

Tassos bolted straight up in the chair. "What, who?" He looked at Maggie pointing a finger at him. "You're awake, my love. Thank God."

"What are you doing on Ikaria?" Maggie realized she sounded more aggressive than she intended.

"Well," said the nurse, "if you're strong enough to begin an inquisition, I'll take that as a sign you're strong enough for me to leave you two kids alone to play together. But don't overdo it. You had a close call."

"Thank you," said Tassos as the nurse left the room, closing the door behind her.

"I'll ask the same question without so much emotion, and a little differently. What were you doing on Ikaria when someone tried to kill me?"

He reached for Maggie's hand and squeezed it gently. She squeezed back.

"Your cryptic message to me about when I could see you and when I could call you set me to thinking you were up to something. And when an old sea captain friend of mine called last night on Syros to say his freighter was in port, but only for an hour before he had to sail for Ikaria and points east, I took it as a sign from the Fates and hitched a ride with him."

Tassos cleared his throat. "The only problem was, the freighter stopped in Agios Kirykos at two in the morning, and left twenty minutes later for Samos, but the captain arranged for one of the dock workers in Ikaria to give me a ride to Yaya's. I got there around three. I wanted to surprise you, but decided knocking on your cottage door at that hour was not likely to endear me to you. Besides, it was a beautiful moonlit night, and so I picked out one of those comfortable chairs in front of your cousin Spiro's house, figuring I'd wait there until his family was up. Then I'd surprise you."

"So you were there when someone tried to kill me?"

"Not someone, Tom and Jerry."

"Did you catch them?"

Tassos squirmed in his chair. "Let's just say they're not going to bother you anymore."

She stared at him. "I see. Why don't you tell me how *that* happened?"

"It was so quiet I feel asleep in the chair but woke to what sounded like a motorbike engine coming from the direction of your cottage. No motorbike had passed by me, so I knew it didn't come across the orchard from the new road. I thought it might be someone coming up the old way by the gorge, and what I'd heard was the sound of an engine echoing up the gorge, or perhaps a chainsaw. I never thought for a moment it actually was coming from in front of your cottage. Then I heard the sound of breaking glass."

He shook his head. "Thankfully, I didn't ignore that sound and go back to sleep. Something didn't feel right, but not being familiar with the area and neighbors, I didn't want to just run off in the direction of the noise and stick my nose in other people's business. Instead, I decided to knock on your cousin's door and tell him what I'd heard."

"You woke up Spiro in the middle of the night?"

"He greeted me with that same thought in mind. I apologized, gave him a quick explanation for why I was there, and told him what I'd heard. He pulled his phone out of his pants to show me the time, in what I'm sure was a gesture meant to emphasize just how crazy I must have sounded. But that's when he noticed your message on his phone. He played it and raced back inside the house, yelling for Yianni to come quickly because someone was trying to kill you. Spiro came back out with a shotgun and headed for the steps leading down to you with me behind him and Yianni bringing up the rear. He yelled down the steps to a guy standing in the moonlight and, when the guy shot at him, Spiro let him have it with the shotgun. Both barrels."

Tassos took his time telling Maggie everything that happened between then and the ambulance's arrival.

"You are my Prince Charming."

"At your service, my love." He stood up, leaned over, and kissed her on the forehead. "But what honestly saved the day was the quick thinking on your part that got your butt into that hidden passage."

"Bless my *yaya* for telling me about it. And bless adrenaline for triggering old memories in a time of need."

"For sure. The ambulance driver told me most people never wake up from carbon monoxide poisoning. It's tasteless, odorless, colorless, and capable of passing through the drywall used in modern construction. Luckily, you ended up sealing yourself in a stone-and-oak chamber and found a source of fresh air. Otherwise..." His voice trailed off.

She smacked his hand. "Don't get all teary-eyed on me."

Tassos bit at his lower lip. "What, me? Never."

"I have one question. What in the world made Yianni think tossing plates at my door would draw Jerry to look outside?"

Tassos burst out laughing. "I asked him the same question. He said it came to him as a variation on a classic home-invasion ruse that's been around Athens for years. Bad guys will come to an otherwise secure home and pour enough water at the front door to seep inside. Then they wait for some curious soul on the inside to open the door to see where it's coming from. *Voilá*, they're inside. Yianni figured it was worth a try to see if curiosity would lure him out. It did and bye-bye, Jerry, though we do owe Spiro's wife a new set of dishes."

Tassos leaned back in the chair and stretched through a yawn. "All of which proves the adage that curiosity killed the cat."

"Correction," said Maggie. "In this case it killed the mouse."

Tassos smiled. "I'm glad to see you're returning to form."

"Where's Yianni?"

"On his way back to Athens. Once we knew you were out of danger, Andreas told him to get back to the office. Something about going at the problem in a different way." He kissed her hand. "But I'll be here to protect you for as long as it takes."

"From whom?"

"All threats, foreign or domestic."

"I take that to mean Andreas still isn't sure who was behind the attempt on my life?"

"Or the rest of what he calls a big mess. He told me to suspect everyone, so I'm not letting you out of my sight until he and Yianni get to the bottom of what's going on."

"That could be a long time."

He smiled. "If we're lucky."

———

When Yianni walked into the domestic arrivals area at Venizelos International Airport, Andreas was waiting for him.

"This is a surprise. I thought I'd meet you in the office. Is everything okay?"

Andreas gestured for Yianni to follow him down the wide hallway leading to baggage claim and the airport exit. "Do you have any bags other than the one you're carrying?"

"No."

"To answer your question, personally, everything is fine. Professionally, not by a long shot. The media is sniffing around for the story behind the deaths of Tom and Jerry. They're not sure yet whether to paint them as hero cops killed in some major gun battle with leftists on Red Rock or crooked cops getting what they deserved. The press doesn't care which story they run with, as long as it sells."

"But why did you come to the airport to tell me that? You could have waited until I got to the office, or called me."

"It made more sense to pick you up instead of wasting time waiting for you to get to the office, since we'd only be heading straight off to Korydallos."

"Why are we going there?"

"Because there's a prisoner for us to see." Andreas steered them toward wide glass doors marked 10.

"I'm parked just outside. I'll tell you everything once we're in the car."

Korydallos lay west-northwest of the airport, but the fastest way there was also the longest, forty-five kilometers, mostly on the National Road. A brief jog out of the airport to the southwest, followed by a wide loop north and west to avoid central Athens, and a turn to the southwest by Marousi toward Piraeus, brought you to Korydallos in thirty minutes.

Andreas planned on using every minute to bounce his ideas off Yianni.

"As I see it, now that Tom and Jerry are no more, the only

chance we have at learning who sent them after Maggie, and why, is if, by some miracle, Stavros's killer knows more about them than he told me."

"I thought Tom and Jerry were working for the Chens."

"Logically, it looks that way. All the reliable evidence supports that, and by reliable I'm excluding Papa George's alleged confession." Andreas tapped his hands on the steering wheel. "But one thing keeps gnawing at me. How did Tom and Jerry know where Maggie was staying and how to get there? They must have had local help. The perfect fit would be if we could prove they delivered the cooler to Papa George on Ikaria, and he used that opportunity to fire them up for going after Maggie."

"But all Spiro overheard Tom say was that they had *delivered* the cooler. Nothing about to whom or where they made the delivery. They could have been following instructions from the Chens to deliver it somewhere in Athens, and then left for Ikaria to do away with Maggie."

"I understand Ikaria doesn't have street addresses. If that's true, how could they have found Maggie on their own?"

"Mm." Yianni nodded. "Well, I'm hardly a supporter of Papa George, but according to Maggie, virtually everyone on the island knew where her *yaya* lived. It wouldn't have been hard for Tom and Jerry to get that information and even directions from any number of local sources."

Andreas let out a deep breath. "Which brings us back to my original point. Stavros's killer looks like our last realistic hope at getting to the bottom of this."

"So, what's your plan?"

"I'll put it to you this way: I get to play the good cop."

Yianni smiled and smacked the dashboard with a fist. "You just made my day."

———

"I bet you're feeling all warm and fuzzy at the thought of seeing me again," said Andreas, walking into the interrogation room. He sat down in one of two chairs across from the prisoner.

The man said nothing.

"How's the shoulder?"

The prisoner lifted his sling-set arm high enough to give Andreas a middle-finger salute.

"Well, if that's how you feel about me, I can't wait for your reaction to who else has come to see you." Without looking away from the prisoner, Andreas raised his voice. "Detective, come in and join the party."

As Yianni strode in, the prisoner snarled and tried to come up out of his chair. "You crippled my fucking arm, you asshole."

Yianni kept coming straight at him, and when reaching the table, leaned in toward the prisoner's face, "If I had to do it over again, I'd have aimed for your head. That was my friend you murdered."

The prisoner struggled against his shackles.

"Chief, would you do me a favor and ask the guard to take off that dirtbag's shackles and handcuffs? I think he wants to give me the chance of sparing our nation any further cost other than for his funeral."

"Now, Detective, you know we don't do that anymore. Besides, we're here to bring him good news."

"What sort of news?" said the prisoner, turning his head away from Yianni's glare.

"News you don't deserve, dirtbag."

Andreas grabbed Yianni by the arm and pulled him down onto the chair beside him. "Detective, enough." Andreas turned to the prisoner. "I'm sorry, but you killed one of his best friends."

Andreas paused. "Maybe you don't know how that feels, but that's sort of why we're here today. I'm sorry to tell you that two of your dear friends have also passed away: Tom and Jerry."

The prisoner's jaw dropped. "How?"

Andreas shook his head, "They made a very bad decision. Last night, they tried to kill someone near and dear to the detective and me."

The prisoner sat up in his chair. "You're not scaring me."

"I'm not trying to. I'm trying to help you out of a bigger jam than you were in before they died."

"What sort of jam?"

"You might think that with them dead, you don't have to worry about them eliminating you as a loose end, which is understandable, considering their past behavior. However, their death does screw up your defense that you never knew the man you murdered was a cop."

"But I didn't."

Andreas shook his head. "I always knew you were lying about that, but it didn't matter before. We'd have gotten all the answers we needed from Tom and Jerry about why they arranged the murder of our friend. We didn't think we'd need you for anything more than what you'd already given us."

Andreas smacked the table. "But now things are different, and without knowing *why* they wanted our friend killed, the only person left for us to go after for what we need to know is you."

"Where's the good news?"

"I'm not done with the bad. You'll be prosecuted as a premeditated cop-killer and convicted. You're not going to do well inside with guys like him," nodding toward Yianni, "always looking to get a piece of you."

"Come on, already, what's the good news?"

"Something the detective doesn't agree with," said Andreas.

"Damn straight, I don't."

"Lucky for you, I'm his boss."

"Just tell me."

"I know that you knew your target was a cop all along. That bothers me a lot. More than you can imagine." Andreas leaned forward, "But like I said, we need you now. You're at the very bottom of the food chain on this, and if you give me the information I need to get to the top, I'm willing to go along with your claim that you didn't know he was a cop."

"How do I know I can trust you?"

"Did you find a new lawyer yet?"

"No."

"Do you want a lawyer before we go further? If you do, that's fine, but just so you know, this conversation is off the record, so whatever you tell me you can deny, and your admission that you knew he was a police officer will never reach the prosecutor or judge's ear."

"Are you taping this?"

"No. So, may I begin?"

"What the hell…ask away."

"Did Tom and Jerry know the person they were asking you to kill was a police officer?"

He shut his eyes and exhaled. "Yes. That was the reason they asked me to do it. I knew it had to be something big for them to be looking to me to do a hit for them. So I pressed them until they told me the truth."

"A hit for *them*?" asked Yianni.

"Yeah, who else?"

"What he means," said Andreas, "is was there anyone besides Tom and Jerry who wanted Stavros killed?"

"Not that I knew of."

"Jesus, Chief, I told you we couldn't expect the truth out of him."

The prisoner looked surprised. "I don't get you. They were scared shitless that the drug cartel who paid them to protect their operation on the docks would find out that a cop had infiltrated their organization and blame them for screwing up. That's the sort of screwup that gets you killed."

"Are you saying they killed him on the orders of a drug cartel?" said Yianni.

"Hell, no. The last thing they wanted was for the drug cartel to learn he was a cop. Then they'd be dead for sure."

Andreas sat quietly staring at the prisoner.

"Honest, they wanted him dead to protect themselves...no other reason."

Yianni leaned in across the table. "How did Tom and Jerry find out he was a cop?"

"Purely by accident. They told me someone had approached them on a different deal having nothing to do with the cartel. Something about smuggling some product out of Greece. The new people were looking for someone who could arrange to transport their product onto the docks and out of the country without any official interference. So—"

"When you say 'new people,' was it more than one person offering the deal?" interrupted Andreas.

"I've no idea how many were involved. It could have been one or a hundred. All I know is Tom and Jerry complained about having to deal with big-money people who didn't trust anyone. The new people wanted photographs of anyone who'd have anything to do with getting their product to the ship. So Jerry got copies of IDs and passed them along to the new people.

"Tom and Jerry shit their pants when they heard back from the new people that one of the IDs turned up a cop. That's when they put the arm on me."

"Do you have any idea what that product was?"

"Not a clue."

"What about where it was coming from?" asked Yianni.

"Some island."

Andreas held his breath before asking, "Do you know the name of the island?"

He gestured no.

Andreas put on a disappointed look.

"Hey, I wish I could help you, but they never talked about those details with me. I just remember hearing them bitch among themselves about the jam they were in. You'd think they'd be glad they stumbled onto that information before the drug cartel did. Instead, they worried that someday they'd be found dead in a container bound for Hong Kong."

Andreas jerked straight in his chair. "Hong Kong? Why Hong Kong?"

"Because that's where the new people intended on shipping their product."

———

For the first minutes of their drive back to the office, neither Andreas nor Yianni said a word. Andreas followed a hodge-podge of city back streets that took them through a cross section of the sorts of shops, homes, institutions, and history typical of the more than three million souls living in Greater Athens and Piraeus, an area half the size of New York City.

Less than two decades earlier, Greece had proudly celebrated its history with the world by hosting a wildly successful 2004 Olympics. Three years later, the nation fell victim to the world-wide financial crisis, followed by strict European Union fiscal constraints that crippled its economy and triggered a massive brain drain. Yet Greece persevered, and just as its economy had nearly struggled back onto its feet, the pandemic hit, knocking it back down harder than before.

Times were tough and people were desperate, so opportunists pounced, both foreign and domestic. Villainizing ensued, with foreigners by far the easiest target of the frustrated and angry.

Andreas was beginning to understand why so many felt that way.

"I'm pissed," he said, breaking the silence.

"You've got company. What do you think the chances are of getting the Chens back here to stand trial?"

"Stand trial for what? Our prisoner just pinned everything linked to Stavros's murder on Tom and Jerry alone. As for the elderly victims on Ikaria, everything supports Papa George's version and points directly at the Chens. But the only living witness we have against them is Papa George, and the Chens' lawyers will have a field day with him and his so-called confession."

"You're forgetting about Anna. She's doing well."

"Thank God. Though I'm sad to say that, based upon all the wonderful things virtually everyone on Ikaria has to say about George, I doubt whether Anna's testimony would inspire a prosecutor enough to go after the Chens and their battalions of lawyers, or Papa George and his Church."

"Are you suggesting we just give up and walk away?"

Andreas bristled. "Go to hell." Then, "Sorry, Yianni. I'm just as edgy and angry as you are. It aggravates me to my core to think that true evil is escaping responsibility for the premeditated genocide of our oldest and most vulnerable citizens."

Andreas drew in a deep breath. "I'm not prepared to let that happen on my watch."

"What do you have in mind?"

"Not sure yet. I've got to step back from my anger and take a long, hard look at everything we know. If I'm lucky, I'll find where the bad guys outsmarted themselves and take it from there."

"From the way things are going, I'd say we'll have to make our own luck."

"I'm working on it. Starting now."

———

The day after Yaya's *enniamera* memorial service, Maggie and Tassos left Ikaria to spend a week at Tassos's home on Syros before she returned to work in Athens.

Despite the bitter anger she held for Papa George, and her frustration with a system that allowed him to escape responsibility for whatever role he'd played in Yaya's death, she owed it to her family and friends who'd stood by her not to dwell upon the injustice of it all, but to move on with her life.

But before leaving Ikaria, she and Tassos paid an unexpected visit to Papa George. In a calm, level voice, she told him to immediately discontinue his ministry to the elderly. He refused graciously, saying that he felt an obligation to the Lord to continue caring for his flock. Maggie told him if that's how he wished to proceed, she had an obligation of her own to fulfill: sharing her recording of his hospital confession with the world, which she began playing for him at that moment.

Papa George's cool demeanor crumbled as he cried, "*That's blackmail!*"

Maggie said, "Have a nice day."

Chapter Sixteen

Three months had passed since Maggie'd returned to work at GADA. The holidays were over, the weather had turned decidedly wintry, and she hadn't been back to Ikaria except for the *mnimosino* memorial service held forty days after Yaya's passing.

Maggie longed to return to Ikaria again, but each time she sought to plan a visit, her anger surged at the thought of running into Papa George. She bore him resentment she could never forgive; she struggled daily to keep her rage from consuming the many wonderful things in her life. Her solution was simple and heartbreaking: She barred herself from visiting the one place on earth she loved most, in the process making her yet another victim of Papa George. But she saw no other choice.

She heard Andreas's voice come through their intercom, "Maggie, please find Yianni. I'd like the two of you to join me in my office."

"What's up, Chief?"

"I'll tell you when I see you." His voice sounded serious. Her first thought was, *Who died?* That showed where her head was these days.

Two minutes later, Maggie and Yianni walked into Andreas's

office, closed the door, and sat together on the sofa, leaving the two chairs in front of Andreas's desk empty.

Andreas picked up a document from his desktop and walked to the front of his desk. He swung a chair around to face Maggie and Yianni and dropped onto it.

"You look serious, Chief," said Yianni.

"Very," agreed Maggie.

Andreas quickly ran his tongue across his lips. "I just received a telephone call from Nikolaos Lombardos."

"The criminal defense lawyer?" said Yianni.

"Yes. He said he represents a client who wished to meet with me privately. I asked about what, and he told me it would be obvious the moment he identified his client. So I asked for the name."

Andreas paused to look at the document in his hand.

"So, who's the client?" asked Maggie.

"Chen Jin Wei. The father of Chen Li Ling and Chen Bo Heng."

"The brother and sister tied into Papa George?" Maggie said.

"The same."

"What does he want to meet about?" asked Yianni.

Andreas waved the document in his hand. "My letter to him."

"What letter?" said Maggie. "I never typed a letter to a Chen."

"I sent it before you returned to work."

"Why did you write him a letter?" asked Yianni.

"A day or so after Maggie told me of her final conversation with Papa George—"

"When I told him to stop working with the elderly?"

"Yes. What struck me was how you described his reaction when you threatened to go public with your recording of his supposed confession."

"It's the only time I ever saw him lose his cool."

"Precisely. That got me to thinking why, of all the harsh words, inferences, and downright accusations you and Yianni had tossed at him, he lost it over what you might do with a recording portraying him as the innocent victim of ruthless, heartless manipulators."

Andreas held up the document again. "That's what led me to write this letter. I gambled that what Papa George feared most were the Chens, and the last thing on earth he wanted was for that recording—of him throwing the brother and sister under the bus—to somehow find its way back to them. So, I decided to shake things up and send it."

"The recording? To the Chens?" asked Yianni.

"It seemed the only shot we had left. But I sent it to the father, not the children. And by diplomatic channels, to make sure it reached him. Billionaires don't generally pay attention to letters from cops. They have lawyers to do that."

"And you just heard back today?" asked Maggie.

"Frankly, I'd given up on ever hearing."

"What did your letter say?" said Maggie, leaning forward on the sofa.

"It starts off with his name and address, followed by a line introducing me and picks up here:

"I write to you not as a policeman, but as the father of a son and a daughter of whom I am as proud as you must be of your daughter, Li Ling, and son, Bo Heng.

"I never had the honor of meeting either of your children, but in the course of an investigation into the deaths of six Greek elders ninety to one hundred years old, your children have been identified as complicit in their deaths.

"I apologize for delivering such a stark statement to a loving father, but those aren't my words, nor are they as harsh as the actual accusations made by a Greek Orthodox priest well-known to your children, blaming them for morally reprehensible, if not criminal, acts.

"Whether or not your children have committed a crime is not my decision to make. Nor is it my place to tell another father how to deal

with his children. But I do consider it my responsibility as a father to alert you to such serious accusations against your children.

"I do not expect you to take my word on any of this, which is why I enclose an audio recording of the accusations asserted against your children in the voice of one they know well.

"Whether or not I hear back from you, I offer you my sincere wishes that none of what your children are accused is true.

"Respectfully...and so on."

Andreas sat back in the chair.

"Oh, my God," said Maggie, "that's quite a letter."

"I felt I owed it to you to take the risk."

"What risk?" said Yianni.

"Take your pick, anything from being accused of a shakedown, or attacking the Church, to defamation, or a bullet in the head."

"Why didn't you tell us about the letter?" said Maggie.

"I saw no reason to get your hopes up of anything coming of it until I heard back."

"So, what did the lawyer say his client wants to talk about?" asked Yianni.

"He didn't. All he said was that we couldn't meet in our office or his. It had to be in some out-of-the-way, neutral location, one that wouldn't raise suspicions should some reporter learn of his presence in Athens."

"So, where are you meeting him?" said Yianni.

"Not me, the three of us. No way I'm going into a meeting like that without witnesses."

"Okay, I'm with you on that, but I repeat: Where?"

"In my apartment tomorrow at nine in the morning, after the kids are off to school."

"Just the sort of address where a Chinese billionaire would be expected to be visiting friends," said Maggie.

"Sure beats my apartment," said Yianni.

Andreas rolled his eyes. "Okay, once you're done with the jokes, I want you two getting back up to speed on everything we know about the Chens."

"Don't forget Tom and Jerry," added Yianni.

Andreas nodded. "This may be our only chance at ever getting answers."

"You do realize," said Maggie, "that all this drama could be nothing more than a buildup to the lawyer smacking you across the face with some massive threat of what will happen to you should you ever again breathe a word about what's on that recording."

"That's possible, but somehow I don't think so." Andreas pointed a finger in the air. "But I do agree with Maggie on one point."

"What's that?"

"The lawyer has some sort of big surprise in store for us." He paused. "It's the nature of the beast."

———

Lila and Andreas's penthouse apartment occupied the entire sixth floor of one of downtown Athens's rare, old residential buildings. It was among the city's most exclusive addresses, next to the Presidential Palace, across from Greece's National Gardens, and offering unobstructed breathtaking views of both the Acropolis and its majestic sister hill, Lykavittos.

At precisely nine, the intercom linked to the concierge station in the lobby buzzed in the apartment.

"Our visitors are right on time," Andreas told the assembled group, picking up the handset. "Hello?"

He paused, then said, "Send them right up, please."

Lila stood. "Well, I'll leave the three of you to do your business."

"Stay. You're more than welcome. This could be quite a show. Besides, as soon as they leave, you'll be pumping me for details on what happened."

"Yes, please stay," said Maggie. "I could use the sisterly support, if only to calm my anger. Your presence might even help me hold my tongue."

"If only that were true," chuckled Yianni.

The doorbell rang.

"No need to bother, Marina, I'll get it," said Andreas to the maid.

He drew in and let out a deep breath, readying himself for whatever surprise might be coming. He opened the door with a poker-faced smile on his face, one that he hoped hadn't faded when he saw who stood in the foyer—three immaculately tailored Chinese people, and one far-less-so Greek lawyer.

"Chief Kaldis, I presume," said the lawyer, not extending his hand.

Andreas nodded to the group, "Please, come in so that we may make proper introductions in more suitable surroundings." He waited for the four to enter, closed the door and led them through the apartment to the main sitting room.

Yianni, Maggie, and Lila stood from the sofa as the group entered the room. Andreas shot each of his crew a stern look, hoping it might discourage them from displaying the sort of surprise he'd felt upon recognizing the two unexpected guests. He stopped next to Lila and turned to face the lawyer.

"Permit me to introduce my wife, Lila; my chief detective, Yianni Kouros; and my personal assistant, Maggie Sikestes." They smiled as Andreas said their names.

The lawyer pointed toward the older Chinese man, "This is the Honorable Chen Jin Wei, his daughter, Chen Li Ling, and son, Chen Bo Heng." The father stepped forward to shake Andreas's hand, and then the hands of Lila, Yianni, and Maggie. His son and daughter followed their father's lead.

The lawyer made no effort to shake anyone's hand.

Guess he's going to be the bad cop, thought Andreas.

"If you'll excuse me for a moment," said Lila pointing to a coffee table set with china and silver for six, "I must inform my maid that there will be eight, not six of us."

The Chens nodded.

"Please, make yourselves comfortable," said Andreas, gesturing for the father to sit in an upholstered wing chair featuring a clear view of the Acropolis. The son and daughter chose seats to the father's left, while the lawyer sat to his right.

Maggie and Yianni dropped back down onto the sofa, leaving room for Lila.

Andreas pointed to a chair matching and across from the father's. "Doesn't anyone want to sit there? You'll be more comfortable."

The father answered in perfect English. "This is your home, sir. Please sit there."

Andreas responded in English. "Thank you. Do you speak Greek, sir?"

"Not as well as my daughter or my son, so I prefer we speak in English. That is, unless you would prefer to speak in my native dialect." He smiled.

Andreas laughed. "I'm a bit rusty on that score. So English it is."

The lawyer cleared his throat. "May I speak?"

Lila walked into the room followed by the maid carrying a tray bearing a hammered-silver tea service and two additional place settings. Behind the maid came the nanny, carrying a tray filled with a variety of Greek pastries.

"I apologize for the casual service," said Lila, "But it seems easier to let everyone serve themselves."

"We're not here for social chitchat," said the lawyer, plainly piqued at the interruption of his planned opening.

Lila ignored him and turned to the maid. "Marina, please take away the gentleman's place setting. He's not here for any of that."

Lila dropped onto the sofa, next to Maggie, flashing what Andreas knew to be her best forced smile straight at the lawyer. Andreas struggled to keep a straight face.

"Yes, please do begin," said Andreas.

The lawyer appeared poised to say something to Lila but caught himself and cleared his throat again.

"The Chen family has asked me to represent them in connection with matters raised in your letter to Mr. Jin Wei and the recording included with your letter. The recording purports to be a conversation between your colleagues," nodding toward Maggie and Yianni, "and a Greek Orthodox priest known as Papa George."

He shifted in his chair. "Though I advised my clients against meeting with you in Greece because it posed the risk of immediate arrest of the son and daughter, all three insisted on meeting with you in Athens. I also told them to assume that everything they said would be recorded. They said they did not care. I have only one question to ask of you on that score. Are any of you recording this conversation?"

"I can speak for all of us on that point," said Andreas. "The answer is no."

"Good."

"I have the same question for you, sir," said Andreas.

"I'm not, but I told them I thought it would be prudent for them to do so in order that what they say isn't later misquoted or—"

"The answer is no," interrupted the father, glancing at the lawyer. "I appreciate your professional efforts to protect our interests, but I think it's best that I take it from here." He looked directly at Andreas. "Are your children here with you?"

"They're at school."

"Too bad, I wanted to meet them so that I could tell them how blessed they are to have a father possessing such an informed view of his responsibilities to them, and to the preservation of their family name."

Andreas felt he might be blushing. "That's very kind of you to say."

"You and I descend from powerful ancient cultures and share a deep reverence for our respective histories. We who live today have a duty to preserve the honor of our families in order that our descendants be respected in centuries yet to come. It is a virtuous commitment we carry, one to be cherished and praised—and never neglected."

Andreas nodded. "Understood and agreed."

"I was deeply disturbed by your letter. At first, I felt anger directed at you for daring to send me such a letter. I could not believe my children would ever in any way be involved in such acts as you described."

He paused to reach for the teapot, but his daughter reached for it faster and poured her father a cup. He left the cup untouched. "Then I listened to the recording."

He lifted up the cup and saucer and took a sip. "It took me two days to summon up the will to confront my children over the priest's accusations. Not that I distrusted them, but to process my own anger at the man identified as Papa George. I needed to do that for myself if I hoped to help them manage their inevitable anger at this serious defamation of our family."

He put down the cup and saucer. "Two days later, I flew to Hong Kong and arrived at their offices unannounced. I apologized for interfering with their day but told them I had something of grave importance to discuss with them immediately. The three of us sat alone. Without offering a word of introduction to the audio recording, I played it for them. Waiting to observe their reactions was one of the most difficult moments of my life."

He sighed. "They said not a word while they listened, but from their expressions I knew they were as shocked as I was when I listened to it. After they'd heard it all, I read them your letter. Then I asked them a single question: Is any of this true?"

"They answered *yes*."

He patted his fingertips together. "I spent the rest of that day, and well into the night, going over every detail of their involvement with Papa George, from the first moment they met, through the last contact they'd had with him—or anyone on his behalf."

He looked at his children. "They will tell you in their own words what they told me. But let me assure you of one thing: I did not only take their word on what they are about to tell you. I spent months sparing no expense to verify every detail. All of that is available to you if you wish to see it."

"I do," said Andreas.

"I'll have it delivered this afternoon to your office."

"Mr. Chen, I have to caution you—"

The father raised his hand to silence the lawyer. "Older Brother will speak first, followed by Little Sister. Please feel free to interrupt them at any point."

Brother nodded to his father. "Ladies and gentlemen, I have had months to reflect upon what Little Sister and I are accused of. So please do not confuse any lack of anger in my words as a measure of the deep disgust we carry for the accuser and his accusations."

"We have been betrayed, misled, and simply speaking, framed by one we thought a trusted friend," said Sister, sitting ramrod straight in her chair. "George, as we knew him when we first met on Santorini, was a jeweler—engaging and fun to be with. He made a point of spending as much time with us as we had available to be with him. And not just on Santorini. He kept up with us by email, and on occasion, when we mentioned we'd be Greece, he'd meet us where we planned to be. Once, he even came to visit us in Hong Kong. Yes, he was a jeweler, and we were his very good customers, but Older Brother and I thought of him as a true friend."

Brother nodded. "We confided in each other about our goals and interests. We told him of our desire to do good for the world through our pharmaceutical business. He said he'd once thought of becoming a priest and helping the world through service to God, but soon realized he liked living the good life, which came at a price no priest could afford."

"And certainly not at the level we lived," said Sister. "We're used to people quietly envying our wealth, but George never hid his envy, nor was it a big point with him. He'd simply remark in good humor that he needed to find a way to live our lifestyle." She locked eyes with Andreas. "Approximately three years after we met George, we lost track of him. No more emails or phone calls, and when we returned to Santorini, no one seemed to know where he had gone. We worried something bad might have happened to him." She lowered her eyes.

"A little less than five months ago, I received a letter from George," said Brother. "He wrote as if we'd never lost touch. He said if it seemed as if he'd dropped off the face of the earth, well, he had. He had decided to finish his priesthood studies and had since been serving the people of Ikaria."

Sister spoke next. "Up until this point, what he described on the recording is essentially accurate. The rest of his words, though, are not only fiction, but evidence of his premeditated plan to make my brother and me appear the perpetrators of criminal acts committed solely by him."

Brother nodded. "On receiving George's letter, I called him to extend my congratulations. We spoke like old friends, and he said how blessed he was to have a ministry that tended to the oldest people on Ikaria, an island famous for how many of its locals lived to beyond one hundred years. I said Little Sister would be thrilled at the news of our reconnecting, and we both looked forward to seeing him again soon."

"A few days after Older Brother told me of his conversation with George," said Sister, "I called him to say hello and extend my congratulations on his elevation to the priesthood. He asked me when we'd next be in Greece, and I said we planned to be in Athens in a couple of weeks. He said he'd like to see us in Athens if we had the time, and I said we'd make time." Sister paused. "We did *not* invite him to come to our hotel, he invited himself, and at no time in either Older Brother's call or mine was there any mention of anything having to do with business of any sort."

"That is until he walked into our hotel suite," said Brother. "Even dressed as a cleric, he was the same salesman we knew as George. From the moment he arrived, everything he told us about his new life and his precious flock was aimed at the sale he'd come to make. In fact, in retrospect, we believe George saw the priesthood as a step toward amassing the fortune he'd always wanted."

Andreas leaned forward, "Excuse me for interrupting, Mr. Chen, but that's a rather explosive accusation."

"It was hard for us to believe too," Brother said. "But once you've heard all that we have to say, I think you'll agree with us."

Andreas leaned back in his chair. "Sorry. Please continue."

Sister shook her head, "No need to apologize, Chief Inspector. As Father said, feel free to interrupt."

Brother continued. "When we met him at our hotel, it was as if we'd not seen each other in four days, not nearly four years. We reminisced and caught up on each other's lives, but as usual,

George—now Papa George—did most of the talking. He told us how he'd gone back to his seminary and finished up his studies in near record time, and how he'd specifically requested an assignment to Ikaria, so that he could 'tend to those closest to their approaching time in heaven.'"

Sister interrupted. "He said those actual words, and then went on about how Ikaria was filled with people living significantly longer than anywhere else on the planet."

Brother nodded. "He asked for our views on the recent pandemic, and spoke of how miraculous it was that Ikaria had so many residents who'd survived both the recent pandemic and the Spanish flu."

"It sounded quaint at first," said Sister, "as if he'd become a cheerleader for his adopted island's tourist board. Then he steered Older Brother and me into a discussion of the different vaccines that had come into prominence around the world to battle the 2020–2022 pandemic and asked whether we'd been involved in any of that. When we told him no, he said, considering the trillions spent by nations around the world to get vaccines into the arms of their citizens, why hadn't we?"

The brother resumed. "I explained that we were not equipped to manufacture vaccines, and with the world debating whether China was the source of the COVID-19 virus, any effort to import vaccines from the West carried political risk that could impact, if not destroy, our business."

Sister nodded. "That's when he came to what we now believe was his real but unstated reason for meeting us in Athens. He said he had an idea to spare the world great suffering. He described it as one that would allow his flock in their final days to safeguard generations yet to come from future pandemic disasters. It involved nothing more than a harmless blood donation yielding antibodies from which a universally effective vaccine could be developed."

"Sister and I admired his effort to do good work but had to point out to him that the science of vaccines was far more complicated than that and required a vast investment of capital, time, and other costs. When we told him that antibodies and RNA samples derived from pandemics of centuries past already were available to vaccine developers, he became visibly upset. As if we were challenging him by bringing reality into the discussion. I'd never seen him act that way.

"He said when he first came to Ikaria, he planned on financing his mission to the elderly by producing a supplement that would capitalize on Ikaria's reputation for long life. Then, in the most somber of tones, he said he'd been struck with a vision in which he saw in the pandemic a message from God: a way to bring salvation from plague to the world and to give meaning to the final years of his flock."

"According to George," said Sister, "his flock stood ready, willing, and able to help save the world from future pandemics. And now, he said, those who could turn that into reality lacked the courage to seize on this unique but rapidly fading opportunity."

"Sounds like your old friend had turned a bit aggressive on you," said Andreas.

"It didn't bother us as the time." Sister smiled. "We're used to emotional Greeks. Besides, we were sensitive to his disappointment at learning what he thought a grand plan for doing wondrous good for the world was neither a novel or practical idea. At least not in our opinion. As we expected, the moment passed and he apologized, admitting his disappointment at losing what he thought a great opportunity for funding a foundation he'd created to benefit his flock and the community of Ikaria."

This time, Brother smiled. "We thought at the time that he'd finally come around to the real point of his visit. I even laughed out loud, and said, 'You're still a salesman.' He acted disappointed, but only a little. That's when he said it would be a great consolation to his disappointment if we could see it in our hearts to give a sizable donation to his foundation. We asked how much he had in mind, and he immediately said a hundred thousand euros. That struck me as high."

"Me too," said Sister, "but after all, he was an old friend who'd committed his life to doing God's work, so we agreed."

Yianni raised his hand. "Was there ever any discussion that, if you went forward with his vaccine proposal, one percent of worldwide sales would be donated to his foundation?"

"Not a word," said Brother. "I considered his visit an effort on the part of a well-meaning, but clueless, friend to raise money for charity. His ideas on the vaccine made no sense to us from a scientific or business perspective, and we rejected it the moment he raised it. Nothing about compensation was ever raised or discussed."

Andreas stared at the brother. "Are you saying you had no business discussions with him at all?"

"No, I'm saying we had no further discussions with him about his vaccine project. A week later he called me and asked if he produced a product that would have a market in China, could I help him find a way to get it imported there? I told him that if his paperwork was in order, we most certainly would be willing to help him find an appropriate importer."

"What was the product?" asked Maggie.

"He said he was back to his idea of marketing an over-the-counter supplement based on Ikaria's reputation for long life."

"Using Ikariot blood?"

"In some capacity, yes."

"What came of that?"

"Nothing. We never heard back from him. Approximately a month later, we returned to Athens, and I called him to say hello.

He was excited to hear we were back in Greece and literally begged us to charter a boat and come visit him in Ikaria. He seemed desperate to show us the results of his holy work, so we agreed to leave the next day and spend a night in Ikaria."

"What did you do the night before you left for Ikaria?" said Yianni.

"Nothing special," said Sister.

"But what did you do?"

She looked at Brother. "What did we do?"

"We went to a club. I don't even remember the name of it. It was a pretty boring place."

"Then why did you go?" asked Yianni, pressing harder.

The Chens' lawyer raised a hand. "Why are you asking these questions?"

Without taking his eyes off Brother, Yianni answered, "Because I want to hear his answers. So unless you're instructing him not to answer, I expect him to answer my questions, as I was told we were free to ask."

Brother started blinking, "I don't understand why any of this is relevant."

Yianni patted his chest. "I do. So how about an answer?"

Brother shut his eyes, as if straining to remember. "I believe George may have sent us there."

"Yes, that's right," said Sister. "He said his friends had an interest in a club and we should check it out. But I don't remember its name."

Brother shook his head. "I don't either."

Yianni kept his eyes fixed on Brother. "It's called The Buzz Club."

The siblings' mouths dropped open.

"That's right," exclaimed Sister.

"How did you know?" said Brother.

"You're not the only ones who've spent time over the past

months looking into your former friend Papa George and his associates." Yianni let that sink in. "Are you ready to answer some questions about your evening at The Buzz Club?"

They looked at their father, who looked at the lawyer.

"Is there a place where I can speak with my clients privately?"

"Sure," said Andreas and he led them into Lila's office. As Andreas walked back to where the others were seated, he winked at Yianni, leaned down, and whispered, "Nice move, Detective."

"Let's see if it shakes up their carefully rehearsed routine."

"It already has. Now let's see where it takes us."

———

Fifteen minutes later, the Chens and their lawyer returned to the sitting room. The father's lips were tightly drawn, his children's expressions chastened.

After they'd resumed their seats, the lawyer spoke. "Chief Inspector, if you'll assure me that your questions have nothing to do with an investigation of recreational drug use, and that you will not pursue a line of inquiry intended to implicate any of my clients in any such activity, then I'm prepare to allow you and your detective to continue."

Andreas fought to maintain a serious expression, all the while thinking of how pissed off the father must be to learn that his prized children were doing drugs in a nightclub. He looked at Yianni. "What do you say, Detective?"

Yianni shrugged, "That's fine with me." He looked back at the siblings. "So, on to your night at The Buzz Club. Who did you meet there?"

Sister gave him the real names for Tom and Jerry.

"And what was their connection to Papa George?"

Brother said, "All George told us were the names of the two

men, that they were involved in the club, and they expected us. I never heard the two say anything about their connection to George beyond some vague involvement in arranging for the export of his product."

"You mean the supplements?"

"They didn't say."

Sister jumped in. "One had a little too much to drink and told me George had brought them in on a deal they could retire on. Then he thanked me and Older Brother for making it all happen and kissed me on both cheeks."

"What did you say to that?" asked Andreas.

"I had no idea what he was talking about and thought he might be hitting on me. But they both seemed so nervous around us that I thought it best just to nod, smile, and change the subject. The rest of the evening was uneventful, and the next morning we had a very pleasant voyage to Ikaria."

"Did you ever ask Papa George what the man meant by thanking you?" asked Andreas.

"No. I'd forgotten all about that evening by the time we reached Ikaria."

"What about you?" said Yianni to Brother.

"Until today, I never knew any of that. Little Sister never mentioned that exchange to me."

"Have either of you had any other contact with the two men you met in that club?" asked Andreas.

"Absolutely not," said Sister.

"None," said Brother.

Yianni leaned in toward the siblings. "Do either of you recall being asked to provide details on the identity of a man pictured in a photograph?"

"I assume you mean in the context of something related to George or those two men?" said Brother.

"Yes."

"George knew that we had access to sophisticated software capable of searching the Internet for information on whatever face we scanned into the system. I don't remember the precise date, but a week or so before our last trip to Athens, I received a telephone message from George asking whether I could arrange to scan a few photos through our system. He said they were of men he was considering for a position at his foundation. I arranged for one of my assistants to take care of it for him."

"Did you ever learn the results of the search?" asked a grim-faced Yianni.

"No, as I said, I turned it over to an assistant to handle. I never even saw the photographs."

Andreas cleared his throat. "I don't want to mess up your storyline here, but I think you should know before we go any further, that information you provided on one of the photographs you scanned for Papa George led to the assassination of the person in that photograph."

"*What*?" shouted the lawyer. "I insist on talking to my clients immediately. And in private."

"Easy does it, Counsel. I'm not yet done with the surprises." Andreas turned to face the father. "The software program your son employed as a favor to Papa George identified a man in one of the photographs as a police officer. He was working under-cover seeking to expose a drug-smuggling operation on the docks in Piraeus. The smugglers were protected by two corrupt drug enforcement agents, the same two men your son and daughter met with at The Buzz Club. They arranged for the assassination of the police officer shortly before your children showed up at the club."

The father began to blink uncontrollably as the blood drained from the faces of his children.

"I had no idea about any of this," said the father.

"N-nor did I," stuttered Brother.

"Nor I," said Sister, breathing rapidly.

"Easy there, Miss," said Andreas. "We don't want you hyperventilating."

"This interview is over," said the lawyer, bolting to his feet.

Andreas stared up at the man. "It is, if you'd like me to arrest your clients right here and now."

"On what charges?"

Lila chimed in for the first time: "I never went to law school, but even I can answer that question."

"I suggest you sit down and allow your clients to finish their story. I just want them to know in advance how serious the situation is, and how carefully they have been set up to look guilty."

"Assuming they actually aren't guilty," added Maggie.

"Seeing how they came here voluntarily to speak with us, I'm willing to give them the benefit of the doubt. But we need the unvarnished truth."

Brother shut his eyes and breathed deeply to calm himself. "I swear to you on the soul of my father that everything we have told you is the truth."

"The unvarnished truth," said his sister, who appeared to be on the verge of weeping.

"Then with your father's permission, please continue."

Father nodded to his children to proceed, and the lawyer silently slunk back onto his chair.

Brother spoke first. "George told us to meet him in the port village where he lived. He said not to anchor, because he'd be waiting for us on the dock, and with such calm seas we could better appreciate the beauty of the island from the water. We've since learned that this was yet another step in his scheme to make Little Sister and me appear guilty for his crimes." Brother shook his head. "He insisted we order from a restaurant quite a distance from where we'd anchored for the evening. He knew that the restaurant would deliver an order of that size in a cooler and made certain that the order and payment was in my name. Neither of us thought anything of it. We'd always paid for George, and we certainly planned to now, with him being a *humble* cleric." A tinge of anger slipped through Brother's otherwise business-like delivery. "After dinner, and a bit more wine than we should have had, he suggested we go straight to bed so that we'd all rise early, and he'd take us to see his *prize* first thing in the morning."

"I asked him what he meant by his prize," said Sister, "He answered with a pun, saying it was a 'sur*PRIZE*.' We left it at that, and George told the captain where we wanted the boat to be at sunrise.

"The next morning, we woke up in Karkinagri and disembarked for shore on what was looking to be an unpleasant and unnecessary adventure. We'd not slept well and awakened in a godforsaken part of the island that had nothing of any interest to either of us. On top of that, the only available rental car was hardly adequate. Bottom line: we were cranky."

"And George was anxious," said Brother, "but we had no idea why. Then came the drive up into the mountains. The views were lovely, but what kept running through my mind was, Is this trip really necessary? When George finally parked the car, we were in the middle of virtually nowhere. The only possible thing of any interest, beyond the view, was a small church. We couldn't imagine we'd gone through all of what we had, just to see another Greek church. I was irritated now, and I asked George why he'd brought us there. He answered, 'To meet someone who is going to make me very, very rich.'"

"Then he grabbed the cooler he'd put in the back of the car," said Sister, "and led us down a path to a tiny stone cottage. He knocked softly on the door, announced 'It's Papa George,' and entered before receiving a response. He motioned for us to follow him inside. There on a simple daybed lay a frail, very old woman, barely awake."

Brother drew in and let out three quick breaths. "George set the cooler down next to the bed, reached down to hold the woman's hand, and said something along the lines of, 'My dear Anna, I'm here with people who've come from far away to honor you as a savior of humanity.' What happened next, shocked me so deeply that..." He stopped, seemingly speechless.

Sister reached over and patted Brother's hand. "As traumatic as it was for me to see what was happening, it was far worse for my brother."

"What happened?" said Yianni.

"George reached down and opened the cooler. We thought he'd brought something for the poor woman to eat or drink. Instead, he pulled out paraphernalia used for obtaining a blood donation. I was horrified, and Older Brother began to shake, so I grabbed hold of his arm and led him out of the house into the fresh air."

"Did either of you go back inside?" said Yianni.

"Absolutely not," said Sister.

Maggie glared at her. "Papa George said you're the one who drew Anna's blood."

"While your brother encouraged you," added Yianni.

"As Papa George screamed at you both for what you were doing to her," said Maggie struggling to contain her anger.

Sister smiled. "I know it seems most inappropriate for me to be smiling at this moment, but, considering all the great care George has taken to make us appear guilty for whatever crimes he might be accused of committing, I cannot help but smile. I say that because with that one simple lie involving my brother, George has outsmarted himself."

"I don't see how," said Yianni. "It's your word against his."

"Not quite," said Brother. "You see, I suffer from vasovagal syncope."

"Huh?"

"I faint at the sight of blood. I always have, and my medical records show that I've been that way since I was a child."

"You've got to be shi—" Yianni caught himself.

"Shitting you?" asked Brother. "Absolutely not."

"If you and your sister weren't there to draw the blood, then who drew it?" asked Maggie.

"George, of course," said Sister.

"What do you mean, of course?" said Andreas, leaning forward.

"George was a medic in the Greek army."

Andreas leaned back.

"He said you'd provided him with a nurse to do the blood draws," said Maggie.

Sister shook her head. "He said a lot of things that weren't true."

"But I spoke with people who saw him visit members of his flock, accompanied by a nurse he claimed to be a nun."

"I'm sure they did see that," said Sister. "Investigators hired by my father to unmask George's lies located the woman. She was not a nun. She was a refugee with nursing experience imprisoned in the Vathy refugee camp on the neighboring island of Samos. George went to the camp, learned from those in charge the identities of female refugees with nursing experience, and convinced the authorities to release one into his custody so that she might help him better the lives of his flock on Ikaria.

"The woman spoke virtually no Greek but enough English to communicate with George. He told her that if she did not follow his instructions to the letter, he would send her back to the camp."

"Where is she now?" asked Maggie.

"Back in the camp," said the father. "Apparently, once he

realized my son and daughter were out of Greece, and that the police were suspicious of him, he returned her to the camp, taking care to describe her to the authorities as a thief and liar who could not be trusted."

"What a horrible human being. He's a disgrace to the Church," said Lila.

"I have a question," said Maggie, turning to look at Sister. "What did you and your brother do after you left Papa George alone with that frail woman in the cottage and a bag full of blood-drawing implements?"

Sister lowered her eyes. "I can tell from your tone of voice you think we should have done something to stop George. If I were in your place, I would think the same thing. But we were strangers in your country, in the middle of nowhere, with a priest of the church, doing something we understood he was doing *with* the consent of the woman. We had no idea then how deranged he was."

"But we did pray for her," said Brother. "And when we saw you later at the port in Agios Kirykos transferring her to an ambulance, we thanked the spirits of our ancestors for having sent you," pointing at Maggie and Yianni, "to save the poor woman."

"Didn't you hear what I was shouting at your boat?"

"As you waved a cross at George? Yes, every word is indelibly etched into our memories."

"*May you rot in hell,*" the siblings said in unison.

"And we shared your sentiment after all that we'd witnessed." Brother paused. "Until that morning, we had no idea of the horrifying devil we'd once considered a friend."

"Frankly," said Andreas, "I find it hard to see why you were so horrified to learn that Papa George was doing the very thing he told you he planned to do. Namely, drawing the blood of very old people."

"That's not what horrified us," said Brother. "That happened later, back on the boat."

"On the way down the mountain, George did not say a word to either of us," said Sister. "We'd never seen him so lost in his own thoughts. It was as if he'd flipped a switch, changing his personality from extrovert to introvert."

Andreas shook his head. "You two sure do know how to tell a suspenseful story. I can't help but wonder how much of a hand your lawyer played in its development."

"Conversations with my clients are privileged, Kaldis," snarled the lawyer. "You know that."

"Thank you," said Brother to the lawyer, "but there's no reason to be concerned." He turned his attention to Andreas. "Of course, we went over what we've told you today with our lawyer. It would be foolish not to. But I swear, not a fact has been changed."

"Or shaded," added Sister.

"So, let's get on to that boat ride." Andreas crossed his legs.

"When we got back to Karkinagri and dropped off the car, George spotted our boat's tender tied up alongside a jetty. He carried the cooler to the tender and the three of us went back to the boat. The first thing George did onboard was fumble around, looking for tape to seal the cooler shut. After he'd done that, he told us to call the captain and tell him we wanted to leave ASAP, and that he should find someone to ferry him back to our boat because we'd taken the tender."

"When are we going to get to the horrifying part?" asked Maggie.

"Now," said Sister. "It started when I asked George what he intended to do with what was inside the cooler." Sister paused to pour herself a half-cup of tea, her hand shaking as she did.

"Oh, let me get the maid to bring us a fresh pot. That must be cold now."

"No, thank you, Mrs. Kaldis, please don't bother. I just need something to moisten my throat." She took a sip before continuing. "George sat perfectly still for a full minute staring straight at me, then burst into laughter, the eerie kind we think of as madness in poor horror movies. Yet there he was, laughing and pointing at each of us. Then, just as quickly, he turned serious and said that even though we lacked the vision to see a once-in-a-hundred-years opportunity to gain wealth and power beyond imagination, he *forgave* us."

"For not joining him in his vaccine plans?" asked Maggie.

"We assumed so," Sister nodded. "He said we'd already cost him trillions, but he'd nevertheless found a way to amass billions without our help, and no longer wanted or needed our help finding an importer in China."

Brother said, "It was as if he were angling for one of us to ask how he proposed to do his business without our help. But we didn't bite. We just let him go on as if everything was fine."

"He sounds insane," said Lila.

"Which is precisely why we simply let him talk," said Sister. "He began to gloat, and without our asking, began telling us his plan. It was simple. And would likely work. For it has in other parts of the world. All one has to be is amoral."

Andreas fidgeted in his chair. *And this story might take another hundred years to finish.*

"George said arrangements were underway to have his product distributed across China, Vietnam, and other East Asian countries. It would all happen within a matter of weeks and without red tape to slow things down. Distributors were clamoring to outbid one another for even a single molecule of what he had carefully amassed over time. Now all he had to do was prepare it for market."

"Sounds like a drug deal," said Yianni.

Brother nodded. "But far worse, because his business model killed the sources of his drug and could kill untold others who'd be misled by his false claims." He swallowed. "I'm sure you're all familiar with the horrible fate of the Southern African rhinos illegally slaughtered for their horns. On the black market, powdered rhino horn is worth more than gold, and the closer to extinction they become, the more valuable their horn."

Sister added, "Some practitioners of Chinese medicine claim rhino horn cures a plethora of common maladies, like headaches and vomiting."

"And erectile disfunction," added Yianni.

Andreas lowered his head and rubbed at his eyes with his thumb and index finger, not daring to look at Yianni.

"Yes," nodded Sister, "There is the widely held belief that it also serves as an aphrodisiac, though the specific effect you describe, when achieved, is not because of the horn, but the surreptitious addition of sildenafil to the compound. The worst thing is, these false cures become valuable *because* of their high cost, and the prestige that comes with possessing it."

"It doesn't take much imagination to see the potential market George had in mind," said Father. "With so many already paying extraordinary sums for concoctions that claim to cure a headache, or achieve an erection, can you imagine what those same people living in a part of the world hysterical over when the next pandemic will strike would be willing to pay for something that promises healthy old age and a lifelong resistance to plagues."

Brother added: "Especially with every source of that miraculous cure disappearing from the face of the earth in less than a decade. It might not bring in the trillions that a legitimate vaccine would, but if marketed correctly, certainly hundreds of millions, if not billions, stood to be made." Brother poured himself some tea and took a sip. "That's *if* it's marketed correctly. And by marketed correctly,

I mean through the international black market that traffics in rhino horn, bear gallbladder, and so on. A market that is tightly controlled by highly organized and violent criminal syndicates."

"Sounds risky," said Andreas.

"He's playing with fire," said Father. "We know who the players are in the black market, and they know who we are. We keep a respectful distance from one another. George is embracing a tiger, for if even one drop of what he offers is as valuable to the traffickers as he hopes—and if they accept him as their only source—then his value lasts only until his supply runs out."

"But what's to stop him from passing off any old blood as coming from an Ikariot centenarian?," blurted Maggie.

"There are ways to test that the blood is at least in part as he claims," said Brother. "And, yes, even in the black market there are counterfeits, but for an item of this inestimable value, I've no doubt the syndicates will ruthlessly root out any who seek to tarnish their brand with counterfeits."

"How did he get tied in with the black market?" said Andreas.

"He said that the men we'd met at The Buzz Club were his connection to what he called his *distributors in the East.* The two apparently had worked with the syndicates before."

"Those two have been dead for months, now. Do you know if he's found another connection?" asked Andreas.

"We have not yet made such inquiries," said Father.

Andreas looked at Brother and Sister. "Did he tell you any more about his proposed deal with the syndicates?"

"At that point, a fisherman came alongside with the captain in his dinghy, and George said not another word on the subject. He acted as if we were three old friends out for a boat ride and went on and on about how happy he was at our paying him a surprise visit and pleased that he'd been able to fulfill our long-held desire to meet dear Anna.

"None of that made any sense to us, but we just let him ramble on. Frankly, we couldn't wait to drop him off and be rid of him. Looking back, he obviously said all that for the benefit of the captain. It was the same sort of ploy as he'd pulled when he boarded the boat in Evdilos, and told Older Brother to have the captain disconnect the ship's GPS to avoid us being tracked by paparazzi. That was just another step in his plan to make it seem that we'd been the ones behind the attack on that poor woman."

"Thank God she survived," said Maggie.

"Yes," nodded Brother and Sister.

"So, what happened next?" asked Yianni.

Brother answered. "We planned on dropping George off in Evdilos, where we'd picked him up, but as we neared Agios Kirykos, a boat came racing up behind us. George's attention and subject of conversation switched to the boat, how fast it must be going, and how crazy its captain had to be. When the boat drew close enough to see some of the people on it, George fell back into a deep silence, his eyes fixed on the boat as it passed us, speeding toward the port. Next thing we knew, George started shouting for the captain to follow the boat into the harbor."

Brother looked at Yianni and Maggie. "We reached the port just in time to see you and the police help transfer Anna into an ambulance. At that instant, George underwent yet another transformation. He was back to being our best friend, worried for our safety and deeply concerned about a wave of bad publicity he saw heading straight for our family. Police were now involved, and there undoubtedly would be an investigation into what had happened to the old woman. Though as a cleric, he'd undoubtedly be spared any scandal, we being foreigners––"

"Excuse me, Older Brother, but the way he described us was, *'Chinese, who are not well-liked in Greece.'*"

"Correct. And he went on to say that for this reason we'd be targeted by the police and press. He urged us to get out of Greece immediately. He also suggested we leave all our luggage on the boat and tell the captain to arrange for it to be delivered to our hotel in Athens. The hotel would ship it to us in Hong Kong, along with the rest of our things."

"And you believed that you should flee?" said Yianni.

"After the craziness we'd witnessed that morning, what he suggested seemed his only sane suggestion yet. Who wouldn't flee such madness in a foreign land for the security of home?"

Sister bowed her head. "We were frightened, and when we returned home, we decided to put the entire affair out of our minds. And George out of our lives, forever."

"We're ashamed to say that we did not tell our father," said Brother, lowering his head like his sister.

Father looked at Andreas. "To their credit, I must say that when I confronted them with your letter, they disclosed every detail without any effort to excuse or avoid blame for their poor judgment." He looked at his children, then back at Andreas. "For that I am proud of them. I am also aware that even though I am assured by our attorney there is no criminal risk or civil liability for their part in any of this, a great wrong has been done to innocent people by a criminal who's used my children and our good name in an attempt to hide his own sins.

"Whether or not you believe that my children are innocent, and without regard to what formal action you may seek to take against them, we are prepared to make financial amends to the families of those harmed by Papa George." He leaned forward. "But just so there is no misunderstanding as to the purpose of this meeting or this offer, I am not going to mention a sum or the means of achieving our goal. Only once you're satisfied that such an arrangement is lawful and workable will we discuss the specifics of what we have in mind. Again, if you wish to arrest my children, they are prepared to go through that process, and if you choose to follow that course, we shall not modify or rescind our offer to aid those who were victimized. We'll be at our hotel for the next three days. I assume that's an acceptable time frame within which you are able to reach a decision?"

Andreas thought for a moment. "It's acceptable to me." He looked at Maggie and Yianni. "Do either of you have anything to add?"

Yianni gestured no.

Maggie sat up on the sofa and looked Andreas in the eye. "I do."

Andreas blinked.

"You should write more letters."

Chapter Seventeen

"So, who wants to be first to give your take on what we just heard?" Andreas dropped into the wing chair, having shown the Chens and their lawyer to the elevator.

"No one touched a single pastry," said Lila.

"They were too focused on reciting their lines to think about eating," said Maggie.

"Well, I'll make up for that," said Yianni, reaching to put a strawberry fruit tart on his plate.

"Now that we've got that major issue under control," said Andreas, "perhaps you could let me know whether you believed them."

Yianni talked through a bite of his tart. "I thought I'd cross them up on The Buzz Club because they'd obviously left that visit out of what they'd told their father."

"And their lawyer," said Lila.

"Do you actually think the reason they never told their father about any of that was because they feared he'd learn of their recreational drug use?" asked Maggie. "To me, it seemed more like a convenient ploy conjured up by their lawyer in Lila's study to give his clients an angle for squirming out of something far more incriminating."

"Good point," said Andreas. "But everything they told us about that evening squares with what Yianni saw, and if they really were into something more with Tom and Jerry than that one visit to their club, it's hard to imagine they'd risk voluntarily coming back to Greece now."

"But their father *made* them come back," said Maggie.

"True, but let's be real. As tough as it may be to accept that your children aren't perfect, do any of us believe their father would have done that if he didn't honestly believe his children were innocent? If he felt differently, my guess is he'd have found a way to discipline them at home, not turn them over to the Greeks for a carnival prosecution."

Maggie sighed. "But if the siblings knew Tom and Jerry were dead, even today they might not have told their father the whole truth. After all, they're the only ones left alive who know what the four of them talked about that night at the club—and any other links they might have had."

"You're forgetting Papa George," added Yianni, reaching for another tart.

"A person they've gone to a great deal of trouble and expense to discredit," Maggie shot back.

"That works both ways," said Andreas. "Remember that part of the story where either Tom or Jerry told the sister of some deal Papa George had brought them in on that would enable the dirty duo to retire? And how profusely he'd thanked her brother and her for making it all happen? The sister dismissed that as weird, but it struck me as surprising she would tell us such a potentially incriminating detail unless she honestly didn't understand what he was talking about then."

Yianni jumped in. "And the reason she didn't understand is because Papa George had told Tom and Jerry that the Chens were behind it all. Papa George wanted everyone he'd involved in the scheme to think he was only a bit player in what was going down."

"Precisely. That way, if Tom and Jerry were caught, they'd roll over and point to the Chens, not Papa George."

"That also explains why Tom and Jerry appeared so nervous when I saw them meeting the Chens in their club. They thought they were meeting the big bosses behind their new deal."

"What a cunning bastard," said Maggie.

Yianni nodded. "If you believe the Chens, Papa George launched his plan to incriminate them the moment they rejected his proposal to manufacture and market his miracle vaccine. Right then and there he set up the Chens to appear as the powers behind it all, starting with their hundred-grand donation to his foundation. From that point on, he took every opportunity to implicate them more deeply, culminating in the visit to Anna."

"Hell hath no fury like a hustler scorned," said Lila.

"Well, is it time yet for us to answer the ultimate question?" asked Andreas, reaching for a custard tart.

"Let's hear it," said Yianni.

"Despite your personal feelings, do any of you believe a prosecutor will think there's enough evidence of wrongdoing to bring charges against the Chens and/or Papa George?"

"Innocent people have died," said Lila.

"Yes," said Andreas, "but we've confirmed that Papa George possesses signed, legally binding consents from each of those poor souls, releasing everyone involved from any responsibility for what cost them their lives."

"That can't be right," said Lila.

"Morally, I agree. Legally, it's a different story."

"Someone *has* to be held responsible," Maggie protested.

"Perhaps we'll find something in what the father promised to deliver this afternoon to the chief's office," said Yianni.

"I doubt we'll find a smoking gun in anything that their lawyer's reviewed," said Andreas. "He may be full of himself, but he's sharp and thorough."

"What do you think about the Chens' financial proposal?" asked Lila.

"They're trying to buy us," said Maggie, dismissively.

Yianni waited a moment. "*Or* they're simply trying to do as the father said. Redeem the family for his children's bad judgment in befriending Papa George."

"I thought you were on my side," Maggie said to Yianni.

"I agree someone should be held responsible. The problem question is who?"

"I'm afraid Yianni's right. From what we know so far, the only ones who can truly answer that question are the suspects. And we know their stories. Papa George blames the Chens, and the Chens blame Papa George." Andreas swallowed. "I know this is hard for you to hear, Maggie, but even if we knew which of them was morally responsible—even legally liable for damages of some sort—I doubt an adjudication of guilt or innocence would ever make it to a criminal trial."

"Are you saying we accept the Chens' proposal?" asked Maggie.

"I'm not sure what the terms of their offer are yet, but it appears the Chen family is willing to pay an as-yet-to-be-disclosed amount for the benefit of those harmed, without regard to who may or may not have caused that harm. We've got three days to take another hard look at all the evidence, firm up their proposal, and decide how we proceed."

"I don't like it. I want *justice* for my *yaya*."

Yianni said, "And despite what the father said, I'll be very surprised if, at the last minute, assurances aren't insisted upon by the lawyer that the children won't be prosecuted."

Andreas exhaled. "I agree with you both. *But*, based upon the facts as we know them, I fear justice for Maggie's *yaya*, and all the others who've suffered, may have to await a heavenly tribunal. As for your point, Yianni, I'm reminded of advice my father-in-law once passed on to me."

"Huh," said Lila. "I've never heard you quote my father before."

"I'd never needed to before."

"I hope it's flattering."

"So, what's the advice, already?" said Maggie.

"Never turn down a deal you haven't been offered."

———

Maggie walked into Andreas's office under full steam, followed by Yianni, who shut the door behind them. The pair plopped onto the sofa across from Andreas.

"Let me guess, the two of you went in as partners on a winning lottery ticket, and you came to tell me you're out of here."

"We'd never tell you that, Chief," said Maggie.

"At least not the part about being out of here," said Yianni.

"Good. And Maggie already did hit the lottery, kind of."

"You mean my *family* hit it," she corrected.

"How's that working out?" asked Andreas.

"The father kept his word. The Chen family established a foundation on Ikaria to tend to the special needs of Ikariots ninety and older. And as embarrassing as it is to say, they entered into a very generous long-term lease of Yaya's property that preserves it from development. It's now the foundation's headquarters, with my cousin Spiro serving as its resident executive director." She cocked her head at Andreas. "By the way, did I mention that Spiro said, per this deal, Yaya's cottage is mine to use as I see fit, for as long as I live?"

"You don't say?" Andreas smiled.

"Funny how that happened *after* I'd spoken to you a couple of months back about how worried Spiro was at the thought of having to sell Yaya's property to developers, and you had me convince him to wait until the real estate market turned around."

"Amazing, isn't it, how the Lord works in mysterious ways?"

"You didn't happen to have a conversation about any of that with Mr. Chen while you were discussing the terms of his offer, did you?"

"As I vaguely recall, the subject may have come up in passing in the context of some general observations on how Greeks, as well as the Chinese, value their ancestral homes. And, of course, there was some incidental mention of how you almost perished in your late *yaya*'s cottage at the hands of his children's buddies from The Buzz Club."

Maggie smiled and rolled her eyes. "But only vaguely and incidentally."

"Of course," said Andreas. "The primary focus of my discussion was making clear to Chen that whatever he offered would have absolutely no influence on the prosecutorial outcome."

"I was with him," said Yianni, "and all we agreed to was forwarding the file to the prosecutor without a recommendation one way or the other. Whatever happened next was up to the prosecutor, not us."

Maggie shrugged. "I do have to admit that the father kept his word. He fulfilled the terms of his offer well before learning that the prosecutor had decided not to prosecute."

"Anyone, including Papa George," said Yianni sourly.

Maggie feigned spitting at the floor at the mention of the priest's name.

"Okay, so when will one of you tell me why you marched in here?"

Maggie pointed to Andreas's phone. "Tassos called me to tell us to have you phone him. He said he has something important to tell us."

"Maybe he's calling to propose?" Yianni winked.

Maggie turned on him. "Oh, yeah? And how is Toni these days? I must remember to give her a call."

Andreas waved them both off and placed the call, putting it on speaker.

"Hello?"

"Tassos, it's Andreas. I'm here with the other two members of your summoned audience. So, where's the fire?"

"Ten minutes ago, I got off the phone with the Ikaria chief of police. He said he had news that might be of interest to my girlfriend and her colleagues at GADA."

Andreas leaned in toward the speaker, picking up a pencil as he listened.

"Papa George hasn't been seen or heard from for weeks. It's as if he's vanished off the face of the earth."

Andreas's expression turned grim.

"Given what the chief knew about what you all have been up to, he did some checking around to make sure Papa George hadn't fallen victim to what he called foul play. And lo and behold, this is what he discovered."

"Tassos, get to the point," said Maggie.

"Yeah," whispered Yianni, "propose, already."

Maggie smacked his arm.

"Among the things the chief did was call the travel agents on the island, on the off chance Papa George booked something through one them. What he learned was that three weeks ago, a third party had purchased a round-trip ticket for Papa George."

"Round trip to where?"

"You're going to love this. Beijing."

"You can't be serious," said Andreas.

"Please don't tell us the purchaser was one of the Chens," said Maggie.

"No, it was purchased anonymously through an agency in China. But the local agent remembered how excited Papa George was when he picked it up. He kept going on about how his dreams had just come true and he was off to consummate the opportunity of a lifetime. She thought that a rather strange way for a priest to speak, but then again, it was Papa George."

"When was he supposed to be back on the island?" asked Andreas.

"A week after he left."

"So he's overdue by roughly two weeks?"

"Yep."

"And no one's heard from him since?"

"Not a peep."

Andreas looked at his watch. "I've got to make a call. I'll get right back to you."

"No problem."

"Beijing is six hours ahead of us," said Andreas. "It's still early enough for me to call."

"Call whom? As if I haven't guessed," said Maggie.

Andreas put his finger to his lips as he dialed. It rang five times and, as Andreas was deciding whether to leave a message, he heard, "Hello?" come across the line.

"Mr. Chen, this is Andreas Kaldis, calling from Athens."

"Oh, yes, Chief Inspector, how are you and your family?"

"We're doing well, thank you, and you and yours?"

"My children are back to their business, stronger and wiser than before."

"That's all we can hope for as parents." Andreas paused. "I'm here on the speakerphone with my assistant, Ms. Sikestes, and Detective Kouros. We have a question to ask you, but you need not answer if you prefer not to."

"I understand."

"I've just learned that three weeks ago Papa George took a flight to Beijing and was supposed to return a week later, but he has not come back. I'm wondering whether you have any idea what happened to him?"

Silence.

"Mr. Chen?"

"I am deciding how best to share this news with you in a manner that will not lead you to the wrong conclusion. Yes, I am familiar with his fate, but not because I—or my children—had any part in it." He paused. "Days after he arrived in Beijing, I received a surprise visit from the authorities, asking me about a man who'd been arrested for trafficking in forbidden medicines. He claimed to be a Greek national, a priest, and a business partner of my children. The officers then showed me a photo from the accused's passport. I told them that, yes, my children knew the man, but they had absolutely no business dealings with him, had no idea he was in China, nor could they confirm that he was a priest." He cleared his throat. "They accepted my explanation and left."

"That's it?"

"As far as my family is concerned, yes." He paused. "But I must admit that curiosity got the better of me, and I did make some discreet inquiries as to what had befallen him. Apparently, the man you know as Papa George entered the country thinking he was to meet with members of that criminal syndicate I mentioned to you when we met. He did not realize he was being caught in a sting operation set up by Chinese security forces who'd been investigating his supplements business for months. They are who paid for his airline ticket. They arrested him the moment he arrived in Beijing.

"At first he tried using my family name to curry favor with the authorities, but when that failed, he gave them what they wanted:

the identities of the syndicate members who'd been smuggling and selling his supplements into China."

"I'd think that could prove dangerous for him," said Andreas.

"Yes, it could," said the father. "Especially since the result was not a reduction in the charges against him, but rather a speedy trial."

"When is the trial?"

"It's done. He's now serving twenty years in a rather difficult prison, filled with people who do not speak his language, any one of whom could be an assassin dispatched by his former syndicate partners to do away with him."

"It sounds like a living hell," said Andreas. He thought he heard a chuckle in response.

"That's why I'm sharing his fate with you and your colleagues. I can think of no one who'd appreciate the irony more."

"You've got that right," said Maggie.

"For sure," said Yianni.

"Thank you, and Godspeed, Mr. Chen." Andreas hung up.

"It's hard not to believe in God when you hear an outcome like that," said Maggie.

"Or the vengeance that can befall one who seeks to destroy a dynasty but fails," said Andreas, tapping his pencil on his desktop.

"Do you think the Chens could have played a part in Papa George's fate?" said Maggie.

"Machiavelli wouldn't bet against it, so why should I?"

"I wonder if we'll ever know which story was true, Papa George's or the Chens'?" said Yianni.

"Maybe someday we'll know, but for now only the guilty do for sure, so I'm all for moving on," said Andreas.

"But don't you wonder, at least a little bit," asked Yianni, "what's going through a guilty party's mind when things don't go as they planned?"

"That's something we'll likely never know in this case, so why dwell on it?"

"Because," said Yianni, "like the man just told you, it's curiosity. After all, isn't curiosity what keeps us working as cops?"

"Well," Andreas told the pair, "if I ever get an answer to your impossible question, I'll be sure to share it with you."

"Me too," said Maggie.

Andreas turned to catch Maggie's eye. "May I suggest that, until that day arrives, we agree to put this matter and all its potential bad guys out of our thoughts? Instead, let us pledge to do honor to those precious souls who perished along with your *yaya*, by remembering a principle that's been hammered home to me by everything that happened in this case."

"Which is?" asked Maggie.

"True loyalty among family and friends is a treasure beyond value."

Maggie shut her eyes, leaned back on the sofa, and exhaled. "Amen."

ACKNOWLEDGMENTS

Mihalis, Roz, and Spiros Apostolou; Zisis Asimomytis, MD; Scott Backus; Michael Bursaw; Antonio Cacace and Sara Yanousi; Kinsey Casey; Mandy Chahal; Beth Deveny; Diane DiBiase; Andreas, Aleca, Mihalis, and Anna Fiorentinos; Alkistis Giavridis; Flora and Yanni Katsaounis; Elena Kefalogianni; Panos Kelaidis; Ioanna Lalaounis; Malina Leslie; Linda Marshall; Terrence, Karen, and Rachel McLaughlin; Kelsey McPherson; Jeffrey W. Moses, MD; Sudha Nair-Iliades; Renee Pappas; Jim Paulate, RN; Barbara Peters; Petros and Frederick Rakas; Dora Rallis; Victor and Carol Raskin; Jonathan, Jennifer, Azriel, and Gavriella Siger; Ed Stackler; Elias Zaoutis; Barbara Zilly-Siger.

And, of course, Aikaterini Lalaouni.

ABOUT THE AUTHOR

Jeffrey Siger was born and raised in Pittsburgh, Pennsylvania, practiced law at a major Wall Street law firm, and later established his own New York City law firm where he continued as one of its name partners until giving it all up to write full-time among the people, life, and politics of his beloved Mykonos. *One Last Chance* is the twelfth novel in his internationally bestselling and award-nominated Chief Inspector Andreas Kaldis series, following up on *A Deadly Twist, Island of Secrets* (first published as *The Mykonos Mob*), *An Aegean April, Santorini Caesars, Devil of Delphi, Sons of Sparta, Mykonos After Midnight, Target: Tinos, Prey on Patmos, Assassins of Athens,* and *Murder in Mykonos.*

The *New York Times* described Jeffrey Siger's novels as "thoughtful police procedurals set in picturesque but not untroubled Greek locales" and named him as Greece's thriller writer of record. The *Greek Press* called his work "prophetic,"

Eurocrime described him as a "very gifted American author…
on a par with other American authors such as Joseph Wambaugh
or Ed McBain," and the City of San Francisco awarded him its
Certificate of Honor citing that his "acclaimed books have not
only explored modern Greek society and its ancient roots but
have inspired political change in Greece." He now lives in Greece.